To Mary, Keep on Keepin' on!

Deadline Zombies

The Adventures of Maxi and Moxie

Teel James Glenn

BooksForABuck.com
2010

Teel James Glenn

Copyright 2010 by Teel James Glenn, all rights reserved. No portion of this novel may be duplicated, transmitted, or stored in any form without the express written permission of the publisher.

Warning: The unauthorized reproduction or distribution of this copyrighted work is illegal. Criminal copyright infringement, including infringement without monetary gain, is investigated by the FBI and is punishable by up to 5 years in federal prison and a fine of $250,000.

This is a work of fiction. All characters, events, and locations are fictitious or used fictitiously. Any resemblance to actual events or people is coincidental

Published by
BooksForABuck.com
ISBN: 978-1-60215-126-0

Dedication:

To Liz Pressman, a reporter heroine if ever there was one

The Reporter Hero

Moxie Donovan is one of a long line of reporter heroes that stretch all the way back to O'Henry's 1905 short story "Calloway's Code". In that story, the intrepid reporter's cryptic wire from a war front is deciphered by the old news-hound to 'save the day' and scoop the other papers thus giving us a two for one journalistic good guy.

It is no accident that Superman and the Green Hornet's alter egos are in the news biz. Aside from giving them a heads up on crimes to stop, it was a profession that their creators knew well. Most pulp writers of the Golden Age had backgrounds as ink slingers in the Fourth Estate.

It made sense; while writers with a literary bent could afford to labor over each phrase and nuance of the next Great American Novel, the guys (and gals) who were in the trenches were slaving away for one-cent a word.

No time there to wait for the Muse to visit inspiration on the writer—the wolf was at the door so they had to just sit their butt down and get their word count out!

Only the world of deadline journalism could teach the discipline and skill set necessary to make a living wage with words in the pulp magazines.

For a good craftsman, the pulps were steadier and less dangerous work than news reporting work and offered a chance to graduate to the 'slick' magazines that paid as much as ten cents a word!

The key to survival and success was volume so it is also no surprise that the axiom 'write what you know' became 'write what you don't have to do too much research on'. Thus the word jockeys drew on their own lives for inspiration and characters and churned out a steady stream of word wrangling wonderboys:

John X. Kennedy (in the MacBride and Kennedy series by Frederick Nebel), Jerry Wade, The Candid Camera Kid, (by Norman Daniels), Daffy Dill (by Richard Sale), Flashgun Casey (By George Harmon Coxe) and Jack Darrell (by Arthur K. Barnes in a science fiction side trip of the reporter hero) are all prime examples of the genre.

The printed word leapt to the silver screen where fast-talking, wisecracking news hounds kept it light and witty. Movies like *The Front Page*, *The Philadelphia Story*, and *It happened One Night* all had newspapermen and women as their protagonists. The mystery sub genre was replete with newsy sleuths like John Forsythe's character in *Captive City*, Torchy Blane (where the hard drinking male John X. Kennedy became the wise-cracking female Torchy). On TV, Charles Bronson's

Deadline Zombies

portrayal of *Man with a Camera* and the TV incarnation of *Casey, Crime Photographer* portrayed by Darren McGavin who came back decades later as another reporter, *Kolchak: The Night Stalker*.

These are the direct ancestors of Maxi and Moxie and the inspiration for their adventures.

So if you, dear readers, like what you see here I'm sure I can find more chronicles of these ink-slinging adventurers.

So stop the presses and get rewrite on the phone-the story goes something like this....

Teel James Glenn 5/28/09

-30-

The Beast of Governors Island

Prologue: The Stag Horned Man

The whole thing with Maxine and my involvement with the Beast of Governors Island started before I came into it directly and it began with a guy named Jonathon Colliers. He was an actor. Not a great actor—he was usually the guy carrying the torch or the spear in the back of Julius Caesar's triumphant march into Alexandria. He wasn't even a good actor—he usually only got one or two lines, his high squeaky voice made sure of that—but he was a persistent actor. He was also a tall muscular man and when he had heard that Producers Distributing Corporation was going to shoot a movie in New York he used contacts he had at the Astoria Studio to wrangle an audition on the film. It was so rare to have a chance at *real films* in New York, any more, beyond the Yiddish cinema and some industrials that he saw it as his only real chance to get *footage* to show to a Hollywood talent scout. He was sure his destiny lay on the silver screen and not the stage.

He was overjoyed when he landed the role, though if truth were to be told it was because he was the right size to fit the costume the production company had shipped out from California.

He didn't care, it was a role and he was going to play it to the hilt to make an impression.

On his lower body, he wore little more than a loincloth and thigh-high soft leather boots. Strapped to his chest and covering his head and shoulders was a magnificent animal's head prosthetic. He was afraid at first that his face would be covered, but he was assured that many shots of him before would be shown and the small space where his face was visible beneath the animal's head would keep reminding people that it was him.

The mask/hat was a golden stag with lifelike eyes that actually blinked and moved; controlled like an elaborate puppet from a device hidden in the long leather fingerless gloves he wore. He had been scheduled for a full day of running around in the woods in the center of the island but the weather had scotched those plans, and the crew had moved to what they called a *cover set,* which allowed them to not fall behind schedule. It was a large cave-like room in the lower levels of the circular fort that everyone called Castle Williams.

It had been exciting in the extreme for Jonathon who got to do his pre-transformation scene with *real* acting and then donned his headpiece.

Deadline Zombies

There had been interminable hours sitting around doing nothing while other shots were done, or readied, but the moments he was on camera were exhilarating.

In between shots he had wandered off into the bowels of the old fort, poking into the dark rooms with the child-like curiosity that kept him pushing at the edges of an acting career.

It was that curiosity that killed the stag.

He was in one cell-like room at the end of a long dark corridor when he happened by chance to find a hole that dug into one of the walls. He stuck his hand into it and pulled out a small piece of metal that had been shaped and worked.

He felt like Little Jack Horner with his plum as he stared at the dirt and grim encrusted object. It was a belt buckle and it had 'CSA' carved into it. I looked like it was actually tarnished silver. He turned it over in his hand and could make out strange scribbling on the back but the light was too poor for him to read them clearly.

He moved around excitedly, in as close to a dance of joy as he could do in his cumbersome costume. It was more than a souvenir, it might be a valuable artifact, one that could bring him enough, perhaps for train fare to the opposite coast and future stardom.

He looked around suddenly afraid someone had seen him take the buckle. The fort was, after all, a government reservation and army base so technically taking anything might be a crime. He stuffed the buckle in his waistband and hurried back into the corridor, not wishing to press his luck and be discovered. He still had two more days on the shoot and with luck he could sneak back to search for more booty.

That was when he heard the growl.

It was a deep rumble of sound that conveyed anger and terror in its base tones. It came from the darkness back from the way he had come.

"Is somebody there?" Surely someone was playing a joke. "Is that you Mike?"

The big jolly special effects man, Mike Drucker, was always pulling little practical jokes.

Ominous silence flowed at him out of the darkness, in waves that were practically tangible.

"Hello?" He tried one more time, and then he heard the growl again in the inky darkness. The sound grew to a roar and two pinpoints of light glowed in the darkness.

Jonathon turned and ran for his life.

He raced blindly down the dark corridor, bouncing off the damp stone of the walls, at one point breaking off one of his antlers. Behind him he heard the heavy tread of *something* stalking him.

He rounded a turn and came to a door that he clawed open.

The cold wind of the harbor blasted into through the doorway, but Jonathon didn't care. He ran headlong into it screaming, "Help!" at the top of his lungs. The sound was swallowed by the wind.

The harbor air hit him like a sledgehammer and the driving force of the wind whipped sleet into his exposed skin like tiny razors. With the fort behind him, he ran straight into the woods, a remarkable park-like space that seemed a million miles away from the lights and sounds and granite towers of New York. It was even more isolated with the storm swirling around him.

He lost the sound of the thing pursuing him but he knew it was there. He pressed on, hoping to find the road or a house of one of the soldiers, but all he kept colliding with were trees.

He hit one of them so hard he rebounded off it and fell to the ground on all fours. The collision knocked the wind out of him and he knelt panting trying to think what to do next.

He never got the chance. The great snarling shape leapt out of the blinding snow and Jonathon Collier's hopes for a career on the silver screen ended in a great bloody mess.

Deadline Zombies

Chapter I: Byline for Murder

"You gotta be kiddin' me, Whitey," I screamed across the bullpen at my editor William 'Whitey' Wilson. "A movie review? What am I, Hedda Hopper?"

"You got better legs than Hedda," my fellow scribe Fran Striker said sotto voce from her desk across from mine.

"It's not a movie review." My baldheaded lord and master emerged from his glass cubical with a cigar shoved in his kisser and a shift of papers in his hand. "It is an assignment to do a color piece on that new movie, *The Faerie Queen*, they are shooting on Governors Island. My brother-in-law is a producer on it and he got that ghoul guy, Lugosi, to star in the damn thing. And the masses love the neck biter."

"I'm a crime reporter!" I wailed from behind my Smith Corona. I had the racing forms strategically hidden under an article on a triple homicide in Yonkers and was trying to scan the nags while creating verbal art out of the carnage.

"You're a two-bit hack wordsmith who takes orders on assignments from his editor or goes to Boise to cover the Winter 'Tater Festival." He puffed till the cigar was red and then turned and headed back into his lair. Just before he slammed the door, he added, "I want it by the evening edition; don't bother with a shutterbug, I'll have Hank pull something from the morgue."

Fran looked at me, flipped her hair back and smiled. She had the homeliest smile of any dame I ever met but was the best back-up a guy ever had on the city room floor. "You really shouldn't piss him off after he saved your bacon from the district attorney."

"Oh come on, " I said as I marked Seahorse for the fourth at Belmont. "That Scanlon would never have gone through on the obstruction of justice charge. Besides, didn't I find the real killer?"

"Only after you let Wentworth get away and gave Mike O'Toole a very bum steer that almost got an innocent man arrested."

"But we got the guy who did do it," I said. "That's all that matters."

She threw up her hands. "And that is the only reason Whitey went to bat for you."

"That and my copy sells papers." I finished my picks for the day and waved to Slip Mahoney the copy boy. He raced over and I handed him the sheet and five bucks.

"Take these to Benny and put the money down across the board," I said. Then I tore my copy from the word-o-rama and handed that to him as well. "And get this to the desk editor."

"Sure thing, Mister Donovan." He dashed off on his two errands.

Yeah, that's me, Mister Moxie Donovan, ace reporter for the *Daily Star*. Some people called me the 'Ace of Spades,' since I ran into more than my fair share of meat puzzles in the course of my work.

I grabbed my hat and my trench coat and walked over to Fran's desk to open her bottom draw and pulled out the Glenfiddich bottle and my glass. She pulled her own glass out and held it for me to pour.

"If I'm going out into that cold I want to be fortified," I said.

"You are a piece of work, you drunk Irishman," she said as we clinked glasses and knocked our shots back in unison.

"That is a redundant statement, dear Frannie." I shoved a thumb back toward the ogre's office. "Tell his highness I'll be back before the storm hits but I'm putting the cab on his tab."

I was as good as my semi drunken word and hopped a hack to South Ferry. It was two days before Thanksgiving of nineteen thirty-six and a Nor'Easter was whipping the streets to froth. I had the cabbie make two stops, one up town and one on Thompson Street in the West Village where I hoped to pick up some background color before I went ghoul gabbing.

"Wait," I called to the driver as I darted out into the wind. "I'll only be a minute."

My stop was the Tome Tomb, a treasure trove of facts and figures that was the *Daily Star's* secret weapon against the bigger papers. The little gnome who ran it was Digger Tome, a scowling cartoon with thinning hair slicked back, who wore thick glasses. He had the manner and wardrobe of an undertaker.

"Hey Quasimodo," I called as I entered with my bribe of the day, a Reuben sandwich from the Stage Door Deli. "How are the bells ringing?"

He inhaled the sandwich while I quizzed him on the Hungarian bloodsucker and Governors Island. He had an amazing ability to ferret out obscure sources for background on any piece and was a living, breathing encyclopedia of the weird and wacky. I knew the marble mouth Hungarian would be right up his alley.

"I heard they were doing a movie of Spenser's *The Faerie Queene*," Digger said, "But I didn't realize Bela was in it."

"Who is Spenser?" I favored the racing form or *Doc Savage* pulps so when he looked at me crossed I didn't feel particularly Neanderthalish, until he rolled his eyes.

"English poet? He wrote *The Faerie Queene* in the fifteen hundreds. Shakespeare ripped off part of it for *A Midsummer's Night's Dream*."

"Did he take old Billy Bard to the mat on it?"

"They all stole from each other back then,' Digger said. "It was before copyright law and they called it 'inspired by' like you tabloid muck-monkeys."

I made to snatch the last of the sandwich from him but the gargoyle moved fast and suddenly pulled a book from behind him and thrust it into my hand. It was an annotated copy of *The Faerie Queene* by Edmund Spenser.

"Does it at least have pictures?" I asked.

Again the eye roll. It is very humiliating to be looked down on by a troll.

"I heard that PDC was going to try a prestige picture but I had no idea they were going after the Warner Brothers' *Midsummer* crowd."

"Hey," I said, at last recognizing something he was talking about, "Wasn't the one last year with Mickey Rooney as the guy with the horns?"

"Puck," he said.

"You don't have to be insulting."

"Lugosi—I have a press book from when he did Dracula on Broadway that has a bio on him." He tried to ignore my comment. He reached behind him in a pile of books that looked completely random and his hand seized exactly on what he wanted. "Probably all lies," he said. "Written by some hack like you, but you can plagiarize it and no one will notice."

I gave him my freeze your heart look but his kept beating. I was losing my touch.

The cabbie was sitting at the curb reading a newspaper (a rival tabloid I'd noticed) on the boss' tab, so I kept pumping my gnome for background.

"And the island they are shooting this movie on?"

"Governors Island is a 172-acre island in Upper New York Bay, approximately one-half mile from the southern tip of Manhattan Island and separated from Brooklyn by Buttermilk Channel." He never broke stride while he chewed and I stood in awe of not only his knowledge but also his ability to take massive bites and not choke while talking.

"First named by the Dutch explorer Adriaen Block, it was called Noten Eylant and later in pidgin language Nutten Island," he continued. "The Brooklyn-Battery Tunnel passes underwater and off-shore of the island's northeast corner, its location marked by a ventilation building connected to the island by a causeway."

The sandwich was gone and he produced a blood red silk

handkerchief to wipe his mouth. "One interesting fact is that during the Civil War, Castle Williams held Confederate prisoners of war. After the war, Castle Williams was used as a military stockade."

I could see the wind picking up out the window so I grabbed the press book on Lugosi, dropped a ten on the counter and called, "See you in the funny pages," as I raced out to the cab.

"Watch yourself," he said as I exited his musty store. "There's a hell of a storm coming in."

There was more than a storm blowing in, but at that point I didn't know it.

Deadline Zombies

Chapter II: The Staten Island Fairy

"Mister Donovan?" The figure that greeted me at the dock on Governors Island looked like Nanook of the North's big brother. He was wearing a parka with the hood up and big boots with fur at the top. The face that peeped out from the hollow of the hood looked like it would have been at home in the Yukon, a grizzled beard and deep-set eyes. "Ah'm Joe Beauford, the caretaker out here."

I was wishing my trench coat was at least as thick as Joe's accent as I climbed out of the motor launch the bobbed violently at the wharf. The wind was whipping up and it had started to sleet again. I hated Whitey Wilson.

'I thought this was a military base," I said as Joe walked me up the pier toward an old Model T flatbed that was parked on the dirt road.

"It is," he said. "But they're all a bunch of paper pushers that all rotate out of here all the time; they need a person who knows how the plumbing and all works and to keep the grounds."

We climbed into the cab of the jalopy.

"I'm going back in an hour," the launch captain called up. "Sooner if this weather keeps getting bad, so get back as soon as you can."

"I'd be going back now if I didn't have a bar tab to pay off," I yelled to him as the Ford coughed to life and we were off.

The truck wasn't much warmer than the outside but at least the wind wasn't cutting me to ribbons. We drove along a wide dirt road that had been graveled irregularly and bumped accordingly. The shocks of the ride could have used work.

"Only have one road," Joe said. "Runs around the rim of the island. The interior is still pretty wild, light forest. I have a horse and team to do the regular hauling—costs too much to bring fuel out for this usually, but them movie people are paying for all the expenses." He laughed in an Ozark-flavored cackle. "I love being paid twice—money is good."

I couldn't argue with the bumpkin on that one, or the view. As we bumped along I got a great look at the lower part of Manhattan with the shape of the Empire State Building dominating the skyline. It really was the greatest city in the world and I reminded myself every time I got another chill or had my spine realigned by Joe's driving that in order to live there I had to take Whitey's lousy assignments. Well, I didn't have to like them.

The fort they called Castle Williams was impressive, a stone round fort with three rows of what I took for windows running all around. As we got closer I could see the windows were actually gun ports. Joe must have seen the look on my face cause he gave me a history lesson to add to Digger's.

"After the beginning of the American Revolutionary War, the Continental Army, under General Israel Putnam fortified this island with earthworks and 40 cannon for anticipation of the Battle of Brooklyn, the largest battle of the entire war. The American's cannon inflicted enough damage to make the British commanders cautious of entering the East River." He seemed to take great pride in the whole thing and I just let him talk, my trusty notebook in hand. I could pad the article if marble-mouth didn't prove talkative.

"The Continental Army forces eventually withdrew from the island as well, and the British occupied it until Evacuation Day at the end of the war in 1783. This circular casemated work was completed in 1811 just in time for the war of 1812."

We were at the door of the building now and close up it was just as impressive though the only thing on my mind at the time was, is it warmer inside?

Thank God it was. As soon as we stepped through the old heavy wooden and iron strapped door, I was hit with a blast of warmth equal to the cold from outside. We had stepped into a huge parking-garage sized stone room that was ringed with tall stands on which huge lights blazed away.

Joe pushed his hood down and revealed regular features and a bald head. In the light of the room, he looked less the mountain man and more the handyman. He held a finger to his lips and pointed.

In the center of the ring of lights a gorgeous redheaded woman in a long green gown stood chained to a post while men and women with animal heads on them—a donkey, a doe, a boar—danced around her. Lording over all was a tall thin figure with long white hair and a wise man beard dressed in black and silver robes.

"You will surrender the secret of the castle to me, Una," the figure said (though it sounded like "Uoo Veel soorander' to my untrained ear). "Or my minions will tear you asunder."

"I will never surrender to you, Busirane," the redhead said. I could swear I detected a Bronx accent coming from the fair maiden.

Graybeard stretched his arms up and there was a puff of smoke and a geyser of flame and maiden Una screamed.

Great hokum.

"Cut!" A little guy in a blue cardigan and wearing a beret yelled and the dancing stopped like magic. "Print it!"

"Okay." Another figure with a thick binder suddenly popped up beside Cardigan and yelled, "Next set up close up for Busirane; everybody else take ten."

The animal dancers scattered like roaches to corners of the cavernous room and more than one off them immediately lit up a coffin nail. A stagehand, or whatever you call him, went over to the redhead and unfastened the chains from her and threw a blanket over her bare and very attractive shoulders.

She hustled over to a canvas-backed chair and settled into it, pulling a binder from a pouch on the side to bury her nose in.

Meanwhile the giant mechanical thing on a tripod that I assumed to be the camera was being moved in toward graybeard.

"Wow," I said in a whisper to Joe, "They sure are a busy bunch of beavers."

"Dangest thing," he said. "They seem to run around all day and I still have no idea what most of them do."

At that point a little guy wearing glasses and a long beige camelhair overcoat came up to me, grabbed my hand and started pumping away like he was hoping to get water out of me.

"Morty Gluckman, PDC promotion department," he said. "You must be Donnelly."

"Donovan," I corrected. "I'm from the *Daily Star*."

"Glad to meet you," he continued. "I know you'll want to chat with our stars but this weather has really put us behind schedule so if you don't mind I'll sort of shuffle you through around their shooting."

I began to wonder if the guy ever took a breath. Normally I like to do my own 'shuffling,' but I was anxious enough to get the heck out of there to let him do the leading.

He grabbed my arm and walked me over to the redheaded dish that was reading from her binder and moving her lips while doing it.

Must be a blonde who dyed her hair to trade up, I thought. When we got closer I could hear her repeating phrases over with different inflections as she did.

"This is Miss Maxine Keller, star of Broadway and the Orpheum circuit," Gluckman hyped as we stepped up beside the flame-haired frail.

She looked up with an annoyed expression on her face and I noticed she had fiery green eyes and a sprinkling of freckles across the bridge of her nose barely hidden under the slathered on makeup. And from her roots and eyebrows she was a natural redhead. I'd heard those could be dangerous. When she opened her mouth she proved it.

"Oh for Christmas sake, Morty. I have three pages of dialogue to memorize for today since they changed the schedule. I can't face another gossip mag hack till I do.

I thought the little guy would wet himself right there. He sputtered and giggled and smiled at me. "This a member of the fourth estate, Maxine, honey," he said. "Your contract says you have to talk to him."

"I will talk to who I want to and my contract also says I have to learn my lines and turn in a good performance. Tell him some more lies like you told the last two newshounds and leave me do my work."

"She's always kidding," he said with a broad smile and patting her on the back. " Maxi-baby is a real trouper and always kidding."

She wasn't. She stood up and went nose to nose with the guy.

"Don't you ever call me Maxi-baby you little twerp!" she said "And if you ever touch me again I will rip off your arm and beat you to death with it."

I suddenly felt sorry for him as she let loose with a string of expletives that would have fried frozen chicken on the spot.

I was starting to really like this dish.

That is until she added, " Take this two bit shopping circular scribe out of here and let me work."

"Hey lady, I—" I was going to tell her what an amazing newshound I was, how much my editor valued me and that I didn't need her stinking interview at all. But then I realized I wasn't and I did, so I just smiled.

"Oh!" She threw up her hands, grabbed her binder and stormed off out of the circle of lights toward a door in the stone wall. She threw it open and a blast of icy air swept in before it slammed shut.

Gluckman stood there, beet-red and gulping air as if it were being rationed starting tomorrow. I had to hand it to him though, three heartbeats later he turned to me and said, "She's just a little high strung, but a great actress."

"I'm sure," I said. "And I'm sure my readers will love—"I never finished my statement because Miss Keller proved that actress or not, she had the set of pipes on her that Ethel Merman would envy. She let loose with a scream that rattled my eyeteeth.

"He's dead!" she yelled. "He's been murdered!"

See what I mean? I'm a meat puzzle magnet.

Deadline Zombies

Chapter III: Lights, Camera, Slaughter

It was no movie scream and everyone on the set knew it immediately. I was second out the door after Old Joe and what we found was not a pretty sight. It looked like Daniel Boone had gone berserk. A big antlered stag's head lay on the ground covered in a spray of gore. Next to it was a man in a loincloth whose guts had been ripped out with a fury that made this hardened reporter a little nauseous.

The redheaded actress was plastered against the stone of the castle hyperventilating, her eyes shut as if to blot out the memory of what she had seen. I felt sorry for the kid—dead people are a pretty abrupt reminder that we are only here on temporary assignment and the great copy editor in the sky can do a rewrite anytime it suits him. I wanted to step over and comfort her (and maybe get a little hug for my troubles), but the newshound in me won out over the hound dog, and I went to examine the body.

It was pretty clear that the dead guy had not gone gently into the night, but from the massive trauma it was a pretty good bet that he had at least died quickly. There were clear rents in his flesh forming a pattern that looked to me like claw marks.

"Looks like an animal did this," I said sagely. I had my notebook in hand and was scribbling details of the scene, even making a little diagram of relative positions. The cops would want all that and I wanted my headline story for the *Star* to be accurate. I saw bonus money in my paycheck, right after my byline on the front page.

"A cat," Joe said as he looked at the wounds on the victim. "But that don't make no sense. Ain't no cats on the island."

"A house cat did this?" I asked.

Joe looked at me like I was a half-wit. "A big cat—puma or mountain lion."

"A lion on Governors Island?" Now I looked at him like *he* was the half-wit. Then I had a thought. "Did the movie company bring one?"

"We have no live animals in this film." It was the Cardigan speaking from behind me. He and many of the cast and crew had followed me and the caretaker through the door from the set. A crew woman had already gone over to comfort the redhead.

Missed that chance, I thought. *But I gotta pay the rent.*

"And you are?" I asked Cardigan.

"Ed Ulmer," he said. "I am directing this film." He was a quiet man and I could see he was doing his best not to be thrown off kilter by this latest grisly interruption to his schedule. "We have no live animals on this production at all."

"And one less live actor, it would seem," I piped in. "Can anyone give me this guy's name?"

"He was John Collier." The redhead stepped up beside me. She seemed to have recovered her wits and despite the biting cold, she made no move to head inside away from the slaughter.

"He was a nice man who played a guard when I was Salome last year at the Broadhurst." Her teeth chattered and her eyes were tearing, but only one was from the cold. Even with red eyes she was a dish.

One of the crew appeared with a blanket and moved to cover the body.

"Don't do that," I ordered in my best imitation of the flatfoot O'Toole's voice. "The police will want everything just as we found it. In fact, is there a still camera around?"

The little guy, Morty, popped up at my elbow and produced a flash camera. "I have this for publicity shots," he said. He looked like he was going to have kittens, his pale skin flushed from the cold. I swear he looked like he was sweating even in the freezing wind. "But the company would prefer that this didn't make the papers."

"Not my call," I said, taking the camera from him. It wasn't the big box that Casey our staff guy used, but it had a flash and it would give me something for my story. The police could have my seconds on this one.

"Let's get everyone back inside," the director said. "We can't do anything here but make a mess. Mister Beauford, will you phone the authorities?"

"Can't do that," the caretaker said. "The line went out after I got the call about Mister Donovan here. Happens in bad weather sometimes."

"What about an army radio?" I was shooting pics of the body, the stag head and the surrounding frozen earth, though the biting snow was playing havoc with the flash. I wasn't sure I'd get anything useful, but I'd kick myself if I didn't try.

"I will drive over to the army base and have them call out." The caretaker headed off around the base of the stone fort at a fast walk.

Ulmer herded the cast inside though I noticed the redhead lingered, looking at the whole scene with eyes not so much reflecting horror, but with a determined squint. I imagined she was fixing the scene in her mind to call up when she testified against the bum that did it. I was sure that had been a Bronx accent on her inside.

Deadline Zombies

I did all I could with the movie company camera, my fingers getting thicker and clumsier as they lost feeling in the cold. Then I hoofed it back inside and slammed the door behind me.

"Man that is cold," I said out loud. I stamped my feet and shook my fingers, shoving the camera under my armpit while I blew on my hands.

"Here." The redhead handed me a steaming cup of java and I wrapped my fingers around it, appreciating the warmth. I sipped from it and hissed at the almost scalding heat. It felt great.

"Thanks." I held the cup close to my face to let the heat of it warm my lips and looked at her over the rim. Her eyes were red rimmed from cold and crying but there was no fear there any more, just determination.

"Are you okay?" I asked.

"Yeah," she said with no vinegar in her response. "I was rattled a bit which is why I made with the siren, but I'm okay now."

"It was a hard break, stumbling on that," I said. "I'm sorry for my part in driving you out there." I got the entire cup of Joe down and saw that she had gotten it from a little table off to the side where the other actors were clustered drinking coffee and conversing in low tones.

"Wasn't your fault," she said. "You are just doing your job. That little twerp Morty just rubs me the wrong way, treats me and the others like commodities. We're artists even if we have to do this stuff for the bread."

"I appreciate that." I appreciated the view just as much as her stepping down off her high horse. Maybe the shock brought her back to her roots. "Let's start over then," I said. "Moxie Donovan, ace reporter from Flatbush." I put out my hand and she took it.

Her hand was warm and soft and I felt a jolt of electricity shoot up my arm straight to my heart. I think she must have felt something too, 'cause her green eyes blinked extra hard as she said, "Maxine Keller, ace singer-dancer-actress from Grand Concourse in the Bronx."

We held the shake a lot longer than we needed to and I know I was thinking about not letting go at all when the guy playing the wizard walked up to us.

"Maxine, my dear," he said with an accent thick enough to smother onions under. "Are you all right?" He had removed his long grey-white wig and had only his chin whiskers on. It was Bela Lugosi, Mr. Dracula himself.

Maxine pulled her hand from mine to turn and accept a hug from the Hungarian. Lucky stiff.

First thing I noticed is that he was taller than I thought he'd be, maybe an inch or two over my six feet with delicate features and long fingers and elegant hands. Nothing feminine about him, but I would have imagined him in a tuxedo even if I hadn't seen Dracula three time. Hey, I liked the female lead, okay?

He also had startlingly powerful eyes, something I had figured was movie magic but was quite real. He had what I guess you'd call presence.

"I'm all right, Bela," she said. "It was just so horrible."

"There, there," he said though it sounded like "Dare, dare." "I saw such things during the war and, though it is vivid now you will be able to make the picture fade like an old painting, if not completely go away."

I was relieved for some strange reason to see that the body language of the hug was fatherly and nothing more. She pulled away from him and turned to me.

"Bela, this is Moxie Donovan from the papers," she said. "Mister Donovan, Mister Bela Lugosi."

He thrust his long fingered hand out to grasp mine and had a surprisingly firm shake.

"I am pleased to meet you, Mister Donovan," he said.

I was beginning to understand his mumbles and that made me concerned—next I'd begin to understand Walter Winchell.

"Though I am sorry for the circumstances," he continued He had an old world charm about him that made me understand his black cape appeal and his manner was gentlemanly almost to courtly. Made me feel like a heel from Hoboken.

"Moxie, please," I said. "Mister Donovan is my dad."

"Then please call me Bela." He laughed warmly. When he did his face suddenly winced and he grabbed his lower back.

"Bela!" Maxine moved to grab him but he motioned her away.

"It is the cold," he said through clenched teeth, "It has aggravated my back."

"Where is your pain powder?" the redhead asked. "I'll get it."

"At my dressing table," he said. "In my valise in the outer pocket.

The dreamy dish disappeared around a shadowed corner and I found myself alone with the 'wincing wampire.' When he saw my eyes follow the redhead out of sight he smiled through his pain.

"She is a lovely girl," he said. "And not just her appearance. She was an understudy to the maid when I did Dracula on Broadway, just starting out. She helped me with my English before each show."

Didn't do a very good job, I thought.

"Uh, yeah, she seems nice enough," I said. Then I put my professional hat on. "Did you know the dead man, Mister—I mean, Bela?"

"No," he replied.

Deadline Zombies

I could see his back was really getting to him and I grabbed a chair for him to sit on from near the food table.

He smiled thanks and sat down. "I had seen him on the set, but we had not spoken. Edgar moves swiftly and I must work hard on my lines. Maxine still helps me."

"Edgar?"

"The director. He directed me in *The Black Cat* two years ago and when he was approached to do this film there was no one else he wished to work with. I am honored, he is a great director."

His statement seemed genuine, not the usual hype-the-boss talk I always heard from showbiz type.

"*The Black Cat* you say?" I said. "Don't that come off a curious coincidence?"

Maxine returned then with a glass of water and a small envelope, the kind pharmacists use for prescriptions. He took both from her and poured the powder into the glass, swirled it around till it dissolved and then knocked it back.

Again he saw me looking and smiled. "I was injured in the war and it pains me from time to time, especially here in this damp place."

I was going to say something witty to try and impress Florence Nightingale Keller when wild man Beauford burst through the door from the outside again.

"The beast has struck again," he yelled. "The radioman's been killed and radio smashed!"

Chapter IV: The Cat's Meow

The groundskeeper trucked me, the director and the little publicity mouthpiece Morty over to the radio shack on the other end of the island. He clattered along the rim road at a crawl because the storm had picked up in intensity to the point where we couldn't see Manhattan or Brooklyn at all. We might as well have been in the middle of the North Atlantic.

I was frozen to the bone by the time we made it to the blockhouse type building that had the aerial on the top of it and I wasn't sure if my teeth would be knocked loose from chattering or the ride first.

Inside was even more chilling. Two soldiers, or rather the remains of them, were scattered all over the inside of the radio room. The communications equipment was in no better shape. I doubt if there was a fragment of the radio bigger than a nickel left.

I tried to push the door closed against the wind, but it wouldn't stay shut unless I threw the deadbolt on it. Once I did, we all stood for a moment drinking in the horror.

"This is bad," Little Morty said.

"I'm surprised you're in publicity with the ability to understate like that," I said. "I'd say we were so far up the creek we'll never make it to the ocean." Suddenly a horrible thought struck me.

"The ocean!" I yelled. "We have to get to the launch to get help from the mainland!"

The four of us ran from the room, but not before I noticed that there was a nice big peephole window on the door and it was slid to the open position.

We wasted our time running to the dock. The launch was gone.

"He can't do that!" little Morty squealed. His camelhair coat was crusted with sleet and his nose was red. He looked like a caramel sundae.

"Well he did," I said. "We are on our own!" I looked around suddenly aware that we were exposed and away from any shelter if the beast should attack. "Where are all the soldiers?" I asked Joe.

"With the holiday coming up, it was just those two to keep the communication open and me out here," the caretaker said. "Don't have but thirty or so here now-a-days anyway." His features weren't visible in his huge parka but I'd have bet he was smiling at the three city dudes freezing their butts off while he was relatively comfortable.

"What about guns?" Morty asked. "It's an army base, right? There should be guns."

Deadline Zombies

The little squirt had a point. I would feel a lot better facing whatever killed those three victims with an elephant gun in my hands.

"The Major locked up the blockhouse with the armory in it before he left. It's like a bank vault. You'd need dynamite to get in to it."

"Mike Drucker!" The director said.

"What?" I asked.

"He's the special effects man on this picture," Ulmer said. "He might have some explosives for the pyrotechnic scenes at the end of the film out here with him."

I liked the idea of dynamite even better than an elephant gun.

"Let's go then,' I said. "We need to get warm anyway. If nothing else, we can all hunker down until daylight or until my editor storms out here to throttle me for missing my deadline on the fluff piece."

"You won't run a story on the movie?" Morty said. Gotta give him that he was persistent.

"About how much fun I had watching you all dance around?" I said as we jammed into the truck cab. "Or how close I came to losing my lunch when I saw the work that monster did to the soldiers?"

That shut him up for the whole bumpy trip back to the castle.

The cast were all huddled in the circle of heat from the big Klieg lights, wrapped in blankets and swilling hot coffee, much of it laced with something stronger from the few whiffs I got.

Everyone wanted to know what we had found but we had agreed not to tell them until at least we had a plan of action. To that end we met with a jolly sort of Santa Claus, complete with white hair and beard, who was their special effects man.

"I don't have anything but sparklers and some smoke pots out here," he said with genuine sorrow for not having the means to destroy a vault door. "I was going to do the forest explosions in miniatures back at the studio in Queens."

I noted he was missing three fingers from his left hand. I hoped it wasn't testament to his proficiency with his craft of demolition.

"That's that, then," I said. "All we can do is circle the wagons until the cavalry arrives."

"We will have to wait for daybreak," the director said. "So let us keep them all busy while they wait—it will be easier." He stepped into the center of the group of actors and waved all their questions to silence, taking charge with quiet determination. "Okay everybody. We will be staying here tonight so let's see if we can get back to work and keep our minds occupied, shall we? We will be fine if we all stay together and in sight of each other, all right?"

He called his assistant director over and the two went off to a corner to plan around the delays the murders had caused—film people are crazy about things like schedules.

I watched the faces of all the cast and crew and realized they needed that bit of normalcy in the midst of the mayhem. Ulmer had made the right choice. The exception was Maxine, who stood with Bela off to one side. She set her jaw and starting toward the director to read him the riot act when I intercepted her.

"Take it easy, kiddo, " I said to her. "I have news for you." I took her aside and explained quietly, and with as little graphic detail as I thought would convey our situation to her, everything we had discovered so far. She took it pretty well and bit her lower lip in a thoughtful gesture that I suddenly found fascinating.

"I see what he's doing," she said when I was finished. " But I can't stand around spouting bad dialogue when the thing that killed Jonathon is prowling around." She gave a little shudder as she obviously recalled the scene outside the castle but she shook it off quickly and was back in fighting trim.

"We'll find the one who did this and their animal," I said to her. It took a moment but I could see the wheels turning as she analyzed my exact words then she got it. Smart kid.

"And 'their' animal?" she said, "You mean John was a put up job?"

I told her about the soldiers in the radio room, ending my story with, "So the door had to be dead bolted to stay closed against the wind. And with that little window they could see any *thing* knocking on the door. Some *one* had to persuade them to open the door and then let their pet monster in! And no animal would be that thorough in destroying the radio, it was too deliberate. A mind was behind it."

She took a moment to let the information sink in then I saw the fire in her eyes ignite and her bow mouth tightened to a grim-but-cute-line. "Okay, shamus," she said. " How do we get'em?"

This kid had Moxie—at least she could have had if she said the word. For that matter, I'd take hand signals or Morse code if she'd take me.

"We can start with anyone you know who would have had a grudge against Collier or maybe would like to see this film stopped."

She knit her brows and then shook her head. "He was one of the nice guys, I don't know anyone who ever had a cross word with Jonathon. As for wanting this turkey put out of its misery, maybe *The Times* movie critic, but that's it. Ed is a genius in making silk purses out of sows' ears and Bela is hoping this will show off his non-horror movie chops."

Deadline Zombies

"Fat chance of that after this animal farm fun." I realized I had said something off kilter when her face darkened.

"It was also my shot at a lead. Bela insisted I play Una and this could have been my ticket for Hollywood!"

"I'd buy you the ticket myself except that that would put you too far away to ogle." I blurted it out before I was aware of it. Her eyes narrowed to see if I was pulling her leg. When she saw the flush I felt, my Irish blood goes to my ears when I get embarrassed, she giggled gently.

"You buy the ticket, ink slinger and I'll send you photos to ogle." She leaned back and made a sly face and gave a little 'meow' noise like a kitten. Then her eyes shot open and her hand shot to her mouth in a gesture that was almost silent movie pantomime.

"I just remembered," she whispered, "Mike Drucker the effects guy. He used to work in the circus as a lion tamer."

I remembered about his missing three fingers and thought, *and a lousy one, too*, before I leaned over, kissed the startled redhead on the lips and then went in search of a murderer.

Chapter V: Who's Lion now?

I asked around the crew for the seven fingered man but no one had seen jolly Mike for a while. The director had Bela in front of the camera doing close-ups while a crew of extras was being arranged in the back of the set for the next 'set up.' They would be dancing behind the evil sorcerer Busirane while he did a long monologue. I gathered from the crew that they expected that to take a long time considering Bela's English language skills were barely beyond Tarzan.

Nowhere did I spot the Father Christmaseque figure of the special effects man.

Maxine trailed along behind me watching my 'technique' as I slipped casual questions about the bearded man's past to the various assistant crewmembers.

"Sure I've seen Mike back in the corridors by the south gate a bunch of times," said one of the men moving a faux cauldron on the set. "I think he stored the roman candles back there to keep them away from the heat of the lights."

"Thanks," I said. Then I turned to my trailing redhead and said, "I think we had better go see if Santa's been naughty or nice, shall we?"

She had a wide grin on her face and bobbed her head in agreement. "But let's bring a baseball bat or something, okay?"

"You got it, Watson." I reached over and plucked a fake wizard's walking stick with a horse's head on it from a stack of props in a wooden barrel. "Duly armed. Let's go hunting."

I'm sure we looked like a vaudeville act as we trouped outside the ring of lights and into the dark corridors of the old fort. Me in my trench with the oversized walking stick and Maxine, still in her princess gown, but with an old horse blanket wrapped around her shoulders.

Princess-in-a-blanket; that's a snack I could go for.

The moment we passed the ring of lights, the temperature dropped and the creepy factor rose by a few degrees. I went first feeling like a bizarre Babe Ruth and wondering how this was going to get me a Pulitzer and how I could avoid the cat food menu at the same time.

I took considerable courage from the fact that I had the Bronx spitfire at my heels but also worried that I wouldn't be able to do much to protect her if things went bad. An odd feeling for the Lone Word Arranger, let me tell you.

I put a hand back and grasped hers in mine and felt reassured that she was there, as if she could give me the strength to tackle the king of the jungle single-handedly to see her smile.

Deadline Zombies

I was not in my right mind. I was chasing a killer lion with a stickball bat in a dark maze of tunnels with only a slip of a girl for companionship and back-up. Right mind? *I was nuts!*

As we went deeper into the maze of tunnels, we became aware of a light ahead, a dim glow that flickered and made it pretty clear someone had lit a touch a few turns away. The grit of the old stone floors made it hard to move quietly and as we got further from the noise and bustle of the film crew our footfalls came to sound like elephant stomps.

Great, I thought, *Lions don't attack elephants, maybe I can confuse tabby!*

A last, the light ahead made it clear we were just around the corner from the torch and we could hear the sounds of someone moving ahead.

I turned to glance at Maxine and saw that her pretty mouth was set in a tight, grim line. I flashed her a smile and nodded then stepped around the bend ready to swing for the fences.

Mike Drucker was there, all right, on his knees and bent over a gapping hole near the foundations of an inner wall in a side cubicle off the corridor. It had probably been a cell at some time past, but the iron bars, the remnants of which I could still see at floor level, had been removed or had rotted away.

We might as well have come in singing and dancing because the corpulent crook was bent over the hole and so engrossed in what he was doing he wouldn't have hear the Marine Corps Marching Band.

"Okay, Clyde Beatty," I said in a gruff voice to impress myself and Maxine as much as him. "Get what's left of your hands up and turn around."

The chubster jumped a foot when he heard me and whirled faster than I thought possible with a gun in his hand that trumped my stick. So much for my home run.

"You can't have it." His pupils formed little pinpoints in seas of white. "I found it and its mine!" He pointed the gun at the two of us, wavering between the girl and yours truly. His hand was shaking badly and there was a quiver in his voice.

I suddenly felt like a target at a Coney Island shooting gallery and didn't like it. Strangely, I felt more fear for the redhead at my side than myself and that was new one on this cynic's blotter of experiences.

I tried to block her body with mine as I spoke.

"We don't want anything you have to sell, give away or trade," I said. "Except your confession and surrender. Did you really think you could kill somebody and get away with it in the middle of New York harbor?"

His frightened features became confused ones. "I didn't kill anybody. I found the treasure just now when I came here to get my pistol from my safe box."

I looked past him and saw a pile of boxes against the wall of the cell with *EFX* labeled on them. There were also a bunch of fake animal heads scattered about, a donkey, a boar and zebra, all carved in detail in rubber with glass eyes shining eerily in the torch light.

"Don't give me that." I slid a little more in front of Maxine. "You had the perfect cover to smuggle a cat onto this island in your gear. How long have you planned this killing spree, Mike? It must have taken some time to train your cat?"

"You're insane."

"That's the pot calling the kettle black," I said. "I mean, luring those soldiers to open the door for you so you could let your cat in to get them might have made a nice mystery if the latch on the door wasn't broken so I figured it out."

"Figured what out?" His confusion was becoming anger. "What soldiers? What are you talking about?" He waved the gun toward the hole and a little pile of objects that he had obviously just pulled from it. They looked like jewelry and coins, but crusted with dirt and tarnish.

"I found all this just a couple of minutes ago when I came back here. I remembered I had this pistol from my last picture in the prop box and came to see if I had any live ammo for it. I didn't kill anybody."

His denial was adamant and shrill and considering he was waving a boom stick at me, I was just about to believe him, apologize and try to back out when the growl from behind me made my blood freeze.

Deadline Zombies

Chapter VI: Taking a Bite out of Crime...

The growl belonged to the biggest blackest panther I have and ever hope to see. It had to have been four foot at the shoulder and had to have been six feet long excluding the tail.

Its head was down so that it looked at me from under thick bony brow ridges and snarled, its mouth agape to show teeth that looked like scimitars.

I pulled Maxine to behind me (which put her between me and Mike, but right then he was the lesser of two evils) and brandished my walking stick at the cat.

It ignored me.

The ferocious feline growled again and crouched to spring.

I stared frozen like a cigar store Indian as the beast launched itself toward me. It would have taken my head off if Maxine hadn't grabbed my coat and yanked me down to my knees.

The monster flew over my head as Mike discharged his pistol at it. It also ignored that.

The cat landed on the screaming man and then the screaming stopped.

Just as Mike stopped yelling there was a thunderous explosion from the direction of the set.

The whole of the Castle shook and debris and dirt rained down on us. Somehow I had reversed position with Maxine and was on top of the beautiful redhead, wrapping myself around her as chunks of rock thudded into my back like shotgun pellets.

"We have to get out of—" I began. Just then a rock the size of Baltimore hit me on the bean and I went lights out between eye-blinks.

When I came to, there was something very wrong.

My hands were tied behind me and my mouth was wedged open with something that was an effective gag. I moaned through, or around, it and tried to figure out how I got there. I was in the stone cell, propped against the wall and I was not alone.

I swiveled my head. Right beside me was my own personal princess tied up like a Christmas present.

She was as angry as a wet cat and frustrated by a gag that kept her from spewing the invectives she wanted to. She was squirming and hopping up and down with her eyes directed to the other side of me. This made me turn my head and my eyes almost popped out of my head when I did.

Across the little room there was a human figure crouched over the gory form of Mike Drucker like a hideous gargoyle: it was Joe Beauford.

As I turned my head, he looked up with a mad grin on his face. "Nice to see you back with us, Mister Donovan. I was afraid you'd miss all the fun."

He rose from the dead special effects man and picked up the small handful of objects that were spread around the dead man. They were jewels and coins, all of them crusted with the grime of age and now Mike's blood.

"I should have known," I said but it came out a muffled "AH SHH AVE KNNNUWN". And I should have. Who else would have had access to the whole island? Who could move freely about in either the movie crowd or the army barracks? The soldiers would have opened the door to him with no hesitation. But why?

"I'm sure you are wondering why all this," he said in answer to my puzzled expression. "It is because I want what is rightfully mine by birth—this." He held up the trinkets in his hands. "The valuables of the Civil War prisoners who were detained here. One of them was my ancestor, Thaddeus Beauford, a colonel who hid among the enlisted men so the Yankees would not know they had so important a prisoner who had vital secrets about troop positions and strengths. He also had something even more valuable." He held up an elaborate silver buckle that had CSA on the front and odd writing on the back. "On his buckle he carved secret teachings meant for the rest of the family, but all the personal property was stolen from the men and hidden. I got me the job on this island to look for it. I've been searching for two years, quiet like 'til this damn movie company come along and almost discovered my diggings—had to cover some holes hastily. That Collier fellow found one of them, my mistake."

The rambling groundskeeper walked across the room to stand directly over me. I saw, to my horror, that here were flecks of blood around his mouth and on the fur of his parka. Had he been kissing his cat after it did its work? *Nice kitty, such a good murderer for daddy!*

I wondered where the big cat was, nervous that I might be on the menu for the eight o'clock feeding.

I tried to get thought like that out of my head and glanced over at Maxine.

The stunning redhead was still snarling mad but also seemed appalled at the casual evil of the bumpkin. I caught her eye in a glance and tried to make a reassuring face but whatever he had gagged me with made that impossible.

Deadline Zombies

"I'm kind of glad you stuck your nose into things, though," the caretaker killer continued. "I made sure to silence that film crew. I dynamited the entrances to the chamber they were shooting in so they won't be able to bother me in my getaway. I hid the boat on the other side of the island after I killed the captain and the radio men as well, but that old horse of mine just won't be up to doing the work I need to get this to the boat."

He went past us to a shadowed corner of the room and touched a particular stone. There was a rumbling sound and at first I thought the roof was going to go in some sort of aftershock, but then a section of the wall swung aside to reveal a dark cavity instead.

Joe held a torch down so he could illuminate what was within, and Maxine and I gasped. Two large trunks, like treasure chests, were visible in the space. Both brimmed with jewels and coins.

Joe laughed in a very unsettling way. "I'm gonna need some help hauling all this, and you are just the guy for me, Donovan."

He stepped over to Maxine and reached out to touch her hair. "And I wouldn't mind some company from you on my trip to Mexico to spend all this and study great grandaddy's secrets."

When he touched her hair she yelled through her gag and tried to launch herself at him.

He just laughed again and stepped back. "I like a woman that lets the animal come out in her. Us Beaufords know all about letting the animal out in us."

He said that last cryptically like it was some big secret. If I hadn't been so angry for him touching her, I might have guessed at what he meant. As it was, he started to hum to himself and went over to pick up one of the rubber donkey head props from the movie. He ambled over to me and started to slip the thing on me over my head.

I squirmed and struggled, but tied as I was, I was no match for him. He fitted the thing on to me so that my face stuck out through the neck and I wore it as if it were a hat.

Joe stepped away and pulled up a small mirror from Mike's gear to let me see myself. I looked like a real jackass, literally. What I had thought was a gag was teeth like children's blocks shoved in to my mouth and secured with a strap around the back that looked like horse's teeth. And the donkey head made me look like someone from the dance scene I had seen earlier in the afternoon.

"Now that I have great grandpa's formula's I can change more than just myself. He was a great alchemist, but I still find that sympathetic images help it along, ya'know?"

No I didn't. I had no idea what the mental case was babbling about but as long as he was talking he was not hurting Maxine or me so I nodded my donkey head, feeling the equine head bob above me.

"You'll be a good hauler for my goods and the little lady," he chuckled.

He stepped back and began to mutter something under his breath and then my world changed. I felt a strange pull on all my muscles and looked at Maxine.

Her look of terror told me something was going on, but to this day, I'm not sure what really happened.

Chapter VII: How Did I Get *Here*?

I felt the strangest sensation in my body as the ghoulish groundskeeper muttered in his arcane language. It's hard to describe, but the closest I can express it is to say that my whole body was being rebuilt from the inside out or like a suit of clothes being re-cut while I wore it.

My chest felt like an ape was sitting on it and my heart pounded like a Gene Krupa drum solo. My belly felt odd and began to swell and round and I felt myself fighting the urge to double over—not exactly pain but a discomfort with sitting in a normal position. I ended up rolling to my side and contorting as waves of muscular tremors washed over me.

I was vaguely aware of Maxine at my side making unhappy noises and squirming to try to get over to me. I wanted nothing so much at that time then to get my hands up to hold her in my arms and say, "Hey kiddo it ain't so bad," but I would have been lying. It was bad. Real bad.

I convulsed as my muscles knotted and my joints started to ache. My head felt like it was swollen, my temples throbbing to that Krupa solo's rhythm. Distantly I could hear Joe still muttering his strange words but there was a second sound under his words that had the tone of a taunting chuckle.

A pressure behind my sinuses and against my upper jaw pushed just beyond discomfort to the edge of pain. I felt as if I were filling the mask itself with my face, as if I were growing into it. A sound came from me that was half moan and half cry of pain that moved from my chest to stick in my throat till I thought I would choke on it.

Maxine's face strained with the horror of my circumstance, her emerald eyes going wide with concern.

I wanted to yell, "We'll get out of this," but I could barely make the whispered moan of despair that was overwhelming me.

"You will carry my future on your back," Joe said though I barely heard him. "Across the island where the truck can not go. The road is impassable already from the snow."

I couldn't care less about his truck but I was darned if I was going to help him get away after he killed all those people from the film company. I shook my head violently from side to side but the action made the earthquake of a headache I felt jump up a few decibel points.

My arms ached and then my legs started to cramp even worse than they had before. As I watched, the skin on my arms crawled and spasmed visibly. My limbs began to transform to something other than what they had been. My hands balled into fists inside the rubber shapes on the end of my arms. Then my fists twisted into misshapen lumps of flesh at the ends of my arms.

My hands! What is he doing to my hands?' That's when I finally figured out what was happening, He was transforming me to his own thing—a beast for him to use.

The changes continued throughout the whole of my body—arms, legs, back hips, and stomach. Worst of all, my clothes split and shredded as my form grew inside them. I'm shy, okay? This was not how I wanted to be disrobing with a great looking dame like Maxine.

Maxine was crying now, really crying as my body was twisted and deformed in front of her. I moaned then and it came out as a whiny-like sound.

The inhuman sound frightened me and I moaned again, this time a louder more braying noise that echoed off the damp stone of the cell wall.

Meanwhile my body had been elongating and bloating as I enlarged in front of the luscious redhead.

I rolled to all fours and my body gave one more great shudder and the transformation came to an end.

Maxine shook her head from side to side and the tears flowed as she looked at me standing before her. I was taller now and looked down on her. I knew without seeing that my whole form would match the donkey head that encased and had become me.

Joe was real pleased with himself and strutted like a bantam rooster. "I got me sledge right out back we can take across to where I hid the boat and the captain's body." He leaned in to grab my gorgeous redhead by her chin. "You and I will be living it up on Broadway before anyone even discovers the bodies out here."

He made two mistakes in doing that: For one, Maxine was a dancer (I found this out pleasantly later). Tied up or not, she was like a coiled spring. When he got close and then touched her, it pulled the trigger on the spring and she shot up and rammed her head into his expanding gut, sending him backward to careen off the wall.

That's where his second mistake came into play. A donkey who had fallen in love with the gal stood six feet away from her.

I spun around and lashed out with a back kick that slammed him into the wall again, hard enough to daze him.

Maxine stared at me for only a second, yanking off the gag with her still bound hands. She ran to me to nuzzle her head into my now overlarge one and moaned, "Moxie, what has he done to you?"

Deadline Zombies

I enjoyed the contact with her, even if it was filtered through my own donkey hair coat, but I didn't have much time to appreciate it because Joe came out of his stupor and he was angry as an Irishman on the Queen's birthday.

"You will pay for that insult, you tramp!" he bellowed.

I bellowed back, a wild, loud neigh—*Nobody says that about my girl*—And made to shake free of Maxine' embrace.

That's when he began his own transformation. And that answered the last piece of the puzzle about the beast of Governors Island.

His changes were different from the ones he had put me through. First off, he did it willingly. Second, his was not into a sidekick for Gabby Hayes. Beauford's metamorphosis was subtler and more refined, if such a thing was possible. I could see some discomfort on his face before the features became unrecognizable, but there was a feral grin on his face as well and an animal enjoyment of the change. For him this was like slipping on an old a jacket that was little too tight.

While me and the pippin watched Joe Beauford, the caretaker turned into a snarling sleek black cat that looked like a panther but was the size of a tiger.

The change left him dazed for a moment as if his overworked nervous system needed time for the new body to reconnect all the switches and dials in his head. That was our chance to move and we did.

Maxine ran out the door of the cell yelling, "Come on!" and I trotted after on my own unfamiliar limbs.

Maxine slammed the rusty metal cell door behind us and then pointed toward the door at the end of the corridor "That way!"

Even with my four legs, she beat me to the door and flung it open to let a blast of icy air into the hallway. She waved me out and then followed, slamming the second door shut just as the sound of the cell door being smashed echoed over the howl of the wind.

She looked around confused and then to me for some kind of guidance.

Like I would know? I was wearing a horselaugh, naked in the worst blizzard since the Donner party and being chased by the King Kong of cats—how should I know what to do?

But the cute kid needed saving (as did I) so it was time to make like Ken Maynard's Tarzan and save the day. I threw my head and sidled around to indicate I wanted her to get on and she nodded her head in understanding. She hiked up her long gown, *What a set of gams*, and leapt up gracefully on my back.

"Okay, big fella," she yelled over the howl of the storm. " Let's head'em off at the pass."

Then I was off like Seabiscuit but with no idea where I was heading for.

Chapter VIII: The Horseshoe's on the other foot

"Move it you jackass Romeo or we are both going to be cat food," the redhead on my back yelled. She dug her hands into my mane and her heels into my back and clung to me for dear life.

The wind off the bay was cutting and drove the snow at us horizontally. The ice crystals hidden in it were like frozen grains of sand cutting into my exposed side. I had to squint my big eyes and keep my long head bent down to try and see anything that would let me find the trail back to the dock where Joe had tied up the boat.

"Come on, Moxie," she yelled again. "I can hear him."

And so could I—the roaring cry of a great cat where there should be none. And it was getting nearer.

He had made his way out of the Castle and was stalking us. At least he couldn't track us by scent with the wind, but then he didn't have to work too hard—he knew where the boat was, I was guessing.

I was new to my form and could barely see, but the great beast chasing us was familiar with its killer shape and didn't need its eyes to find us even in the driving sleet.

I pushed on despite my feeling of hopelessness because the pippin on my back deserved better even if I was dumb enough to qualify as feline fodder.

It all made a hideous sort of sense now. The radiomen would have opened the door for the groundskeeper and then gone about their business. While their backs were turned, he could have made his change and killed them. I also remembered the dirt on the fingers of that first murder victim—it was the same as the soil in the cell. I was betting the poor guy had found some of Joe's treasure and paid for it with his life.

None of my figuring was in time to rescue me and Maxine from the would-be Lon Chaney so I didn't feel very good about putting together the clues. All I wanted to do was save the girl on my back. If I could do that and get out of it all with my skin intact—man or donkey—I'd be happy.

The roar came through the frozen dark night again, this time nearer and I pushed on, my hooves slipping and sliding in the accumulating snow and on the frozen dirt. There was a moon out, but it was little more than a vague illuminating glow diffused through the swirling flakes. More than once I bounced into a tree or blundered into a thick bush but I couldn't let it stop me.

I felt the weight of the girl on my back as she hugged tighter against the wind. *How the hell did a guy from Brooklyn get here?*

I heard the surf.

It was a clear and distinct sound above the roar of the storm and it was a little off to my left and ahead. My dead reckoning had not been far off. An un-amusing person would have called it horse sense. I would not have laughed.

"The ocean," Maxine called from on my back. "Up there. I can see it."

Sure enough the quality of light was different when we broke through the trees, and in between the gusts of wind the roiling surf was visible. And so was the motor launch. It was tied up to a small dock that jutted out from a sheltered cove. By dumb luck, or great skill and logic as I would write it in any story I lived to pen, we had come out exactly where we needed to be.

Just then the roar of the caretaker cat cut through the night. A dark shape leapt between us and the ocean and I lost hope.

I whined and brayed in annoyance and bucked up to force Maxine off my back. She slid off with a startled protest and landed on her feet.

I turned my head to look at her, hoping that my equine features conveys some of my thoughts: *You and me could have been a great team, cutie; sorry it has to end this way; 'member me!* is what I wanted to say. I think "Neeghyawwh!" came out.

I spun at the next roar from Beauford and charged.

"No, Moxie, don't," she screamed after me, but my mind was made up.

I was annoyed, yes, but I was even more angry at the big southern witchman that had made my life miserable and endangered the sweet kid who had just jumped off my back. I was gonna make him pay for that even if it cost me full measure.

Joe wasn't shy about reacting to my charge. The great cat lowered his head, fixed me in his eyes and sprang.

I'd dodged guys that seemed as big when I played football for Brooklyn College so I faked right then spun and kicked him where it hurts as he arced over me.

The cat roared in pain and did a jig in the air, twisting and falling on his side to writhe in pain.

I didn't let him recover. I raced in and stomped down hard with my front hooves in the jackass equivalent of a one-two punch. One of the blows hit him on the bean with a satisfying crack and he snarled again in pain.

"Go get'em Moxie!" Maxine yelled from the sidelines.

Deadline Zombies

No guy ever had a prettier cheerleader. I would have loved to bask in the glow of her praise, but I had to get her out of there.

I turned to try and communicate to her to run for the boat. I'd realized by then I would never fit on it, so she was leaving solo. That pause gave Joe time to get his bearings and he rolled to his feet and attacked again.

This time he sprang on my right side, sinking his claws into my shoulder and flank and ripping at me with his massive hind legs. It hurt.

I bellowed in agony and tried to dislodge him by spinning first clockwise and then counter clockwise, but he hung on and tore. I figured sure that this was the end of it all and cursed the luck to meet a dame like Maxine and then get turned into cat food. A jackass, I expected a gal like her to make me, but feline fodder was a bit much.

Vaguely I heard Maxine shouting, "The jackass is Moxie, be careful" and wondered, *what the heck is she talking about?* Then the thunder of two rifle shots exploded in the night air.

Suddenly the weight of the dark beast was off my back and I was aware of the sting of the wind on the wounds.

There were more shouts, male voices this time, and the thunder of explosions again.

I fell to my knees, all four of them, and turned my head to witness the finish of the whole affair.

Fanned out around the snarling, bleeding cat were four or five of the film crew members, Bela Lugosi included, with rifles to their shoulders. At a command from the Hungarian matinee idol, they fired a volley of bullets that slammed into the beast and spun it on its back.

It snarled in rage and pain and tried to get to its feet again but at a second command from Bela the guns erupted again. The bullets ripped into the body of the monster and its snarl became a death scream.

'Once more," the Hungarian said, though I swear it sounded like 'vunce muur," and this time the only movement from the animal was where the slugs tore into it.

After the gunfire, the howl of the wind seemed whispered. I could feel the wounds on my side and was pretty sure I was done.

While I watched in a stunned, detached state, the men moved in and Bella fired one last *kill shot* into the head of the creature to be sure and it was all over.

I felt my vision going and remember thinking, *I hope they get Fran to write my obit—she'll lie like a judge and make seem like the best hack since Dickens.* Then I felt Maxine's arms around my hairy neck.

"You were wonderful, Moxie.' She kissed my muzzle and I thought, *what a waste.*

"Are you all right, Maxine, my dear?" Bela stepped up beside the redhead and looked down at her with great concern.

"This is Moxie," she cried, her words hardly understandable though her sobs. "Joe turned him into this!"

"You are distraught," Bela said. "This is not one of my films— " Before he continued with the thought, one of the men yelled from by the body of the great cat.

"Look," he said. "It's changing!"

It was. The great black body shuddered and then, as if frames from a film were superimposed on one another, the process that had changed it from man to beast was reversed. In a few moments the naked form of Joe Beauford, his body punctured by over twenty shots, lay bleeding out on the snow.

When his change occurred, so did mine. I felt all the sensations again as before but telescoped to almost a blink of an eye. In less than a minute, I was naked and shivering on the cold ground of Governors Island.

What's more, when I switched from donkey to just plain me, the wounds went away—as if the magic spell or whatever, had been linked to Joe and the wounds to it. Not that I didn't feel like I'd been on a three day bender, but I was alive and naked and being held by Maxine Keller. What's to complain about a little cold?

Bela threw his coat over my shoulders and I huddled in it as my wits came back to me. I looked at the guns and asked, "how?"

"The base armory had just a simple padlock on the door," he said, "and I had some experience with guns and padlocks during the Great War."

Oh, brother, I thought. *It was Joe who told us that the armory was a vault. He was a liar as well as a psychotic shape changing mass murderer. Who would have guessed?*

Deadline Zombies

Epilogue: Broadway Melody

I write news, not truth—I leave that for the philosophers. So when Whitey read my copy on the murders on Governors Island and started screaming about the cold having addled my brain and that I should take out the nonsense about people changing shape and just write the treasure/wildcat angle or I would lose my job, I knuckled under. His version went out on the wire services and still made quite a splash.

I know, *coward*. But I really needed the regular paycheck 'cause I had a girl to support between her Broadway gigs, at least until Hollywood came calling.

Morty Gluckman was just as happy too. He mined the madness angle for all it was worth for publicity for the picture, and even put, *The Murderer of Governors Island* on the PDC production schedule for next year.

Bela went on to do more of the same, his hopes that playing in a 'class production' would get him out of the neck-biter rut proved in vain.

I kept pounding the keys and was thankful every day for my real arms and legs, especially when I could wrap those arms around the sweetest dish that ever strutted along the The Great White Way. And if sometimes she calls me a jackass. I smile and nod and say, "Yes ma'am. For you, anything."

-30-

John Bull and the Fairy Ring

Prologue: Gone in '21

"For the saints' sake hurry up, Boyd," the tall one yelled. He was dragging the milk cart by the two long handles normally attached to a donkey. It was a crisp fall night with the cold mist coming off Lough Neagh to the east. The moon was just above the horizon and working hard to send a glow through the low clouds.

"I am moving as fast as I can Adair," Boyd snarled. The second man was broad shouldered and deep-chested, with features as rough as the homespun clothes he wore and a tangled mop of black hair. The sack over his shoulders bore down on him with obviously great weight.

"Both of you shut up and keep moving; the hole is up ahead." The third member of the group was behind the cart pushing it over the nodes and bumps in the pasture they were moving through. He was a mean height between the other two, with sandy brown hair and a pleasant face now contorted with the effort of pushing the cart. "If you keep yelling you might as well send an engraved invite for the bloody British troops to shoot you in the head!"

The three of them rolled into the open field out of the shelter of trees, all evidencing a heightened sense of fear. Ahead they saw the hole that they had dug before they drove into Randalstown to rob the bank.

Their eyes glanced all around and now and then behind as if expecting pursuit.

A deer crossing the field ahead of them started at their presence and froze.

When the men kept moving it darted off into the woods on the other side. That made Boyd start as well and he almost dropped the bag on his shoulder. "Oh Jesus!" He cursed.

"Watch your mouth, Billy," the leader of the group said from behind the cart. "You don't need to add blasphemy to your crimes."

"Why not, John," Adair said, "He's got a long way to go to get anywhere near my take on Saint Pete's list." His laugh was deep and echoed across the pasture.

"Will you shut up?" John whispered. "Here it is." He indicated a hole that looked much like a grave in the cool blue moonlight.

Boyd dropped his sack directly into the hole and then sat down hard on the pile of earth beside it. "Who knew being rich was so much work?"

"It'll be all for naught," John said, "if we don't get this buried, hidden and get this cart out of here before the Guardia get their heads out of their arses and track us."

That got the attention of the other two and they moved quickly to off-load the cart. The boxes were heavy, full of gold coins so that it took two men to carry them.

The men lay the boxes in orderly rows in the hole. They worked in silence, saving all their air for the effort of shifting the money. It took them a quarter hour to fill the hole that was just a bit larger than the bulk of the boxes.

"There's a fit!" Boyd said, "Good guess, Johnny." He moved over to the pile of earth and took hold of a spade.

"I don't guess, Billy Boyd," he said, "You should know that; I measured a box at the bank and did the math when I came out here yesterday to dig this." He took the spade from Boyd and began to shovel dirt around the boxes. The other two joined in and soon the hole was level with the earth round it.

"Let's have the sod then," Tommy Adair said. He took the grass sections that had been cut from the surface before the hole had been dug out. It was another ten minutes while he fitted the grass over the hiding place and the other two shoveled the remaining earth onto the cart.

"What are we gonna do about these wheel tracks?" Boyd asked between gasped breaths. "They're pretty deep in the peat."

"Its wet enough that if we go back a different way they should even out after the morning rains." John shoveled in the last of the loose dirt and then went over to kick the remnants of the pile to blend it in.

"I still say this is a far way to go to hide a bit of booty," Tommy said. "We could have hid it in my brother's barn."

"And if you were caught—"

"You know I'd never talk."

"I do, Thomas Adair and that is the truth," John said, "but they'd look in every place you were known to frequent and this money would be lost to the Republic."

"So why here?" Boyd asked. He set his spade on the cart and leaned against it.

"It has no connection to any of us," John said, "and I know they can't plow it so it will stay this way until we want to come get this boodle."

The clouds parted at that moment and the moon, swollen and full glared down at them with an unblinking eye.

"But why here?" Tommy stepped back to admire his work on the sod. In the now brighter moonlight the surface of the ground looked relatively undisturbed. He pulled some brush over it to complete the cosmetic concealment and nodded.

"The *cylch y tylwyth teg*." John said using the old Welsh term since none wished to use the Gaelic term from fear.

"A fairy ring? What are you—'" Tommy's eyes widened and he all but jumped up, staring around him on the ground. "Where is it?"

"Relax, Tommy," John said. "The ring is just north of this spot; exactly ten paces north in fact. That's how we'll find this when all the sod grows back."

"You led us into a field with a fairy ring—" Tommy's tone went shrill. He crossed himself and looked around fearfully. "Have you no respect?"

"Oh, come on, Tommy," John said, "We are not in the ring. It's two meters away from us, but it will guarantee that no one will come to this field. Its one of the reasons—beside the drainage—that old O'Toole will never plow it out."

"Who cares about some mushrooms?" Boyd asked. "You're an old wife, Tommy."

"Oh don't be makin' fun of the wee folk," Tommy said. "Me Da seen them—"

"Your Da was seeing the contents of a bottle of whiskey," Boyd said.

"Me Da was a totaller, Billy, you know that." Tommy said. He was at the tongue of the cart now obviously anxious to leave the treasure site. "Let's get back to the lorry and get back into town before we're missed."

"That, at least, makes sense." John said. "Let's move." He joined the tall man on the other tongue. "Come on, Billy."

"I think its time we brought Tommy into the twentieth century, John. I mean, boyoh, it's bloody nineteen hundred and twenty one years since Himself gave up the ghost for us—all that wee folk, Sidhe stuff is done." He started to move away from their treasure spot, heading due north. "Or hasn't the priest told you that?"

"Don't be jokin' about that, Billy," Tommy said. "It's not to be messin' with the forces of the Tuatha De Danin."

Billy laughed. "You got no fear of British and Ulster bully boys pistols but a bunch of toadstools makes you wet yourself?"

"Come on, Billy," John said. "Stop this nonsense, don't be as bad as Tommy. We have to get back before they know we've nicked the cash."

"You're scared too?" Billy said.

Deadline Zombies

"Oh stop that," John said, "I'm not scared of anything but getting caught if we don't stick to the plan."

"You are scared." He opened his arms with palms up and shook his head from side to side. "You really are!"

"Stop it, Boyd," John said sharply, "We have to get back."

The roughhewn Irishman chuckled to himself and danced backward away from the two at the cart. "Big tough Republicans!" He whirled to look away from his friends to look at the circle ahead of him.

It was clearly visible in the bright moonlight, a circle of mushrooms three meters across. Some of the fungus were almost dinner plate size and all stood out starkly white against the dark green-black of the grass in the field. He stopped on the perimeter of the circle as if it were a physical barrier, and windmilled his arms like a child tottering on the edge of a curb.

"Stop it, Billy," Tommy called, "You've no reason to be doin' this; come away with us."

"I'll be along directly," he said in a jovial tone, " but first I've a mind to take a stroll under the hill, as it were!" As he spoke, he stepped forward into the circle… and promptly vanished.

Gone. As completely as if in a puff of smoke or as if a curtain had dropped between him and the two thieves.

"Billy!" they both screamed and their loyalty made them take a step forward before their fear stopped them.

The two men froze, staring at the empty space where Boyd had stood. The bright moonlight seemed to glint off the white toadstool tops in challenge.

"Billy come back!" they both called. Neither could move forward another step, paralyzed by the arcane occurrence they had witnessed.

"What do we do?" Tommy asked when minutes had gone by with no sign of their friend would reappear.

"What can we do?" John said, "We can't go after him." He voice trembled with fear he had never known before. "We have to stick to the plan." He went back to grab the tongue of the cart and Tommy followed suit.

The two of them hauled the cart back to the lorry hidden by the edge of the road a half-mile distant road. They loaded the cart into the back and drove off toward Randlestown.

They only made it to Castle Dawson before a Constabulary roadblock stopped them. They tried to run and the Ulster forces, mistakenly believing the stolen money to be in the lorry, opened fire.

The bullets ended both lives and with them died the secret of the stolen currency and the fate of William Michael Boyd.

Deadline Zombies

Chapter I: The Cock and Bull Story of 1937

The thing I like about my father country, Ireland is that the pub is not the place where the down and out crawl to hide in a pint of beer and lament the horror of their daily life but rather it is the center of the community, sharing, with the church, the sacrament of confession, albeit over the rim of a tankard.

So it was when I entered Randalstown the small town in County Antrim, in the North of Ireland where my family had come from, I went straight to a little gin mill with the image of a rooster and a bull on the sign called the Cearac *Ba*.

Baile Raghnail, in the Old Tongue was the town my father's father came from and I had promised dad I would visit it some day. I was able to keep that promise when the chance to cross the pond from New York to cover a sensational murder trial in London came my way. I got the chance to make the visit to the Old Sod when the trial ended early with the suicide of the accused. I flew over to Belfast, rented a car and drove the hour and change to the little hamlet that was between the towns of Antrim and Toome.

The village had a population of barely four thousand and most of them somehow seemed to be jammed into the pub the day I showed up. The wood in the dark smoky room looked old enough to have been grown in the Garden of Eden and most of the codgers who were yelling from behind their beer mugs looked old enough to have cut it themselves. The accusations were flying across the suds like a Senate hearing back in the States.

No one even looked my way when I slipped in the door. A skill, I guess, as a newspaperman

I was wearing a beat up old trench coat and a battered fedora against the constant Irish drizzle. In an attempt to keep a low profile I kept the hat on and just settled into a shadowy space near the dartboard and listened.

"How in the name of the dark one are we supposed to pay the taxes at this new rate?" The speaker was an old guy, pink nosed and white hair. It seemed a stiff breeze would blow him over.

"Now stop saying what we all know, O'Toole," the bartender said.

Suddenly a little fellow next to me was handing me a thick warm stout without even looking at me. I sipped the blood of the land and nodded a thank you.

"We are here to come up with some sort of plan." The Bartender continued.

"Plan of what?" O'Toole said. "In the old days we'd just run that windbag of a tax assessor out of town on a rail!"

"You know I don't think anything of John Balfour," another of the patrons said, "But he is the law; what can we do?"

The little guy next to me, a thin faced, sharp-featured fellow with a pug nose and longish blond hair that was almost white whispered at me, "Balfour's the English git they sent to change the tax rates on the lands."

I 'uhhmned' him and sipped my brew, enjoying the show.

"We can call for Mike Collins," O'Toole said, "He'll get his boys to come up here and kick these—"

"Oh don't start that again," a female voice piped in from my left. A petite thing with raven black hair stepped out of the shadows and into the center of the room. "Your bully pulpiting for the Republic cost me my father—"

"Now, Mary," another denizen of the pub said in a calming tone, "We know nothing good come to you out of the troubles but—"

"But nothing, Shamus Flynn," she said, "We have to go to Belfast and deal with those thieves directly instead of their bully boys out here."

"Oh it'll be a bit of a row now," my blond play-by-play commentator whispered. "He's gonna get her goat up!"

"Mary, Mary, Mary," Flynn said, shaking his head. "They aren't going to listen to us in Belfast—they still think we are holding out money on them. All they know are the boot and the bullet!"

"And what are you calling for if it isn't the boot and bullet, Shamus?" she said. She was a spitfire and reminded me of the little Broadway dancer I had been seeing for the last half a year though my spitfire was a Jewish girl by way of Moshalu Parkway in the Bronx. "If we can't do this with the local law we have to get those leather heads in London to listen to us; Baldwin wouldn't but maybe this new bloke will. If now we will go to the press."

My ears perked up with that statement and I set my beer mug aside (relax, it was empty already) and pulled out my notebook to get to work. I fumbled a hand in my coat because I couldn't find a pen.

The little guy next to me held out a pencil to me and I took it with a nod and started scribbling.

"Who is going to listen to a little village like us?" O'Toole asked. "We t'ain't but a mud hole to those Toffs in Parliament."

There was fair amount of grumbling after that one, then another of the pub crowd was arguing for then against the tack of trying to get attention to their plight in official channels.

Deadline Zombies

The girl stepped back to the space beside me and seemed to notice me for the first time hacking away in my notebook. She pointed to me and said, "Hold it, everyone, we have a spy here!"

The temperature of the room dropped a few hundred degrees at that moment as all eyes turned toward me. I stopped writing and looked up to flash my best 'don't shoot' smile. I looked for support from my blond buddy but he had made himself scarce.

"Hi folks," I said. "I'm not a spy; I'm a reporter."

The crickets could have heard a pin drop at that moment.

"American?" The bartender asked.

"Moxie Donovan, New York Daily Star!" I pulled out my press card and held it up like a cross against a vampire. I walked the circuit of the room letting every one of the occupants look at my credentials.

"What'cha be doing here?" One of the codgers asked.

"I uh—"

"Donovan?" Another asked. "Any relation to Old William Donovan?"

"My Grandfather, sir," I said hoping Grandpa didn't owe any of them money. "It is the reason I am here, to see from whence I come."

There was a new round of grumbling from all in the room with the gist of it being "Why trust this newcomer."

"Gentlemen and ladies." I said, "If you will give me the facts as they have occurred I will do my best to make sure the world knows of them. I have a friend at *The Times* in London and will make sure this gets voice there; Even Chamberlain reads the times."

They started to all talk at once but I held up a hand. "I didn't mean right now. Let me talk to you all over the next couple of days: walk the town and see it all for myself. I will tell the story, but I will tell the truth; I won't lie for either side. Fair enough?"

They all looked to one another and then back to me.

"If the gent behind the bar will kindly refill my beer mug I'll step outside while you talk it over. In any case I hope you'll at least not shoot me before I see the family homestead." I held my mug up for the barkeep, who seemed amenable to the refill.

I stepped outside the door of the pub and leaned against the aged wood of the jam sipping my warm beer while the town wags went back to loud discussions. I surveyed the old home sod and reflected on what I recalled of my grandpa's descriptions of the place.

He always called it a 'mud hole' but it looked pretty green and civilized to me. Not an outhouse in sight.

Randalstown was what the tourist types might call picturesque: waddle and daub buildings with thatch roofs. It had a history of linen and iron industries that was commemorated by a memorial in the middle of the town made from the original turbine used to generate electricity for the town salvaged from the Old Bleach Linen Company. I could see the old linen mill chimney from the factory to the west over the low roofs of the town.

The beer went down smoothly. Grandpa came through Ellis Island with more in his pocket than most and started a roofing business in Brooklyn.

"It's a good little town, isn't it?" My little buddy from inside the pub was at my side with a pint in his own hand.

"Yes," I said. "Seems like a hard place to leave but my granddad never talked about it much—not at all really."

"He was a sly one, Willy Donovan," the little man said.

"You've heard about him?"

"They know him here-abouts still." He gave a satisfied sigh as he downed his drink. "Quite a horse trader that one was."

We stood and sipped for a bit and I became aware that the sounds inside had died down.

"I guess the vote is in." I expected a comment from the blond but I realized I was alone again. At least until the girl Mary came out the door of the pub.

"Okay, Tom Mix," she said to me, "The group has given you to me to keep." Her eyes were blue and bore into me with a toughness that could have been from Flatbush.

"Well," I said, "I thought this was a conservative country." I gave her the grin that launched a thousand punches and she shot back a pout.

"I have my Da's room at my cottage out the edge of town." She said. "I know you'll be perfect gentleman 'cause I also got my Da's shotgun."

"Yep," I said, "that's the etiquette I grew up with too." I offered my arm to her. "My car's over there."

I let her lead me and thought again how much she reminded me of my dancer. Maxine would never need a shotgun though, her right hook was good enough to enforce chastity in Barrymore.

Deadline Zombies

Chapter II: Both Sides of a Mountain are Uphill

On the brief drive to the cottage my hostess and guide, Mary Boyd, filled me in on the lay of the local political land.

"This town seems to be cursed," she said with a deep disgust in her voice. "Just before the Republic there wasn't a lot of fighting around here but some splinter groups got it into their head to try and help Collins down south with robberies. One of the groups held up the bank here in Randalstown in twenty-one and got off with over a hundred thousand pounds of coins and notes."

We pulled up in front of a cottage just outside the town proper. It was over a small stone bridge and off to the side of the road backing up to a field of hay. It was a small place, one story of stone and plaster that looked like it was as old and enduring as the land but the thatched roof looked like it could use some work. It reminded me of a dowager trying to keep up appearances.

"My father was in on that robbery," Mary continued, "The other two were killed in a shootout with the Constabulary."

"And your father? Did he get away with the loot?" I had asked those sorts of questions with lots of cons' families. It never gets easier so I just blurt it out and hope they don't swing.

"No one knows what happened to Da," she said with a casualness that told me she had answered that question a thousand times. "Or the money—none of it has ever shown up. My Ma certainly didn't get any of the loot; the shame and the poverty killed her three years after the robbery."

She stepped out of the sedan and was greeted by a setter who came charging around the building and jumped up to lap her face.

"Easy, Fergus!" she called. "It's not a elegant place, but it's home."

There was little I could say so I went to the trunk of the car (they call it a 'boot" over there) to get my suitcases. The pup saw me and raced over to say hello with his muzzle and tongue.

While I was getting some puppy love, another car came down the road from outside of town and pulled up next to mine on the shoulder. Two men stepped from the dark green car and stood in such a way as to block my car if I wanted to leave. Their attitude and ill-fitting suits marked them as flatfeet: probably government rather than local.

They stood unmoving while the passenger side of the sedan opened to disgorge an extraordinary figure. He was barely five and half feet tall and seemed equally as round standing on spindly legs. He had a dark blue suit-coat and striped morning pants and low crowned top hat.

"Good afternoon, Miss Boyd," he said in a high-pitched voice that seemed absurd coming from his bulk. "I see you have a visitor."

The two stone-faced fellows standing near the fender of my car regarded me like a specimen in a zoo. They had more the look of strikebreakers than diplomats. Real old school flatfoot types for sure.

"What do you want, John Balfour?" There was enough venom in her tone to kill a half dozen mongeese.

"Your tone is not appreciated, Miss Boyd," he said. "You are speaking to the Crown when you address me; and I do only what is required." He had a pleasant smile despite his appearance. He waddled toward us and Fergus capered to him, leaping and barking with excitement. The corpulent man evidenced delight with a little giggle and patted the pooch on the noggin.

"What are you doing here, Balfour?" she asked. "Haven't you already told me I live in a palace and have to pay accordingly?"

"Miss Boyd," he said calmly, "I do my job; and you need to allow an actual assessment of the interior of your home." He gestured toward the two men and they moved toward the door.

"Keep out of my home!" Mary commanded. "You have no right-"She moved in to block their paths and one of them grabbed her arms to move her aside.

Fergus seemed to sense that something wasn't Kosher and started to bark and become agitated. The second cop grabbed for the dog's collar and when the dog snapped at him he produced a sap and reared back to strike the animal.

"Hold it bub." I stepped in and grabbed the raised arm.

He reacted like a true officer of Justice and spun to jab me in the gut, knocking the air out of me.

Mary yelled at her assailant and kicked him hard in the shins.

He cursed a blue streak and reached in his own jacket for a sap.

"Stop it this instant!" the squeaky voiced Tweedle Dee called. "There is no need for this violence." He looked directly at me while I was trying to remember how to breathe.

The round man extended his hand to me. "I am Jonathon Balfour, His Majesty's Tax Officer for this district, sir. And you are?"

"Moxie Donovan, *New York Daily Star*." I pumped his arm looking for an oil gusher with my fake enthusiasm.

"A Yank?" He seemed surprised to hear my accent in the hinterlands. And he wasn't pleased that I was a reporter, of that I was certain by the look he shot to the two guards.

"Guilty as charged," I said with my 'I'm an idiot' pasted on smile still sending out the wattage. I enjoyed the fact that the two goons were looking at me like I was roast beef and they were Rin Tin Tin.

"And why are you here-em Mister—eh...?"

"Donovan—" I pulled out my magic credentials again.

"...Donovan. Randalstown is not the crossroads of the world."

"But it is the birthplace of great men," I said. " The Donovans to be exact."

"Ah, returning to the ancestral roots?" The thought seemed to amuse him and he gave a short high-pitched chortle.

"Yep," I agreed. " That and doing a little local color piece for my editor and *The London Times* on conditions in the small towns in Ireland." My manner stayed jovial but I put a very professional spike in my statement. I followed up by pulling out my trusty notebook and my blond friend's pencil. "Could I have your exact name for the article? Was that one 'L' or two in Balfour?"

His eyes went wide and he quickly motioned to his goon squad to get back in his touring sedan. "We shall be back tomorrow after I assess O'Toole's pasture land, Miss Boyd; I expect access to your dwelling."

"You actually scared them off," Mary said. "You may be right about the power of the press."

"Nothing like it," I said as I hoofed my suitcases through the low lintel of her cottage door. "Where do I put these?"

It was a comfortable main room that had a slate fireplace with a cook pot hanging in it and large wooden table. The whole of the place had, like the outside, a sense of age and permanence. Doors led off to rooms that were obvious new additions, and by new, I mean a generation or two old.

"That room there was my Da's," she said pointing off to the right. "You can put your things in there."

The bedroom was rustic like the rest of the home with a bed, chair, dresser and a small window that gave a view of the fields behind the house. On the dresser were two framed photos, one a wedding picture of what must have been her father and mother and one of a miniature version of Mary seated on the shoulders of the man from the wedding picture. I threw my coat and hat on the bed and went back outside.

When I came out of the bedroom I made note of the shotgun hanging ominously over the fireplace and the fact that Mary was standing by it while stirring the contents of the simmering pot.

"Hungry?" she asked.

"For home made stew? You bet!" I sat down at the table and watched her. She was young but there was strain at the corners of her eyes and her hands showed hard work. I wondered how a rural girl had not married already but then I thought about the suitors available—farm boys, mostly out of work themselves most of the time or maybe gone off to the big city to make their fortune; might not be a big pool to choose from. Then again from what I'd seen she was a spitfire and might scare most of potential Prince Charmings.

She ladled out a deep bowl of dark brown stew that smelled like childhood memories of my Grandmother and gave me a piece of coarse bread to go with it. She sat across from me and started to eat in silence.

Fergus sat quietly at the foot of the table, big eyes begging silently and seemed to enjoy my ravenous consumption vicariously.

After a time I felt safe to ask, "So what was that with butterball and the gargoyles?"

She stared at me for a moment, I guess trying to figure out my vernacular (a lot of people seem to do that) and then said. " We've had it hard around here for a long time, a lot of people had to mortgage family lands, me included, just to make due. That pompous windbag showed up here a couple of weeks ago and said he was sent by the Ministry of Transportation to survey roads. He was a miserable liar. It was very clear from the start that he was a tax assessor when the first revaluations of land taxes started to arrive and the bank that holds the notes on most of the land around here gets it all because none of us have more than we barely need to scrap by."

"That sounds pretty straightforward," I said, "you should be able to protest through normal channels, right?"

She made a disgusted snort. "If it were just about the taxes; but they wanted to punish the whole region for the activity at partition and Randalstown particularly for the robbery. And me because they still think my Da has the money somewhere. And the rich Protestants in Belfast, lap dogs of the English get the land as a prize. Land that's been in some of our families for five generations or more."

"Try and force you off the land to make your old man come out of hiding to help you, huh?" I had finished my plate and looked hopefully to her for a second bowl. She got up and ladled out some more that I took to with gusto; she wasn't a bachelorette because she couldn't cook.

"It seems that way." She said. "But I don't know where Da is and I don't have the money. And I can't lose this farm; it's all I have."

She was doing her best to not whine but it wasn't hard to see how deeply this was affecting her.

"Sounds like a Mascot serial to me, Mary," I said, "Evil land baron uses crooked sheriff to drive homesteaders off their land with supposed force of law; enter crusading cowboy journalist to save the day. Which is

Deadline Zombies

why you need Tom Mix here to shine some light under the rock to scare the snakes away. You saw how he reacted today; ghouls like Balfour worry about looking bad with the voters. I'll make some noise, babe, don't you worry."

This got a smile from Mary that was fetching enough to make me worry about my dancer telepathically detecting my roving eyes. "Tonight I'll wander down to the pub for some local chat and start my real notes. Then tomorrow I want to take a tour of the Donovan family estates, or the ruins thereof before I follow Rolly-Polly around to see how he works."

"You can do both at once," she said as she cleared the plates, setting them down for the patient Fergus to lick. "Your grandfather's home was on the O'Toole's field that John Bull's looking at tomorrow."

Chapter III Like a Circle in a Spiral

My evening in the 'Cock and Bull' pub just reinforced what the dangerously charming Miss Boyd had stated, namely that the powers that be seemed to have it in for the locals with increased and arbitrary tax enforcement and harassment. Some of the locals even hinted that some livestock thefts were not the work of poachers but "Government Stooges," to put it mildly and in language that can see print.

A number of the locals, when they found out I was related to 'Old Willy Donovan', had to tell me stories about how he conned this land owner out of a horse or swindled some English Toff out of his carriage money at cards.

Grandpa, who would have known?

I even found a fellow, older than water, who had actually known my Grandfather when he was a child. "Ay, Old Willy Donovan was a clever fellow," the old codger said with the third drink I'd bought him. "He was quiet all right, make no mistake, but when he spoke you knew he'd been thinkin' about what he said." The old fellow chuckled and took another swill of the ale. "He was not wantin' ta be farmin' so he was always on to some scheme about how to get out of here but had no way or no hope till one day that circle appeared in his field."

"Circle?" I asked.

"Aye—the Fae circle-just showed up one day and started to occupy his thoughts. Didn't tell many folks: he told me cause I was sort of a mascot for him, but he swore me to secrecy. Kept a sayin' he was gonna find a way to trick the wee folk out of their gold and get himself over to America—things were bad back then, you know, lots of folks was hungry not least of all Willy. Then one day he come into town sayin' he'd sold his land to O'Toole for a song and was off to America! Nothin' he had but a big pack on his back that seemed awful heavy! O'Toole tried to live in the place but got himself drunk one night and burned the place down in—hmm—Oh nine I think it was. After that just left the field as it was."

I knew my granddad never talked about his time in 'the old country' but he was developing into an interesting fella, a real man of mystery.

Mary had not made the pub trip with me and I'd decided to walk so I slipped on my hat and waved goodbye to the denizens of the pub knowing I'd be seeing most of them in the morning at O'Toole's place.

The moon was up and it was an unusually clear fall night. Somewhere far off a dog was barking. It was an almost perfect night and it made me feel somehow connected to my grandfather. For a moment I found myself wondering why how he could have had the courage to leave so bucolic a scene to cross the frightening ocean and enter the wild canyons of New York to begin a new life.

I hadn't gone twenty feet when I became aware of footsteps on the wet cobbles behind me. I glanced over my shoulder to see the little blond guy ambling along behind me.

"Evening, Yank," he said. "Mind if I walk along with you? I live out this way a bit." He was puffing on a clay pipe. He had on a dark red jacket and wore no hat. "Having fun visiting the old land?"

"It's getting interesting," I said. "It's never as calm down on the farm as it seems." I looked over at him and he had a half smile on his face enjoying the night as much as I was.

"You got a name, bub?" I asked.

"Fitheal Mac Tir," he said. He blew out a smoke ring and poked a finger through it. "You're old Willy Donovan's kin, ain't ya?"

"Yes," I said. "You have more stories about him?" I was beginning to feel like I was related to Jesse James or something.

"Oh I have stories," he said with a shade of vitriol in his tone. "He was a real squirrel, he was." His eyes darkened with a recollection then he gave a short sharp laugh. "Could strike a deal or dance around a word of promise like one of the 'folk' himself. A real squirrel."

"What did he swindle your grand pa out of?"

"Oh, he made a good deal on some land that cost my family some," Fitheal said, "But I have to say he done it with style, Old Willy did."

We reached the bridge at the end of town and I stopped to look back at the village behind us. It looked like an etching in blue and silver, so very different from the neon glow of Gotham across the sea. I hadn't been away long enough to be homesick so I could appreciate the beauty of the little hamlet.

"Maybe it is a little slice of Heaven, like they say, Fitheal." I turned back to look at the little guy but he was gone. All that was left was a lazy 'O' of smoke drifting in the breeze.

"You have a future as a cat burglar, buddy boy," I said to the empty space. I had a sudden creepy feeling and the quiet of the country air suddenly felt a little unnatural.

"Maybe I know why you left now, Grandpa," I said. Then I went into Mary's cottage to get a bit of sleep.

* * * *

Right after breakfast, I drove Mary about two miles out of town, rounding Lough Neagh and going along the main road for another couple of miles to where the road split near O'Toole's farm. There we came on several other cars, horses and wagons pulled off to the side of the road. It was like a mini-carnival with several dozen people, men women and children standing there waiting.

"What are they all doing here?" I asked.

"O'Toole's land is one of the biggest pieces around here, what with your grand Da's land and his joined. If we let that windbag Balfour tax it without protest he'll ruin us all!" She moved off into the group of villagers leaving me alone to pull out my ever-present notebook and start writing observations.

Just then the ringmaster or, perhaps the main attraction showed up in his long green sedan. This time it was followed by a second car filled with uniformed Constabulary. The taxman exited the car to a chorus of boos while the cops and his two 'civilian' guards formed a cordon around him.

"Man I wish I had a camera," I cursed.

"Will this do?" I jumped as Fitheal was standing beside me with a genuine box camera. "I had a feeling things would be pretty photogenic here today, what with old John Bull coming to 'beard the Irish Lion" and all that."

"I could kiss you," I said. "But I'll settle for paying you fair pay for any pictures you get."

"I like money, Yank," he said. "That is for sure."

I was beginning to feel like a real reporter and all as I moved along with the surge of the crowd that followed the portly official off the road up a path through trees and out onto an large open field. The rotund centerpiece of the bizarre parade seemed to pay little attention to the jeers that were coming his way.

I ran up along side of him and started earning my pay. "Mister Balfour why is revaluing this piece of land so very important?"

He regarded me from beneath hooded eyes and crimped the corners of his mouth down in annoyance. "I am doing the Crown's work, sir. A fair assessment of this land is necessary to keep the coffers of the government full for the defense of this nation and the care for the poor." He grinned, very satisfied with his answer and that I was writing furiously to take it all down verbatim.

"But is it not true that you will be making folks poor by excessive taxation? Being from the states I have a fair memory that excessive taxes are what gave the founding fathers reason to kick you English out in the first place."

He stopped in his tracks and his face reddened with a contained anger that flared up. "Sirah," he said, "These rebels hide their assets and then expect to go on the dole to strain the fabric of this nation."

We were standing at the edge of the field now, the crowd behind him in a semicircle, his guards posted at the four corners around us. Lough Neagh was visible off in the distance across gently rolling fields. Fields that were all plowed save for the field we were standing on the edge of.

"This field, for instance," he said, "O'Toole has listed it as un arable." He spread his arms to take in the several acres before us. "It is a perfectly good field; he is just too lazy to work it."

"You snake tongued devil!" Old Man O'Toole yelled as he pushed his way through the crowd. "It can't be worked and that swindler Donovan knew that when he sold it to me; I can't plow it out—the Circle's practically right in the middle of it there!"

"The what?" Balfour said. "What circle?"

Half the crowd pointed across the field where I could see the white tops of some large mushrooms. "The *cylch y tylwyth teg*," several whispered voices offered.

The government officer and myself exchanged confused looks.

"A fairy ring," Fitheal whispered at my elbow. He held up the box camera and snapped a shot of the puzzled look on Balfour's face.

I looked over at him and repeated. "A fairy ring?"

The little blond guy smiled knowingly. "A fairy ring, known as a fairy circle, elf circle or pixie ring. Some folklore says fairy rings are made by flying dragons; once a dragon had created such a circle, nothing but toadstools could grow there for seven years. It's where the Sidhe store their treasure—or so they say—and they guard the rings very jealously."

"You are joking, correct?' I said. "The reason you can't plow this field is a bunch of toadstools?" At that moment the cartoonish tax man and I both looked at O'Toole with the same expression.

"Anyone who steps into an empty fairy ring will die at a young age," O'Toole said, "or worse, be taken by the Wee folk."

"I have never heard such rubbish!" Balfour said.

"Don't taunt the Wee folk," Mary said, "Even you can't be that foolish."

"Foolish is not developing perfectly good land for a crop and expecting a man of my stature to give credence to such reasoning." He moved further out into the field so that he was standing near the edge of the circle of mushrooms.

The crowd hung back, save for me and my blond sidekick who continued to tell me about the rings. "The French say that fairy rings are guarded by giant bug-eyed toads that cursed those who violate them. Mortals entering a fairy ring—anyone who violates a fairy ring- becomes invisible to mortals outside and may find it impossible to leave the circle. Some say fairies force the mortal to dance to the point of exhaustion, death, or madness."

"You should be writing this article," I whispered. "I'll get all that from you later."

"I've got that and more, Yank." He smiled. "I know a bit about them is sure."

"This field is perfectly fine," Balfour proclaimed. "You are a shirker, Mister O'Toole. Let this be a lesson to—"

"You bag of balderdash," the old Irish farmer said, "You want to ruin me!"

"You will be ruined," Balfour said, "but it will be by your own hand because you believe in this childish superstition; just like all you Irish are children who need the strong hand of the Crown to guide you."

The crowd started to mumble and grumble and move forward repeating "John Bull is a fool!" The five men who were detailed to protect the Northern Ireland tax official faced the villagers with knit brows and clenched fists anticipating a rough time.

"I will show you, you idiots how silly it is," Balfour said, "Just watch this." He stepped forward as he spoke, crossed over the white caps of the circle and abruptly disappeared faster than Fatty Arbuckle's career.

Chapter IV: In the Circle of Strange

Things happened fast after the tax man pulled his Houdini: the crowd all gasped and took a step back as if it were choreographed; the guards all whirled and ran to the edge of the circle; and old O'Toole yelled, "Stop them fools!"

The villager surged forward and grabbed the guards before the men could step over the line of the mushrooms just as the corpulent taxman blinked back into existence within the circle of the mushrooms.

"There," Mary called. " He's there!" Even the guards realized this was not a riot and stopped struggling as they stared wide-eyed at their boss.

Balfour stood in the center of the circle with a scared deer expression on his face, his mouth slack and his breath coming is short gasps. He looked around him with evident confusion and not a little bit of terror.

"What have you done to me?" He yelled. He took a run at the circle's edge but the strangest thing happened: he stopped dead at the edge of it as if he'd hit a glass wall and bounced back into it. He fell back on his butt with a high-pitched squeal of terror.

The villagers all burst into an uneasy laughter at the sight that made the official's red-faced embarrassment more profound. "Stop that this instant!" he screamed. "Help me!" He reached up toward his guards who, unrestrained by the crowd made no move toward him.

Many in the crowd crossed themselves even as they snickered at him.

"It's a Fairy ring for sure," O'Toole yelled, "and you a fool for tempting the Wee folk with your arrogance."

The rotund man sprang up and once more tried to exit the circle but with the same comical and frightening result. He stood there pounding on invisible barrier that held him in place and began to scream. "You rebellious devils! Let me out of this thing. This is your doing. This is treason!"

"This is ridiculous," Mary stepped almost to the edge of the toadstools, "You were the one who threw yourself into that thing; nobody pushed you."

"You are a criminal, woman," The portly man was red-faced now and his voice came out as a series of squeaks. "And I will have you brought up on charges. Sergeant," he yelled at one of the uniformed cops. "Arrest this woman and then get me out of here!"

The confused policeman looked at his boss and then at the crowd that surrounded him and hesitated. It was clear the officer knew there was no reason to arrest her and that if he did there *would* be a riot. Mary stared at the Bobbie as if daring him.

"What are you doing," Balfour screamed, "I want her arrested." He was pounding on the invisible barrier now, just a few feet away from us. It looked like a Bugs Bunny cartoon and would have been funny if his fear had not been so real.

The crowd around us was getting agitated from his screams, their long frustration with the government causing them to jeer back at the man's horror and helplessness.

"You aren't so high and mighty now," O'Toole sneered at the official." We ain't such 'simple folk now are we, John Bull?"

"O'Toole," Balfour yelled. His voice was so high pitched now and his breaths so gasped that it was hard to understand him. "I will tax you into debtors prison if you do not get me out of here." His fists were getting raw from pounding on the invisible barrier.

I was writing furiously; I was going to win awards for this story if I didn't get put away for being crazy. "I hope Fitheal is getting some good shots of this," I said to Mary. "I could get front page for this odd ball set up."

"Who is Fitheal?" She asked with a curious expression on her face. The two of us were inches from the red faced Rolly-Polly prisoner. I could feel his breath yet it was like there was a clear steel wall between him and us.

"He's the little guy who I hired to photograph all this," I said to her. "I met him in the tavern. Funny little guy."

She looked at me oddly and all but ignored the taxman inches from her. He was loosing steam anyway, his wheezing yells almost inaudible.

"What's his full name?" She asked me.

"Uh... Fitheal Mac Tire I think he said it was." For the life of me I couldn't see why it mattered with all that was going on around us.

A look of horror came over her face and her eyes darted all around, "That's not a man's name, Donovan, it's a Sidhe's name. It means Wolf Spirit!"

As she said it the crowd behind us seemed to swell and jammed into us and I felt a hand on my back. I was pushed forward and slammed into Mary and the both of us were propelled over the white-topped mushrooms and into the circle.

My first thoughts were anger at whoever had pushed me and worry that I had hurt Mary. Then I came to realize I couldn't hear Balfour yelling anymore, or indeed any sound at all.

The next thing that struck me as odd was that I was lying on the mossy ground in darkness. Not that my eyes were closed, but that it was night.

I couldn't have been knocked out, I thought. I looked over at Mary who was right beside me. Her expression was a horrified one but her eyes were focused beyond me.

I rolled over to see a stocky guy standing there staring at the two of us with a puzzled expression. Beside me Mary whispered, "Papa?"

The guy looked exactly like the image of the guy in the photo on the dresser in the bedroom at Mary's place. Exactly as he had in the photo taken almost two decades before.

"Mary?" The man asked. His coarse featured face went through every range of emotion I have ever seen on a human kisser from confusion to joy. "But how can you be my little Mary—The Ring!"

"The fairy ring, Da!" She climbed over me and ran to the figure throwing her arms around him. She held on for dear life.

I pushed myself to my feet and looked around. It seemed as if we were standing exactly where we had been but it was deep in the night with a full moon looming over all in the sky above us. There was no one else around.

When I turned my attention to the two Boyds, they were still holding each other with both of them in tears.

"Margaret is dead?" Billy Boyd was saying. They whispered forehead to forehead.

"No one knew what happened to you, Papa," Mary said. "The other two were killed. They never told about you or the money."

"We buried it outside the ring," he said, "And then I made a foolish mistake—"

"Could somebody explain to me what is going on?" I asked. "Where are we exactly?"

"You are in the land of the Fae, Yank," Fitheal's voice from at my left elbow made me jump.

"Will you stop doing that!" I whirled to look down at him.

He was a very different little guy from my 'photo-partner of just a few minutes before. His features seemed sharper, his ears poking out from his long hair came to points and his eyes glowed like a wolf's in the bright moonlight.

"Can't help it, Yank," he said with a jovial tone. "You mortals are just not that observant."

"You're a – a-leprec-"I began.

"Don't say it," Fitheal said, "I have to always tell people not to confuse my folk with leprechauns. We're the clurichauns. We're free spirited sorts."

"You mean you're all drunken sprites!" Mary pulled from her father's grasp. "And mean-spirited to keep my Da here."

Fitheal frowned. "Now there is no need to be harsh; I've given him chances to leave!"

"He taunts me with puzzles and tells me if I can solve them I can leave, but they have no solution." The unsuccessful thief said.

"Not so," the little guy smiled wolfishly. "I know how many grains of sand are in the beach because I can take the time to count them; I know how many hairs are on the king's head because I can sneak in and count them. I know where the bodies are buried and the music sounds sweetest!" He did a little jig step then and laughed. "There is no task I can not accomplish, no place I can not go but you—are sadly mortal and human to boot. A sad combination."

"I repeat," I said, " What the heck is going on?"

"You are a lot simpler than your Grandda', Donovan," Fitheal said, "You are in my circle with my gold...." He waved a hand and suddenly a stack of gold coins became visible around the perimeter of the circle. "You have to play by my rules."

"You can't trust a Wee one," Mary said, "They always equivocate like the devils they are."

"Or worse, lawyers!" I added.

"You wound me," Fitheal said. "I always keep my word—else your Grandda would not have left the home land with a sack of my coins."

"That was you?" I asked.

"He was almost one of the folk, that fella. Sharp he was!"

"But why are we in here?" I asked.

"You were the ones that came to my bailiwick," the little guy said, "Particularly you, Yank."

"This is about getting back at my grandfather, isn't it?"

"Would I be that petty?" He smiled in what he must have thought was an innocent way but he looked like Red Riding Hood should be running from him. "Truth be told that is a fine thing, but I also happen to hate those English Toffs as much as you mortals do!"

He waved his hand again and the air around us seemed to crackle with energy. The darkness faded and daylight seeped in around the edges of the reality. Like a double exposed image the clearing as it was when we fell into it appeared and we could see the villagers surrounding the crying Balfour.

"He's in a different time and place," our Fae guide commented, "but you can watch while I have a bit of sport with him; I'll just forward in time to their time. Enjoy the show."

Deadline Zombies

Then, barely before his words had a chance to reach my ears, the little blond was gone from beside me and we could see him standing in the crowd looking at Balfour.

"Oh man," I said aloud, "How the heck am I gonna explain this trip to my editor!"

Chapter V: Horsing Around

The whole situation got stranger and stranger, as Alice said when *she* went through the looking glass. As I stood there watching, the little Fae guy, Fitheal, began to torment John Bull.

It was ghoulish and enjoyable at once.

Balfour was pounding on the invisible barrier with decreasing strength but constant fury. The crowd outside the fairy ring was also taunting the corpulent thug and it appeared to me as if no time had passed at all since Mary and I had been thrust into the Fae ring.

That feeling was reinforced when I saw the stunned look on all of the villagers and heard, "Oh Me God. Mary Boyd's been taken!"

"It's all that John Bull's fault!" Fitheal said, stepping from the back of the crowd. He held up the camera and snapped a picture of the annoyed and frightened taxman. It was strange because it was as if Mary, her father and I were standing behind the taxman but looking through him outward toward the crowd. I could almost swear that Fitheal shot me a wink before he spoke again.

"I think we can get that windbag out of there and teach him a lesson at the same time!"

The crowd looked at him and I was sure I saw some indication in their odd stares that they had some hint as to just who—or what—the little man was. A fact confirmed when Mary commented.

"We all know the stories of A Wee one who wandered the land around Randalstown," she said. "I never really believed it till now."

"You people seem to know a heck of lot about these things and ignore caution," I said. "It's like knowing you have rattlesnakes but just walking barefoot anyway."

"There are no snakes in Ireland, Yank," Billy Boyd said, "Just English buggers slithering around our houses."

"They'll take them all, Da," Mary said. "If we can't find the gold to pay their blood money."

"You could use the bank money, honey," he said, "If we could get out of this circle."

"That is the priority here," I piped in, "But how do we do that?"

"I don't know," Billy Boyd said. "I haven't been able to come up with a puzzle he couldn't solve or a task he could not do." He was still looking at his daughter with amazement, and why shouldn't he? Subjectively almost no time –perhaps a single night had passed—yet here was his little girl sixteen years older.

Outside the circle Fitheal was inciting the villagers with an eloquent argument to 'rescue' the taxman. "This bombast is trapped here because he is threatening the land," he said, "And the land is taking its vengeance; it's Eochu himself coming to help his children."

"Eochu?" I asked Mary. I was still, out of habit, I guess, writing it all down.

"He is the horse god of the ancient Celts," she said. "Lough Neagh, the scientists say, means the Lough of the horse-god Eochu. He was the lord of the underworld, who was supposed to exist beneath its waters. To this day fishermen can hear booming noises called water guns that scientists say are whirlwinds on the surface of the water but others say it is the horse god galloping to the underworld."

"So I think," Fitheal continued, "that since it's not safe to go in the ring ourselves, we haul him like the dumb brute he is." He went to one of the horses that had pulled pony cart up the trail and began to remove the harness from the animal. When he had the whole thing in his hand he approached the circle of mushrooms.

"I'm gonna throw this in to you, John Bull," Fitheal said. "Put it over your shoulders and we'll haul you out."

The British official was so exhausted from the ordeal that he didn't even have the strength to protest the indignity of such a rescue scheme. He grabbed the leather harness and as instructed slipped the straps over his shoulders.

As soon as he did, the little blond man began to pull on the end of the tack and Balfour began to move toward the mushroom ring and the barrier between the world within and the world without.

"Be careful you bog-trotting savage!" Balfour yelled. He was pulled against the barrier, his face pressed flat to it like a child pressing his face to the window of a candy store. "You're hurting me."

"Sorry, M'lordship," Fitheal said with a deferential bow. "I'm just a clumsy clod footed bog-dog." He played to the crowd of villagers, grunting and making faces as he pulled on the leather harness.

"Its not working, you idiot," the taxman bellowed against the wall of nothingness.

"Maybe I need help," Fitheal said. He glanced to the guards of the official who, facing the reality of the 'un-reality' of the fairy ring had reached an end to their ability to absorb shocks. They looked around at the crowd and then back at their trapped 'boss' and broke for the road.

The crowd laughed and hurried them along with handfuls of rocks flung at their retreating backsides.

"Come back here you cowards!" Balfour yelled. The power of his command was somewhat mitigated by the fact that he was still mashed up against the invisible barrier and his words were slurred from the contact.

The guards didn't pay any attention to the command but the townsfolk reacted with jeers and laughter.

"Them's not cowards," someone said. "Them's is the only smart English toadies I've ever seen!" This made all concerned laugh all the louder.

Meanwhile Fitheal kept up the tension on the leather tack harness with a broad grin on his face.

It was all so bizarre to see from our perspective, like a shadow show just for us though we were the shadows to the people outside the circle in the daylight world of what had been our reality.

"Maybe you folks can give me a hand here," Fitheal said, "I'm sure it will go easier."

The town's folk were willing to the task and a tug of war began with the unfortunate taxman at the other end. He continued to be squeezed against the unseen wall as the villagers strained against the harness.

"This doesn't seem a fair tug of war," Fitheal said with a chortling laugh. "I think it needs to be a more even match." He screwed his face up with an effort that had nothing to do with pulling on the harness and then he smiled. "That should do it!" he exclaimed.

Then the taxman moaned with a new tone to his discomfort and a change began. His neck seemed to bloat and his body shivered as if from a blizzard of cold. It looked like he was doing some sort of strange Charleston dance with his legs hopping backward and his arms that were pressed against the invisible barrier looked like he was waving them as part of the dance.

He moaned again but it was a deeper, altered moan as his back began to swell and his already large girth became massive and bloated, misshapen thing.

His legs began to swell as well, so much so that his pants split (to the tittered laughter of the villagers) and the thighs became completely misshapen, or rather, re-shaped into things that soon clearly became equine hindquarters.

A bizarre change but, I have to admit, not an unfamiliar one. I, uh— got turned into a little bit of an equine- a jackass, actually, once—on Governors Island—and so while it was strange to see I sure knew what John Balfour was feeling.

His face showed he had a sense that it was not just pain this body was feeling but something in scope and size, to say the least, unusual. His chest began to re-shape as well, broadening and expanding, bursting through his shirt and jacket. It was clear that his whole being was altering and even the trapped man's expression went from horror to a sort of resignation.

Soon his clothes were gone as his new body enlarged and spread backward from his trapped head. His equine shape became clear in not much time. His back legs bent into hind legs and his feet transformed, as we all watched in awe, into the rounded hardened shape of hooves.

To the tittering, taunting laugher of the townsfolk, his buttocks expanded to the animal rump and a tail soon became visible.

His moans of discomfort were mixed with whimpers of despair. I could almost detect words. "Help me!" he whispered.

I couldn't. No one could. He was too far gone into the world of the equine. He had expanded into a full sized draught horse with the harness now fitting him as if it had been crafted for him.

The body had undergone a full transformation into a large dappled grey horse with a braided mane and magnificent full tail.

I could well remember that feeling and I felt sorry for the fat slob—not so sorry that I didn't want to boot him in the keister—but still it didn't endear me to the little Fae who had us prisoner as well.

Would he let us go? Could we fight or trick our way out of the circle? Is this what happened to my grandfather so long ago?

The crowd outside the circle was gripped by a fascination mixed with horror as the transformed official slowly passed through the barrier between the worlds. With a sound like a popping noise, the new 'horse' that had been John Balfour was suddenly standing in the daylight field in County Antrim!

Fitheal stood up and ran a hand along the neck of the transformed man and smiled. "There, now," he said, "I told you I'd get you out of the fairy ring, didn't I?" He laughed and the horse-bodied man snorted and whinnied in horror.

Chapter VI: Horse Trading

Mary, her father and I watched the strange show before us with sickening chills running through our bodies. I looked over at the two of them.

"I think there is spit all chance of fighting our way out of this fungus-Alcatraz," I said, "So I expect we're gonna have to fox ourselves out. Either solve one of his riddles, give him one of our own he can't solve or some task he can't do."

"Easier said than done, lad," Billy Boyd said. "He's come to me every hour and poised one puzzle after another and never did I even come close."

"I suspect it was more like once a month in real world time," I observed, 'I'm guessing time works differently here and out here."

"Right you are, Yank" Fitheal said. He was suddenly beside me again and it made me jump.

"Please wear a bell or something," I whined at the little man. "You're gonna give me a heart attack."

"I thought you Donovans were made of sterner stuff, "he said. "With ice in your veins."

"I have only enough ice to kept the whiskey cold," I said, "the rest is all water, that's the reality of it."

"Reality is a multileveled thing like an onion, Yank," Fitheal said. He had a smirk on his face and I felt like he was explaining geometry to a pet cat. "The layers are so close that sometimes even mortals can see through one to another, hence your ghosts and such. Each layer is governed by its own rules and realities. We Sidhe can travel between at will and bring through, within reason who and what we want. But it gets so boring." He pouted like a school kid. "So most of us like to liven things up with a game or two now and then. Even that gets boring because we almost always win."

"Except with someone like my grandfather." I piped up. This made his smirk twist sideways into a frown.

"Yes," he said, "Old Willy asked, 'How long did the reign of each King of England last.'"

"Until it was over," I said. I remembered my grandfather telling me that riddle when I was five. Now I understood why he laughed so long and loud at his own joke.

"Yes," the little Fae said with a sour look. "So I was obliged to not only set him free—but by the terms of wager to give him as much of my gold as he could carry." It was clear from his grimace that the thought of parting any of his filthy lucre still irked him. But the time worked differently for him—it might really be a fresh wound though in my reality it was over sixty years ago.

"So what will it be, Donovan Spawn?" He asked in a suddenly jovial tone. "Riddle, task or offspring?"

"Offspring?" I asked.

"I've heard of bargains where a man would promise a child to the Fae to take his place," Billy Boyd said. He looked pointedly at his daughter. "Never such a thought occurred to me, my little light," he said. It was clear he was still amazed at the woman she had-to him- suddenly become. "My reason to leave this place was you and your mother."

"I know, Da," she said.

I thought about the horrific show Fitheal had put on for us and realized some of it was for my benefit. He did indeed think we Donovans were something special because of my grandfather and it made me wonder if anyone else had ever conned the little guy. Maybe not—so he was trying to intimidate me with his show of occult power, transforming that tubby taxman right before me.

"The riddle," I asked before I committed myself. "Do I ask it or do you?"

He made an exasperated face. "*Please*. Your mortal puzzles are so very boring... 'What walks on all fours in the morning, etc. or 'A plane crashes on the border of Germany and France-where do they bury the survivors?"

He snorted. "You all think you're De Vinci—well, even he was no De Vinci some days." He giggled at some memory.

"I think I'd rather go for a task then," I said and stuck in my own psychological warfare bid. "I like the idea of telling you what to do."

This made him giggle. His annoying high-pitched giggle again "Oh you are Willy's kin for sure, Yank."

"But I want the terms of the wager set out clear," I said." This escape is not just for me but for Mary and her dad as well."

"Oh that's rich," he said, "All well and good for you if you win—"

"When I win," I said. "'Think positive,' Grandpa always told me."

"But," he continued as if I had not spoken. "What do I get when I win? And not the offspring, please I can only stand so much humanity and I really don't' want any little Donovans running around my mushroom patch."

"Gold," I said. I knew that would perk him up and it did.

"Gold?"

"I am offering you the proceeds of Mister Boyd's bank robbery-"

"Hey!" Boyd said. "That money is for the cause!"

"Zip it Boyd," I snapped. "There's already is a Republic since you were put in cold storage. That money is our bargaining chip to get us out."

"He's right, papa," Mary said, "All that pound Sterling is tainted anyway. They can trace it—we couldn't spend it. And Papa, we have to get out. We have so many years to make up for."

Her father nodded to me and I knew they would back any play I made at that point.

"So is it a deal?" I said to Fitheal. I held out my hand. "Our unconditional release at the time me and Mary were brought into this fungus jail if I can assign you a task that you cannot perform?"

He looked at me from under his brow with an animal suspicion. Then he looked down at my offered hand as if it were a snake ready to bite him.

I counted twenty heartbeats then he smiled and thrust his hand into mine.

"A deal, Donovan," he said. "All terms agreed."

"Okay then," I said. I remembered something else my grandfather used to say all the time. I knew now it had been his holdout if he hadn't solved the little Fae's puzzle.

"All right then, here is the task I expect you to perform for me: Go chase your shadow on moonless night-and catch it!" When I repeated that puzzle-task my grandfather had told me I watched Fitheal's jaw drop.

The little Fae made a low grunting sound and then muttered, "Drat!" so low it was a barely heard exhalation.

Mary and her father both let out a little gasp as they realized that the little guy was staring at me with the shamed defeat. After along moment he nodded his head slowly up and down.

"Willy would be proud, boyoh!" he said. "You can step over the ring anytime you want and you'll be a moment after you entered—and Da here' will be with you as he is."

I gave him a wining smile and acknowledged his 'good sportsmanship'. And he acknowledged that I could have put it to him a lot worse.

"I appreciate you not trying to fox me into throwing some of me precious gold in for good measure."

"About that gold," I said as I ushered the other two over the ring into the real world, "I have a little business proposition for you before I go and a question to ask; do you know what a fence is?"

Epilogue: One Fungus Among us:

Needless to say, the homecoming of Billy Boyd looking exactly as he had sixteen years before sent a major ripple through the fabric of the village of Randalstown. More of a ripple was the sudden appearance of enough money to pay all the taxes and outstanding mortgages in the surrounding county.

Fitheal had proved very amiable to an exchange of Boyd's hot marked money for nice cool, untraceable Fae gold at a rate of sixty-five cents on the dollar.

It more than made up for the money my forebearer had foxed him out of so long ago.

As for me, I ended up with a new appreciation for my sainted grandfather and the myths of my ancestral land, and a story I couldn't print (or else Boyd would go to jail and I'd have been put in a loony bin).

And Old Man O'Toole got himself a sturdy plow horse that answered to the name John B and had an intense and understandable dread of mushrooms…

-30-

Teel James Glenn

News flash: you are not seeing double! The story that follows appears in the weird adventure book *Weird Tales of the Skullmask* but the publisher and I thought that you'd like to see all the Maxi/Moxie stories in sequence in one volume—so this is a bonus. If you've read the Skullmask book you can skip ahead—or have a warm and fuzzy moment re-visting...

The Deadly Puppets

Prologue: Death of a Skullmask

The whole thing with the deadly puppets began before I got into it, and it went something like this:

On Friday night, October twenty ninth of nineteen hundred and thirty seven, while an early snow was falling in New York City, murder happened. It was not your ordinary garden-variety murder, though to the poor schlemiel that passed over to the other side, it didn't make a heck of a lot of difference what variety death was visited on him that night.

He was the doorman for the Cobalt Club, that upper eastside watering hole for the elite of the city—half way between the Explorer's Club and the Ritz in clientele and character. Which is to say, revered but not so stodgy that they couldn't throw a heck of an early Halloween Party.

Joe Chambers was the working stiff's name, a regular guy who lived in the Bronx, was a vet of the Big One, and liked to have a good time. He made a comfortable living holding car doors and hailing cabs for the power brokers of New York who were members of the club. He had for many years. Everyone who knew him liked Joe.

The guy who drilled him through the bean probably had never said two words to Joe.

The doorman was in his red and black uniform coat with peaked cap, but had added a skeleton mask as his costume for the night. He had just gotten a great tip from Chicago's *Daily Sentinel* publisher, Reid, who was in town for a publishers' convention, when gunfire broke out down the street.

Joe looked up and saw this guy in a skull mask running down the block firing behind him with a Broomhandle Mauser semi automatic handgun. The masked man was being chased by three guys dressed respectively as a pirate, a clown and a Keystone cop. (I got all this dope from other witnesses).

All three were firing guns at Skullmask, a fusillade that had everyone on the street diving for cover but the sounds of which were curiously muffled. Joe, who had done his share of diving for cover in the trenches, tried like blazes to get out of the way of the lead hailstorm. He had been twenty or thirty pounds slimmer when he dodged whistling death the last time, so he didn't make it.

The poor slob from the Bronx took two whispered slugs in the back that slammed him against the granite front of the club and a third through the thought box that put his lights out for good.

That didn't stop the gunfire: far from it.

The still-breathing Skullmask spun around not ten feet from the dead one and made his stand. He seemed to have been able to reload almost as fast as he shot, for he returned as good as he got, bullet for bullet at the trio chasing him.

And he was a damn sight better at the game then they were—he hit what he was shooting at. The Clown went down first with a roaring Mauser slug through his ticker, his Roscoe flying from his dead hand.

Keystone Cop dodged behind a Ford truck, trying to avoid the same fate, but Skullmask dropped to the ground and fired under the truck, clipping the cop in the ankle. When the fake Bobbie slapped face to the pavement, the death's head gunman winged a shot straight through his kisser.

That left Captain Crook with a loaded revolver and a bad attitude. He fired his oddly silenced gun twice at the Skullmask, but the lone defender had good cover behind a decorative planter, and the rubber tree took the hits for him.

By this time, the real cops had been called and the sirens were singing a swan song to the violence on the way up Lexington. Skullmask didn't seem to care, but the buccaneer did an about face, scooped up the guns of the other two and took off at top speed into the falling white stuff.

Skullmask stopped long enough to check old Joe to see if there was any life in him, a finger to his neck to feel for a pulse, but he got nothing and took off just as the panda cars pulled up.

I came into the picture about fifteen minutes after all this.

My name's Moxie Donovan and I pound keys for living. That's right, I'm an ambassador of the fourth estate: a newshound. I got the call while I was at my girl Maxine's place—yeah—say it—Moxie and Maxi—too cute for words. Anyway, I was trying to do a little masquerading of my own as Casanova when my editor at the *Daily Star* got me on the squawk line. Maxi's place is only five blocks from the Cobalt Club, so I straightened my tie and hoofed it over there.

What a mess. Joey C had left a red spot the size of a bathtub before the slab jockeys loaded him in the meat wagon. The crime scene boys were starting to do their evidence collecting and there's where it started to go curveball.

O'Leary, the butterball flatfoot from the Detective Department, was the first to turn over the clown and yank the mask off him to glim his

Deadline Zombies

kisser. I was standing right next to him when he pulled the rubber mask off.

"Saint's alive!" he said. "It's a dummy!"

Sure enough, Smilo the Clown was a blank faced wooden form! We quickly went to the Keystone Cop and pulled his rubber mask off as well to be greeted by another knotty pine placeholder.

Poor Joe Chambers had been killed by two life-sized wooden puppets!

Happy Halloween!

Chapter I: Out on a Limb

"I can't print this hogwash, Donovan; where'd you learn to write copy? The horoscopes page?" My editor, William 'Whitey' Wilson, had all the subtlety of a Mae West come-on line and none of her charms. Though his bald head did remind me of one of her highlights.

His lesson in literary style was being dispensed in his office at nine am on Saturday, and even though All Saint's Day wasn't till the next day, I needed the patience of a Saint to take his lecture.

"I've got four witnesses to back it up, Whitey," I said, "And I was there when they took the masks off the wooden gunslingers!"

"Then you were drinking the same stuff as the witnesses," Wilson said. "And don't call me Whitey!"

"The kicker, Whitey," I insisted, "is that the bullets they dug out of the oak outlaws were silver!"

"Now we have the Lone Ranger running wild in Gotham?"

"And the slugs they took out of the doorman were wood!"

"Wood bullets?"

"Teak wood to be exact; Lafferty at the lab said that it's a hard enough wood to survive the muzzle velocity a thirty eight throws out." I was feelin' pretty happy with myself for trumping his objections. I'd written a slam-bang lead piece about mystery werewolf murderers based on the silver bullet angle and the fact that last night had been a full moon —I was never one to let lack of 'verifieds' stop a slam-bang story. He couldn't kill this like he had the article on the Nazi Bund-protection racket I was sure was happening out there in the hinterlands. He screamed bloody murder when *The Times* trumped us on *Das Amerikadeutscher Bund's* activities back in March, but still canned my article in May on the basis of 'not enough verified facts.'

"All that bullet nonsense means is that either your Skullmask shooter was target shooting at these dummies that the real crooks were hiding behind or your witnesses were soused or near sighted," Whitey said.

"Or the werewolf killers couldn't use lead bullets for some reason and the good guy was—"

"This is funny page stuff," he shot back. "And if you believe any of it you belong on the funny farm."

I leaned in and put my size twelve brogans up on the seat of the chair by his desk, makin' like I was all confidential. "Of course *I* don't believe it, Whitey," I whispered. "But the public just might, at least enough to sell papers!"

Deadline Zombies

His baldhead took on a rosy glow as his blood pressure shot up and he jumped up from his desk and screamed, "Get out of my office and hit the rewrite desk before I boot you back to Boise!"

I beat a strategic retreat to my desk, picking up a cup of Joe on the way from Mickey's food cart. I settled down to the work of punching up an article on a German husband-wife murder suicide in Yonkers to go on page two of the afternoon edition.

"You tryin' to kill the old man?" The accusation came from Fran Striker, girl reporter for the same great metropolitan newspaper I worked for. She was older than dirt, tougher than a nickel steak and a good egg all around.

"Naw," I said, "Just testing to see if he could spell 'ridiculous.'" I offered her a coffin nail and the two of us smoked up a cloud while I beat the facts into a presentable story.

She picked up the piece I had done on the shooting the night before and read it.

"I don't see why you had to hook the hairy horror on this one," she said through the fog of smoke, "It's way out there on the bona fide facts anyway." She got a curious look on her less than beautiful face. "Say, I remember some joker with a skull mask back in–I think thirty five or thirty six—had a shootout with some Satanist cult in the Pine Barrens. Wonder if it's the same guy?"

I rolled a new sheet of foolscap into the metal word factory and shrugged my shoulders. "I think I remember that. *The Post* gave it a 'Jersey Devil' headline—bunch of bodies and no killer. No one ever caught, I remember, but nobody missed the skunks he offed so not much came of it. I'll hit up Digger for some background and try to convince Charles Dickens in there to give me two columns in the late edition." I stopped pounding the keys long enough to look up at her.

"Its just that as far as the public is concerned there has to be a why with the story, Frannie—you know; who, what, when, where and what the hell!"

I came across a piece on the desk for clean-up, which was the official version of the shooting. It was all roses and lace—pure nonsense about a robbery gone bad.

"This is a crime!" I yelled as I shot up and headed back for the boss' office. Fran jumped in front of me and did a Slingin' Sammy Baugh-style body block.

"You know better than to call Whitey on a thing like this," she said. "That is the story that will go out because that is the story Commissioner Weston wants to go out and we cooperate with the police, capeesh?"

I stared down at the little troll in his office and took a deep breath to let my Irish settle back into my feet. I bent to kiss Fran on the forehead.

"How many times is that?" I asked.

"That I saved your job?"

"Yeah."

"Fourth time this month." She settled into her desk across from me as I went back to the next clean-up piece.

"Copy!" I called out.

A fresh faced kid named Slip Mahoney came racing up to snatch the Yonkers piece from me while I dove into a clock shop robbery on the west side. Routine stuff about a shipment of watch innards stolen. For this I learned to spell?

"Donovan!" Whitey shouted my name like a bell ringer hitting the gong—loud and with the intention of imitating the voice of God.

I walked calmly to his glass walled temple to receive my holy tablets from the burning bush himself.

"I need a piece on this toymaker guy that the society pages are all fluffy on." He held out an assignment sheet without looking up from the layout sheet on the mess he called a desk. "Put on a clean shirt and get me three columns worth for the Sunday edition; chop-chop. Take Casey."

I stared at the shiny dome of his think box for a moment ready to say something, and then I remembered I needed a job in order to eat- and anything was better than the rewrite dungeon, so I took the hand-scrawled notes and nodded, " Right, Chief!" I backed away from the sacred presence with a smile on my mug.

Casey was the on-the-spot shutterbug who worked the bullpen and was ready for anything. He and I'd been a team on a couple of front pagers in my two years on *The Star*, and a lot more back pagers. He was little gnome of a guy with a broad chest and a face like the loser in a shovel fight, but a reliable guy and a good 'snapper. Casey was a corruption of his name Kasadorvisch. Nobody knew what his first name was and he didn't feel the need to share that little fact. Homely as he was, he always had a dame or two on the line and a straw hat on his noggin.

We made quite a pair; I'm a hair over six foot and soaking wet burden the scale with about a hundred and fifty pounds. He's a hair under five-five and a good two hundred pounds, all solid. A regular Mutt and Jeff team.

"Okay, Rembrandt," I called as I passed the secretarial pool where Casey did his trolling, "We're going to Santa's workshop."

Deadline Zombies

The pippin he was chatting up giggled and waved goodbye as the swarthy 'snapper grabbed his gear and followed me.

We hoofed over to the Independent Subway at Thirty Fourth Street at Sixth Avenue since it wasn't really a rush job and *The Daily Star* was cheaper than your Aunt Martha. The toy shop we were going to had apparently become a hot spot for the four hundred to visit in the last half year. According to the background sheet Whitey had handed me, it was run by one Rudolf Krafft, a Swiss-Deutch toymaker who specialized in elaborate mechanical whatzzits. The background said he came from a long line of toy makers that had made mechanical toys for the crown heads of Europe. *Brother!*

I felt like a stringer for a boonie rag as I left the train at Fifty-Ninth and walked over to the toyshop he maintained across from the Plaza. Me, who had been there when the Hindenburg went down, covered that gun fight on the pier that bronze guy had with those silver-suited guys and taken lead in the shoulder when the hunchback in the fright wig stopped the take-over at Grand Central, writing a fluff piece on a gizmo tinker. Talk about low!

The shop had a picture window front with a colorful display of a miniature amusement park with a Ferris wheel, roller coaster and parachute drop, imitating the one from Coney Island. All a clockwork copy of the full sized rides complete with tiny figures that waved or looked shocked like real folk. I had to admit it was impressive.

I had Casey get a nice storefront shot for the cover and then stepped into the mechanical wonderland that was "Krafft Creations."

Inside, the shop was even more fantastic than the window display. The lighting was low and mysterious, not the bright flashy lighting I would have expected from a toy store, but then it was like no toy store I had ever seen.

First thing inside the door was a full sized butler carved in wood and dressed in real livery. As I stepped across the threshold, the wooden Jeeves swung around to face me and bowed at the waist.

"Good Afternoon," the faux footman seemed to say. "Welcome to Krafft Creations." He then straightened up and rang a little bell in a perfectly sculpted right hand.

I pushed my fedora back on my bean and shook my head. "Holy Moley," I said. "Frankenstein is here!"

"Not Frankenstein's monster, my friend," a voice from the shadows at the back of the shop said. "More like der Golem, I vould say."

Chapter II: Wheels within Wheels

Rudolf Krafft looked like a central casting Geppetto. He was slightly stoop shouldered (one could imagine from long hours at the work bench) and white haired with little watchmaker half glasses across the bridge of his prominent nose. He even wore a leather apron over a white shirt and tweed trousers.

"Uh-Gol-who?" I asked, showing my complete lack of classical education.

"Der Golem." The old man said. "A medieval legend from the Jewish Warsaw Ghetto about a man fashioned from clay with the secret name of God written on his forehead that imbued him with animation." He walked up to the pseudo servant and opened the front of his jacket to reveal a complex array of gears, wheels and tubes. "I am afraid the only secret here is air pressure and pulleys."

Casey snapped a shot of the mechanical guts and I did the introductions. "I'm Donovan from the *Daily Star*, Mr. Krafft," I said, laying on the charm, "And my editor thought our readers might like a feature on your marvelous toys for the weekend edition, being it's Halloween and the start of Christmas season is just around the corner."

The old man smiled warmly and I felt myself going all Currier and Ives.

"Of course," he said, " I love to share my children."

'Children?"

"My creations are all one of a kind items," he said, motioning me to follow him.

Casey wandered off to shoot some background stuff and I pulled a pad from my jacket. Moxie's rules of reporting. Number One: don't rely on your memory!

We walked past miniature scenes of ice rinks and faire grounds that he activated with a twist of a key. The tableaus came to life with a degree of realistic movement—a skater twirling or a rider on horseback rearing —that amazed even this cynic. I could imagine the effect it would have on a kid and understood why he had gotten the reputation with the blue bloods that he had.

His workshop at the back of the store was in many ways more fascinating than the front of the house. Half completed mechanical horses, giraffes and steam engines lay like war casualties across the broad workbench. Blocks of exotic wood were stacked along the back of the bench and wood carving tools were scattered about. Another butler like the one out front was in the early stages of assembly and it gave me a chance to really appreciate the number of parts that made it up.

"Excuse the mess." He eased himself onto a stool in front of the bench. "I have no helper at present; my apprentice, Dieter, had to leave suddenly for a family emergency." He started to tinker with the arm of a foot-high metal soldier while he spoke, as if his hands could not bear to remain idle.

"Uh, I'd like to get a little background for our readers, Mr. Krafft, if you don't mind?"

'Not at all," he said, "I will tell you anything but my craftsman's secrets; much of what I do is handed down from generations past and are family secrets."

"About that, Sir," I asked, " Just how far does your business go back."

"The art of elaborate toy making goes back, I suppose, to the pyramids," he said with genial laugh. "The Sphinx, they say, was an elaborate puppet. Or the Colossus at Rhodes, a great mechanical man. But my family interest goes back to the Wars of Napoleon, when all Europe rose against the little Corsican. My forefather was a clockmaker who made special devices for partisans fighting on the side of Wellington and then, after the war, turned his attentions to mechanical amusements. Five generations now."

"So would you say this is more an art than a business?" I asked

He laughed. "Yah—sometimes I think it is not so good a business. I have had many want to mass-produce some of my amusements—who have asked me to simplify or change them—but each piece is unique, like a sculpture or moving painting. I cannot bear to make them less than what they are. One should always strive for perfection, to reach the ideal."

I was writing furiously, barely aware of Casey flashing away around the shop behind me. The old goat waxed poetic about the history of toys and mechanical men for a while, then I figured I had enough for a Sunday section lead.

"So to wrap it up, Sir," I said, "You decided to come to New York, why?"

His gentle features darkened. "We live in uncertain times," he said. "There are clouds in Europe that many of you Americans have not taken heed of—and with the violence in China, the Orient was not a choice. Only here in your wonderful country are there are still hearts light enough to appreciate what I can create for them."

"Wow," I said," that's a great way to end the piece, sir. You got a little poet in you as well as a little Da Vinci!"

He enjoyed my comparison and gave me a grandfather's Christmas smile.

"Before you go, let me give you something. "He stood and reached across the table to remove a ballerina doll from a rack. It was delicately sculpted and lifelike in every detail. "Here."

"Oh I couldn't," I said.

"No please, he insisted. "Surely you know some child who would love it?'

I smiled, "Not a child, but she's a kid at heart."

* * * *

Before I went back to the paper to do a rough of the article, I felt a bit light on facts—And even though it was not a piece that would win me a Pulitzer, I do have a professional pride in doing a good job, so I went down town to 'thicken the stew' with a few facts from *The Daily Star's* secret weapon against the big tabloids; Digger Tome.

The Lord of the Stacks and Facts held court in a little bookstore on Thompson Street in the heart of Greenwich Village called "The Tome Tomb." As usual, he was seated behind the desk near the entrance. He was a scowling gargoyle of a man, with thinning hair slicked back, wearing thick glasses and dressed like and with the pallor of an undertaker.

Aside from his amazing ability to ferret out obscure sources for background on pieces, Digger was a living, breathing encyclopedia of the weird and whacky.

Rumor had it he'd done the carnival/vaudeville circuit with a memory act until he'd saved up enough to open his bookstore. Now he was a spider at the center of a web of information and the best thing about him for a newsy like me he got a vicarious thrill supplying info and worked for simple perks.

"Hey, Digger," I called as I entered the book lined room. "How's the sunshine in Argentina?"

"Just what you're not," He said without looking up, "Bright!"

I set down a cheeseburger and a vanilla shake on his desktop in the two square inches of exposed surface area and his homely face lit up.

"So what's the news on the doorman shooting up at the Cobalt?" he asked while he inhaled the burger. "I know your rag didn't print the Jake on it."

Deadline Zombies

I looked around as if being conspiratorial, but there was no one else in the store to overhear. "You got big ears, Digger, "I said with a smirk. Then I filled him in on the real facts as I'd learned them so far.

"Wow!" he said, "Killer puppets!" I could see a movie playing behind his eyes of last night's events and it probably starred Bela Lugosi. "I wish I'd seen that," he concluded. "And the shooter was wearing a skull face mask you say?"

"Well, it is almost Halloween, Digger."

"Samhain, the time when the veil between the worlds of the living and dead are the thinnest," he quoted from somewhere. "All Hallows Eve to the unwashed; but I think that the mask had nothing to do with that." He spoke, as he always did, with authority.

"Okay, Mr. Know-It-All, I'll bite: why does the mask have nothing to do with the holiday?"

"I've seen clippings on a guy wearing a Skullmask going way back," he said. "Kind of vague; the survivors of wherever he shows up seem to be glad he was there and so won't spill much, but we're talking way back; There is an account of a colored man in a skull mask rescuing a wagon train in the eighteen seventies—"

"Oh come on," I said, "And I thought my werewolf angle was way out there."

"I'm just repeating what I've read, Moxie," he continued. "Another report of a guy in a Skullmask off Madagascar in the eighteen nineties saved a ship from pirates. This one was a white guy. That much the witnesses agree on. And there is an account of a pilot in the Great War who wore a skull mask, flew in a rogue plane against the Boche."

"What a lot of hooey!"

"But great copy."

The shake and burger were gone already, seemingly between blinks. He was all business then, ignoring my skepticism, rubbing his pudgy hands together in anticipation of tackling some assignment. "So what's the piece you need background for?"

"How do you know this is not just a social visit?"

"You're a newspaper hack," he said with no rancor. "You don't have any social tendencies that don't sell papers!" He gave a gallows grin and had me pegged to the wall, so I recounted my time with Old Krafft.

"Hmm, Swiss clockmaker turned toy maker to the social elite— hmmm!" Digger seemed to pause for a moment in deep thought and his face took on the aspect of Hindu Holy man off on a trance journey. Abruptly, he took a deep breath and shot up from his seat faster than I'd ever seen him move and walked back toward the dimly lit back of the over-piled store.

He squeezed between stacks of books I could have sworn he'd never make it through and went straight to a bottom shelf. Then he did a little ballet turn and reached up to ease a book out from between two others on a topmost shelf.

Then he was back behind his desk, his pasty skin aglow from the sudden exertions and a smile on his face. "Here you go, Moxie," he said, "These should be enough dope for a Sunday feature."

The two books were "*A Short History of Swiss Clocks*" and "*Oddities of the Napoleonic Wars.*" Both were out of print and probably only sold ten copies apiece when they were readily available. Trust Digger to have them and know it.

I looked at the books, then up at him, and my expression must have revealed my dark past of late or badly written book reports in high school. He took pity on me.

"The clock book has an index and you can get a family history: Krafft is a fairly famous name in old Swiss clocks" he said. "That's why it rang a bell for me—and then I remembered one entry in the Napoleonic book." He steepled his hands and spooled the images from the book on the screen of his mind as he gave his lecture.

"Seems there was a unit of Swiss rifle men—snipers—who used specially constructed air rifles to pick off old Nappy's officers. Demoralized the troops and drove the little Corsican crazy. He put a higher bounty on every one of them than on Wellington himself! They never caught any of them, and when the war was over, the guns and the secret of their creation was lost to time. Legend has it that they were created by a master clockmaker name Otto Von Krafft!"

He sat staring at me after the lecture as if waiting for a band to play "ta da!" music behind him, and when none came, he made the sound himself.

"Okay, "I said, "I'll take the clock book then and get it back to you next time I'm through this way." I had no idea how to use the Napoleon stuff in the story, but I could throw some family names in to pad it out and fill the column count.

I slapped a five on the counter to 'rent the book' and picked it up. "I'll have the seat tickets sent down for the fight Friday," I said as I headed out the door. "I got ringside for you this time."

Digger never missed a boxing or wrestling match and between me and two other reporters, we kept him close up in the action.

Deadline Zombies

"Thanks, Moxie—and let me know if you find out anything more about the puppets—that kind of story is my sliced bread!"

'Sure thing, Digger!"

I had no idea I'd have more for him as soon as I waltzed into the city room of the '*Star* and sat at my desk. Everything was in more than the usual state of chaos.

"Have you heard?" Slip yelled to me, "The puppet killers have struck again!"

I never even got to warm my chair before I was out the door and running again.

Chapter III: More Trick than Treat

While I was getting lectured by Digger for background research, not so nice stuff was happening downtown near the Fulton Fish Market.

On a Saturday at lunchtime, trucks had finished their morning runs and the businesses were winding down for the day, having been working since before the sun had risen.

One business that had been housed in a long redbrick warehouse on South Street for three decades was the Arlington Refrigeration Company. Not an icehouse as the name might imply, it manufactured refrigeration equipment and supplied the industry, which made it handy for the icehouses that did operate in the area.

On that day a skeleton crew of three fabricators who were working on a rush order, and a security guard, were all who were on the premises of the firm when the front door was kicked in and the bullets started flying.

Before it was over, the guard and one of the fabricators were dead, shot through the hearts with wooden bullets from silent guns and nearly a mile of pneumatic tubing and copper pipe was taken.

"Oh, I'm sure they made no sound but a little 'pop'" the old Irishman who was foreman for the group that day said. "I used to run a little rum for the New York boys, back in Prohibition and I heard my share of real gunfire."

Despite his calm voice, the old guy, all two hundred fifty pounds of him, was pretty shaken up. He was sweating profusely and his eyes kept darting around the office. The coroner had taken the stiffs out, but he kept looking at where the bodies had been.

"The first one of them just walked in and started shooting," he said. "John—the guard—John O'Malley, he got hit in the shoulder, but he is —was a tough old cuss and he pulled his gun and emptied it into that— that abomination!"

I handed him a paper cup of water and he drank it without really noticing. His shirt was soaked with nervous sweat.

"I swear he hit that first one four, maybe five times, twice in the head, but..." he looked suddenly frightened like a small child in the dark. "It had no face! And it didn't even acknowledge the slugs. We all ran for the back room, but Mike didn't make it."

He got a puzzled look on his kisser, searching my face for some sort of answer. "All they took was refrigeration equipment—tubes and piping; it don't make any sense. The second one shot John again and he went down. Right there." He pointed at the spot that was forever marked by a pool of blood that had soaked into the old wood of the floor and left a dark stain.

"Okay, Mr. Flynn," a gruff voice came from behind me, "You can go now; one of my boys will drive you home." It was Mike O'Toole, my playmate on the force.

"Captain O'Toole," I said sweetly as I turned to face the florid faced giant in the cheap suit. "So nice you could join us at the crime scene."

'Don't give me that, Moxie." He chewed a long dead cigar and had his derby pushed high on his head to showcase his thinning red hair. "You know better than to question one of my witnesses. And how did you get in here—I told Faulkner to keep out news monkeys."

"Can't keep the eyes and ears of the people out," I said as I started to head towards the door—I didn't want the indignity of being physically tossed out twice by the big Philistine (back in June at the Chinatown shootout that Shadows guy was at).

"Is there any truth to the rumor that the guard fired and hit these wooden bandits?"

"Don't start spreading that malarkey," he snarled. "They was just men in Halloween masks, is all—no doubt with bullet proof vests on."

"And shooting wooden bullets?" I threw back.

"How did you—" His face got redder. "Faulkner—throw this bum outta my crime scene!"

I beat the helping hands out the door and sprang for a cab back up to the paper. I knew Whitey would want to get an extra out once I told him what actually went on at the icehouse.

At least I thought I knew. Instead *he* threw me out of his office and told me to have the piece on Krafft on his desk in an hour or pick up my last paycheck and start hitching to the hinterlands!

I had it to him in forty-five minutes and he actually nodded. "Not bad, Donovan; you may turn into a newspaperman yet." Then he told me to get out of his sight.

I took him at his word and went off to a long liquid lunch with the light of my life and chief advocate for the Moxie-is-a-great-guy club, Maxi.

Maxine Keller (the former Maxine Gladys Kellerman of the Bronx) was a drink of cool water in a desert; a redheaded dish with peepers the color of the spring sky, the legs you'd expect on a Broadway hoofer and a smile that could melt the Polar Ice caps. Best part of the whole package is that she blinked those lamps in my direction and flashed that smile special just for me.

We met at a little watering hole that made a decent Rueben sandwich and a high-octane martini the way I liked it. So I'm a booze snob, sue me.

"It makes no sense at all," I said after my second drink evaporated into me.

"I know," she said. "Why steal a bunch of tubes and pipes and air pumps?"

"No," I said. "I mean Whitey not running my werewolf story? I mean, now we have proof that regular lead bees don't sting those walking tree trunks—that makes it pretty clear to me that it has to be silver slugs."

"Moxie," she hissed, "werewolves are hairy, not splintery. You know, like my legs."

She stretched out her silk clad gam from under the tablecloth and ran a hand along the shin as if looking for razor stubble. She knew it was going to drive me crazy.

"Have a heart, Babe," I whined. "I have to go back and at least pretend to keep my mind on my work 'til dinner time."

She gave a wicked smirk. "And a bit after—remember we are going to two different Halloween parties tonight and one tomorrow: the Keppleman's at the Plaza starts at seven tomorrow, but the fireman's fund is at nine tonight and it's midnight at Broadway Mort's-that one will be a rip!"

"Oh, Baby,' I cranked up the volume on my whine. "You know I don't like to put on silly costumes."

She shoved a box across the table that looked innocent enough, but I knew contained her latest instrument of torture for me: a costume.

"Oh, you're not gonna hold me to that? Can't I go as a tired reporter —I have everything I need for that on me now."

She was also a whiz at poker and had won a bet on this week's date —I wanted to go to the racetrack for some pony action and she wanted to do the two-night Broadway party thing. She had a king high flush, so I was playing dress up.

"What did you get me?" I asked, afraid to look, "Nothing with tights, I hope."

She laughed like expensive crystal. "No, those walking sticks of yours could cause blindness in the innocent; what I got you will show off your nice shoulders: but you can't open it 'til you put it on at the paper."

"Oh no," I protested. " Not at the paper."

"That was the bet," she said. "You gonna welch?"

Deadline Zombies

I hung my head in defeat. "I'll do it; but you are crueler than Hedda Hopper!" This brought a giggle of glee from her and it was hard to be angry at that.

"I almost forgot, "I said, "I brought this for you…"

I pulled out the ballerina doll that toy maker had given me and I thought every glass in the room would shatter with her squeal of joy. The hug she gave me almost made up for having to pay off my bet.

Almost.

Chapter IV: Pulling Strings

The night before Halloween was the big party night in the city, and even as I shuffled back to work with the box under my arm, I saw some little tykes in costumes going out to trick or treat.

The city room had calmed down since before lunch and the usual Saturday slow cycle was coming back into play with any political stuff being held 'til Monday, and no major crimes (that anyone would admit) except the 'puppet killings' though, there again, no one but me seemed to want to call them that. I tell ya, it was like the yellow was washing off *The Daily Star* and that bothered me.

I punched out at five and went to the men's room with the box under my arm, hoping I could hide whatever she had gotten me under a trench coat and be out the door before anyone suspected I was dolled up.

No such luck.

My gorgeous, but cruel, lady had filled the box with a blue military uniform jacket, belt and white trousers and knee-high boots. She topped it off with a Napoleon style hat and I knew she wouldn't count the bet paid if I didn't wear the whole get up as I walked out the door.

"Boy am I gonna make our next bet a doozy for you, Maxi." I muttered out loud as I shimmied into the get up. Even the boots fit perfectly, but then my gal had a costumer's eye. *Darn her.*

I prayed no one would walk into the John while I was suiting up but the universe was cruel that day; Whitey came in to wash his hands.

When he saw me standing in the middle of the tile floor adjusting my jacket he stopped, spit into a sink and shook his head. "In my day," he said as he turned to leave, "The screwballs waited 'til they were actually in the loony bin before they got dressed as their heroes."

I wanted to die right there.

Wilson gave an evil tight lipped grin, then added, "Oh, and I'm gonna run your werewolf story in the late addition; it's just the thing for Halloween, but I had Marty add in the new dirt—The coroner got curious and did a 'post mortem' on those puppets and seems those wooden dummies weren't just dummies—they had all sorts of gears and cog wheels in them to make them move. Like something out of Flash Gordon." He shut the door as he called back, " Tell Maxi I still think she's plain nuts for dating you."

And then he was gone.

"They're running my story!!" I yelled to Maxi when she met me down stairs in the lobby. I was so excited by the byline (Marty's rewrite would respect my stuff, I knew) I almost failed to be properly impressed by her harem girl outfit. Almost.

You'd have to be dead not be impressed by Maxine in any outfit, let alone that.

"That's great, Moxie!" she bubbled. "Does that mean he wants you to keep on the story?"

I realized I had been so flustered in the men's room I hadn't thought to ask. "Uh—Just try to keep me off it." I said.

We were the envy of the lobby and curb outside as I held up a hand to hail a hack, though I think most were agreeing with Whitey about Maxi being with me.

The Fireman's Ball was a swinging affair, with the booze and the skirts flowing freely, with hot music and hot women (though of course, I didn't notice with Maxi on my arm) but it paled by comparison to Broadway Mort's shindig.

It was held in a ballroom of the Gotham Hotel on Fifty Fifth Street off of Sixth Avenue. Everyone who was anyone passed through the doors greeted by the little balding guy who was the center of the whole deal, Mortimer Shemel, aka Broadway Mort. He'd run a speakeasy back in the day that had catered to the bright lights of the White Way and now had a legit restaurant down the block from the Gotham.

His parties were legendary and if I had not been preoccupied with the Puppet robberies or dressed like a loony tune I might have been looking forward to it.

"Oh don't be a stick in the mud, Moxie," Maxi said to me as we entered the swanky digs of the Gotham, "You know Morty always feeds strays and reporters."

"Hardy har har," I said back.

Morty was a dynamo at five foot two, a little gnome who had more energy than Hoover's Dam and a cigar in his mouth the size of a submarine.

"Hey Maxi, great to see you!" he said, going on tiptoes to kiss her on the cheek. "I see you got Moxie a parole from the loony bin."

I hate this costume!

Once inside the ballroom it was real showplace, high ceilings with crystal light fixtures and wood paneled walls that gave the place the aspect of a royal court in some far off European country. The crowd was a lot of Broadway royalty to continue the motif, including the Astaires, Champions, Iva Withers, and a bunch of up and comers. All of them had just come from shows and a late snack so their engines were running in high gear.

Everyone was in costume and most masked, so I didn't' feel quite the boob for being in my military get up. There were Cleopatras, Annie Oakleys, Maid Marians, Robin Hoods and Jesse James' galore.

I had to work overtime to not show too much interest in the distaff revelers, but Maxi was an understanding sort of woman, she only kicked me in the shins four of five times in the first five minutes of the affair. At that point I was grateful for the boots.

It may have been a high-class party but the booze was Hell's Kitchen potent, so I had no objections at all. After my second stiff one, Maxi convinced me to step out onto the dance floor with her.

I gotta tell ya I felt like the king of the ball with that dish in my arms. I'm not the worst dancer in the world and she was kind enough to ignore the times I stepped on her feet so we cut quite the dashing image, world conqueror and exotic princess. Everyone seemed to know Maxi and a few knew me, so there were lots of 'hi' and 'how are ya's' as we waltzed around. The fact that the party was held late to let the show crowd make an appearance meant that many were already well lubricated before they put in an appearance, so there was a lot of good cheer all around.

We waddled the full circuit of the floor several times with me showing off my good luck for a couple of dances, then took a break by the punch table. That's when my reporter's eye overcame my roving eye.

One of the costume goers caught my lamp blast, a guy dressed like Lon Chaney's Phantom as the Masque of the Red Death, his skull face a little somber for the gathering and his scarlet robes an eye catcher. He stood alone to the side of the room and seemed to be waiting for someone.

Maybe it was just the strangeness of one person standing alone when there was so much person-flesh to go around or the stories that Digger had filled my head with about the Skullmask guy, but I left Maxi chatting with a girlfriend and sauntered down to the end of the table where the guy stood. I made a pretense to be looking for party snacks and stepped up beside the odd looking duck (like I was so normal in my get up).

"Swell party, huh?" I said with great suave. I kind of destroyed my Gable moment by banging my shins into a folding wooden chair by the edge of the table. I was already softened up by Maxi's boot ballet so I yelped very un-suavely.

"Yah," he said with a European accent that might have been German, "It is a goot party." His eyes never left the door to the room. There was an intensity to them that was more than a Joe waiting for a Jane; his blue eyes were focused like spotlights on an airfield at night, as if to look away would cause a crash.

Deadline Zombies

As I watched, I saw his glims widen in recognition of someone at the door and found myself following his stare to the entrance. Through the dancing and kibitzing crowd, I could see eight figures as they entered. They were all costumed head to foot in elaborate get ups as clowns, sailors, cowboys and a sheik. Nothing unusual in that except that they all wore full face masks that hid their features. They moved in a tight group through the door then spread out in sort of a 'V' formation with a white faced Pagliacci in the lead. There was definitely something odd about the way they moved: maybe it was the precision of their steps, almost marching in unison.

In any case I was about to say something to the skull-faced guy beside me when the lead clown produced a gun and suddenly it was the Fourth of July in October!

Chapter V: Crashers are such a bore!

The clown's gun was a strange one, with tubes and wires wrapped around an amazingly large bore barrel. He waved it in the air, and then the oddest voice I have ever heard came from his unmoving rubber face. "This is a robbery!" he said in a voice that sounded like Rudy Vallee through a megaphone. The inhuman-sounding announcement was loud enough to reach all corners of the room and bizarre enough to catch most people's attention. To show he was serious, the rubber-faced clown fired his weapon and shot the band conductor through the leg. The sound of the gun was strange as well; a whispered cough not at all like any bang stick I'd ever heard.

And I'll bet he fired a wooden bullet, I thought.

"No one move and no one else will get hurt," the clown pronounced. "You will surrender you valuables or be killed. There will be no argument."

Morty stepped forward then waving his arms and yelled, 'Hey, you jokers can't come into—"

The convict clown's pistol coughed again and the impresario went down hard with a bullet through his gut.

There were screams and several women (and a chorus boy or two) fainted.

Maxi darted past me and out onto the dance floor before I could stop her. She went straight to Morty and whipped off one of her veils and began to try and staunch the flow of blood from our host.

The masked men ignored her and fanned out across the room with cloth sacks in their hands, going from guest to guest. They left one of their number standing by the main entrance and he kept a gun leveled into the room.

The robot robbers moved around the room, walking up to the women and snatching jewelry from their throats.

I stood there not knowing what to do, afraid to move toward Maxi for fear of drawing their attention to her, yet wanting to be by her side. Not to mention I wanted to bop the white faced joke monkey with a chair. While I dithered, the red-robed fright-face next to me acted.

Out of nowhere he had a Mauser in his hand and let loose with a barrage of shots that seemed to be magically drawn to the heads of four of the masked men. He fanned his shots across the room, taking out the one at the door first, then moving off to the right.

The crowd all hit the ground at the first shot, the chorus of screams almost drowning out the later shots.

Deadline Zombies

There was a masked cowboy off to my left and he turned at the sound of the Skullmask's gunfire. He dropped the sack of loot he was holding and whirled, reaching for the gun in the holster. He didn't pull a six-gun, however, but another of the weird silent guns the first clown had used.

I didn't let him fire it at the Skullmask's back. I swung like the Babe with the folding chair, shattering it across the masked maverick's extended arm and chest.

There was a sharp crack and the arm of the masked man broke at the elbow, hanging down like a marionette's arm whose string had been cut.

There was no outcry of pain or even reaction to the arm dangling by the sleeve of the calico shirt. Instead, the masked figure just bent down and picked up the gun from where it had skittered across the floor with his left hand.

I was all out of chairs. The best strategy I could come up with was to tackle him and hope there was some way to strangle a life sized Pinocchio when there was an explosion behind me. The cowboy's head abruptly jerked back as a silver bullet from the Skullmask's Mauser hit him dead center in the forehead. The puppet pistolero went over backwards, his mask flying off to reveal its blank wooden kisser. The faux desperado stayed down for the count.

I turned back to see the red cloaked masked man smiling at me. "Thank you," he said, "that was courageous."

"Are you kidding?" I asked. "You're the one from last night, aren't you?"

"Yah," he said.

I was gonna ask him how he knew about the robberies enough in advance to intervene, but a coughing sound from behind me drew me back to reality. My Nappy hat went flying off my bean and my knees turned to Jell-O. I hit the ground faster than O'Leary at happy hour and ducked my head.

The Skullmask didn't move from his spot, just raised his automatic and fired twice. I heard the thud as two more dummy desperados bit the dust.

Then there was the sound of running feet, and I when I looked up, I watched the scarlet skull man race out the door. He paused at the entrance and caught my eye. He smiled from beneath the skull face and then was gone.

I looked over at Maxi who was staring back at me, her pretty face a mask of worry. Beside her, Morty was looking as pale as the skull that had just left.

"Mort," I said, " You sure know how to throw a real shindig; remember not to invite me next year."

I thought Maxi's look of death at me at that moment was a whole site scarier that the wooden puppets had been.

Deadline Zombies

Chapter VI: Second Thoughts

Sunday's edition had an extra on the robbery at Broadway Mort's and I had a byline for the front page about it. Four columns under the banner and five on the following page. It was big. I even used some of the stuff Digger had given me to fill the story out for color about a mysterious secret society of masked men around the globe. Total hokum, but even Whitey couldn't argue with the fact that it sold papers like water in the desert.

Mort's stomach wound was serious but not fatal, the wooden bullet having been less dangerous than a lead slug might have been in the same spot. Maxi almost forgave me for my smart alec remark, but only after I promised to keep our date for the Sunday party: It was being throw by an old friend of hers and I would have been in the hottest water available if I didn't go.

The day was spent tracking down leads that went nowhere and talking to witnesses that remembered forty different versions of Saturday night's events. I tried to find some clue to the German sounding masked man, but all my and Digger's sources were stumped.

Still, it was good day for a news hound like me. Like a hound chasing a fox, I was on a scent and I would not let go.

I had to take a break at five, however, cause my dog handler, Maxi, showed up at the paper and reminded me we had to attend the Keppleman's party uptown.

"But Doll," I protested, "I'm on a hot story—this Skullmask thing—"

"I just came from visiting Morty and he thinks you're the big brave defender for smashing that chair over that death puppet. Am I going to have to tell him a little slip of a girl like me was able to break the neck of such a paragon for going back on a promise?" She smiled like a Cheshire cat when I blanched. "And really, the paper and the story are going to be here in three hours when the party is over; We have to go, Mitsy Keppleman is an old school pal and the dance is for charity." She got *that* look in her eye and added, "and this pays off your debt, Mister."

A guy's gotta know when he's licked, so I punched out and in ten minutes was wearing my Napoleon get up again. The repeat of Maxi's costume had not dulled its effect on me, but the frenzy of the day kept my mind working on the entire ride uptown to the party at the Plaza. I mulled over the little pieces of information on the case looking for new angle on it.

We had a bunch of deadly puppets running around New York, armed with wooden bullet shooting guns that made almost no noise. *Why?* No matter how weird, there had to be a reason for their actions. And why did the guy in the mask have to use silver bullets? Some sort of magic? My rational mind fought that concept, but what I had seen last night seemed to support that.

So what did the robberies have in common? Clock gears, pipes and tubes for the first two we knew of, then last night money.

"It was some sort of supply run," I said aloud.

Maxi looked at me like I had grown a second noggin.

"What did you say?" she asked. "Are you talking shop again."

"Shop!" I said. The timing was just right, because just then the cabbie dropped us off on the corner of Fifty-Ninth by the park. As I helped Maxi out of the car, I looked across the street to see Krafft's Creations store and got inspired.

"Doll, I just gotta do one little thing before we go in."

She gave me that *Oh no, not work?* look, and I had to cop to it.

"Just a little fact check thing I gotta look into," I said, "I did an article on that guy that's running in today's Sunday section." She wasn't buying it until I added, "He's the Joe who made the Doll for you—He's got more inside."

"Okay," she perked up. "As long as I can go with you!"

That was fine by me. We hoofed it across the street and soon I was knocking on the door of the shop. It was closed, but I could see the light on in the back and knew a craftsman like Krafft would be burning the midnight oil. I figured if anybody could clue me in about gears and gizmos, it would be him. I wanted to be able to hit Whitey with a follow up for the Monday morning edition.

A minute or two of knocking got a muffled "Ein moment" from the back of the store and soon the shambling shape of the kindly old toymaker came out of the gloom toward us.

"Ah, Mr. Donovan," he said with an amused smile on his face, "I am afraid I do not have any treats for revelers such as yourself!" He regarded Maxi and her outfit with appropriate awe and delight and looked at me like I was out of my mind.

"Hi, Mr. Krafft," I said, "May I introduce Miss Maxine Keller?"

She did a little curtsey and he went all old world on her and kissed her hand. If he hadn't been a grandfather type, I might have been jealous.

"I came about a story I'm writing on a robbery that happened last night."

"And how might I help you?" He looked a little perplexed. He motioned up into the store and Maxi almost ran me over to get in first.

Deadline Zombies

She immediately started to run from display to display, squealing with delight at each.

"Am I wrong in assuming this is the 'child at heart' you gave my doll to?" The old man asked.

"It was beautiful," she said to him. " Oh my, this is all so amazing."

He beamed as she studied his work.

"Uh—" I tried to cut in. "As an expert on clockwork gears and such, Mr. Krafft, I was wondering if you might be able to answer a question for me."

He watched Maxi as she darted around the store, I think a little afraid she would barrel into his stock, but she moved like the dancer she was, stopping in front of each item with a new expression of astonishment.

"I will answer any question I can," he said.

"In your opinion," I asked, pulling my notebook from a pocket in the jacket—hey Moxie's first rule—"Could a mechanical man be built that was capable of independent action—say, holding a gun or taking aim to shoot someone?"

His face clouded and he knit his eyebrows in thought. "Such a dark topic," he said. "But do come in the back while I think on it." He led the two of us into his sanctum where the workbench looked even more cluttered than it had yesterday morning. Now a mass of tubes and pipes were scattered across it and what looked like an artificial leg clamped in place with a vise.

Maxi spotted the other dolls to match hers and went right to them. One was a little Napoleon and she held it up to show me. "He's already got one of you here," she joked. "And this one is cuter."

The old man laughed at my discomfort, a little chuckle like your favorite uncle has when you snort milk out your nose at Thanksgiving dinner. Well, mine did, anyway.

"Now about your question,' he said, " I do not know of any purely mechanical means where such a thing were possible- a motion such as grasping a gun or pointing it to aim is far more complex than one might suspect." He reached past his work on the desk just as I noticed the tubes on the desk were stenciled with "AR Co." Which I knew with a sickeningly late premonition was Arlington Refrigeration Company.

He turned with an odd looking gun in his hand as if to demonstrate how difficult the action was. Looked pretty damn easy to me.

"Please come to stand by the young lady, Mr. Donovan," the suddenly evil Geppetto said. His voice seemed to have dropped an octave and his eyes no longer sparkled, they glared.

"What's going on, Moxie?" Maxi asked.

"I'm not sure of all of it, Doll," I said. "But Santa over there had something to do with the puppet killings."

Her China blues went wide, but she was a bright girl and kept her exclamations to a minimum.

"You will go down, please." Krafft reached under his work table and pressed a hidden catch that caused a trapdoor in the floor to open. In the darkness below, I could just barely make out some steps. He hit a second switch and the room below blazed into light.

"What makes you think I'll—" I began, but he pointed his pistol at Maxi.

"You will obey, because if you do not, I will shoot the Judean painfully through the knees. At first."

No contest; I obeyed.

The room below was a larger version of his workbench, but on a grand scale. If I had any doubts about his culpability in the crimes, they were sent packing by the sight of half a dozen wooden forms leaning against the wall. There was more of the tubing from the Arlington Company scattered about as well.

The toymaker motioned for me and Maxi to stand across from him in a little set-back in the wall. Then he pressed another hidden button somewhere and bars dropped from the ceiling to effectively lock us in a cell.

"Now, my inquisitive friend," he said, setting his pistol down on the workbench, "You will learn more than you bargained for, I will bet."

Chapter VII: No Corsage for Maxi

"This is a lousy date," Maxi said to me.

"No argument, Babe," I said, "I hope I get to make it up to you."

Krafft, meanwhile, had donned a strange robe incised with strange symbols. He lit a brassier that he set out in front of the cell bars and then began to chalk symbols on the floor.

"What's with the Chandu get up?" I asked.

Maxi punched me in the arm but I did my best to ignore her.

"Bravado is good, my friend," he said. "But make no mistake, your fate is sealed; though not quite what you might imagine." He continued to make marks on the floor and I did my best to copy them into my notebook without him seeing.

"I was truthful with you, Mr. Donovan, when I said that there was no way I knew of for purely mechanical means to accomplish what you mentioned." The old man seemed more spry than he had upstairs and stepped back from the marks on the floor. He raised his hands and began to mumble in a language I couldn't figure.

"Therefore, I turned to older arts than science—Alchemy, using the degenerate arts of the Kabala, much as that Rabbi in Warsaw, thus using the Jew's own arts against them to fully animate my servants as these symbols mixed with the Runes indicate: I have access by such means to older powers." When he saw my look of skepticism his smile became one of the *convinced*. "As our leader says, Mr. Donovan: *We are now at the end of the age of reason. The intellect has grown autocratic, and has become a disease of life. A new age of Magic interpretation of the world is coming, of interpretation in terms of the will and not the intelligence.*" He had the look and sound of someone reciting scripture and it gave me the willies.

"You don't have any reason going for you, I'll give you that, crafty old boy." I put up a front for Maxi, who was looking a bit spooked by all the whacky talk, but I've got to admit I was ready to sprinkle some holy water around the joint myself. I'd heard the same line of balderdash at the Bund rallies at The Garden I'd had to cover, with Fritz Kuhn spouting racist nonsense. I'd almost lost my lunch then with the race baiting I'd had to listen to, and couldn't bear to go back for the second day of the weekend long hate fest. I made no secret of it at the paper when I'd gotten back. Wilson had bawled me out then for losing my impartiality when he read my bund/racketeers piece, but I always figured a good newshound was anything but impartial.

Krafft mumbled a bunch more and before our eyes, the wooden men against the wall began to stand up and walk!

The dummy thugs wore various costumes; cowboy, pirate, clown, and (if only my editor knew) werewolf. Each also clutched the same strange gun in its hand that Krafft had used on us. The pistols were of the automatic variety with tubes running along the outside of the weapon from what looked like a little cylinder they use for oxygen at the hospital. I was willing to bet they were the direct descendants of the guns his granpappy made to shoot at old Nappy! His own ego had compelled him to carve the bullets himself out of the teak blocks I had seen on his worktable.

Krafft put a matching mask on each of the mechanical monsters to cover their blank wooden faces and then pointed to another staircase at the back of the room.

The wooden men obeyed his silent command and they lumbered toward the exit. They paused at the bottom as if getting their bearings and then moved up at a steady pace.

"Losing those two automatons Friday night almost delayed my plans," Krafft said, "as I did not have enough 'spare parts' on hand. But I was able to get all the tubes I needed for the pneumatics yesterday."

'Just like you got the spare clock parts the night before when the Skullmask almost caught your Charlie McCarthies."

He glared at me with virulent hate, then shook himself like a dog drying off and smiled.

He gestured to the rising puppetmen and turned to us with the satisfied smile of a craftsman as he explained, "My children will make enough tonight at the robbery of the rich degenerate Jews at the Plaza to make up for what they missed at last night's party. They are going to finance a much larger army of my marvelous toymen for the Fuhrer. My ancestor made the mistake of rising against a uniter, but I will aid the Reich in rising to true dominance and bringing a thousand year reign of peace to the world." He was in his glory now, expounding on how clever he was, so I did my best to bleed him for more info.

"So you're telling me you make them move by magic?" I asked. Not being the circumspect type, my cynicism kind of showed through. It didn't please papa toyman.

"Sneer if you will, young man," he said, stepping almost close enough to the bars for me to do something about it. "But they, like the Aryan race, are an inevitable force and are unstoppable!"

"Except by silver bullets!" I threw back.

This made him really angry and he took a half a step closer.

Almost.

Deadline Zombies

"Yes, silver is an anathema to them," he said. "And somehow that was discovered by my enemy."

"And that would be old death face?" I was watching his body language and I knew that just one more little annoyance would make him careless. "Just who would he be?"

"I do not know his true identity," he said in a tone that made me think he really didn't. "But he wears a mask with a death's head upon it. He almost stopped me in Europe—where I began my experiments in Geneva, so I moved my base of operations. There are more rich degenerates here in any case. I thought I had escaped him by coming to America, but I was wrong."

'You've done this in the old country?" I asked. Maxi was shooting me the evil eye to shut up, but I wanted to see what I could goad out of the old goat. "So much for a superior race, Pappy, I guess you messed that up pretty bad to come running here?"

"You arrogant—" he stepped too close and I sprang at the bars, grabbing hold of his apron to pull him forward and slam him into the metal uprights.

He made a grunting sound and tried to pull back, but I hung on for dear life.

"Get his keys," I yelled.

Maxi didn't need to be told twice and she moved to reach through the bars and felt in his pockets for the keys.

'I can't find them," she said.

"Try the apron, the main pocket.

"Bingo!" She pulled the keys from his apron just as he jerked away from me and fell backwards onto the floor. Maxi tried to get the keys in the door but fumbled it because she was so excited.

Krafft got to his feet and headed for the table where he had set his gun down. I took the keys from Maxi and had slightly better luck fitting the key in the lock, but I never got to turn it.

A voice from the shop stairs called out, "Step away from the bars, Moxie, or I'll blow your Jew-loving head off." It was Whitey Wilson and he had one of Krafft's air guns pointed smack dab at my kisser!

Chapter VIII: Just Another Stiff

Things went from bad to worse real quick.

In no time flat, Maxine was being strapped down to a worktable and I was hanging by my arms with my feet off the floor. Whitey Wilson was standing there with Krafft like it was old home week.

"I thought when I gave him that last piece of information he would put it together yesterday," Whitey said. "He may be weak and it took him longer than I had thought, but in the end he is a good newspaperman."

He gave me more credit than I deserved, considering I hadn't put two and two together, but I wasn't going to give either one of them the satisfaction of realizing I had just stumbled onto their plan.

"Of course, I put it together," I boasted. "I knew Krafft was behind the puppets as soon as I put together the teak wood on your worktable, the clockwork parts taken Friday night and the pneumatic stuff taken from the Arlington Company; but I have to admit I thought you were an okay guy, Whitey—a real schmuck of a boss, but an okay guy."

Wilson stepped forward and slapped me hard across the face. "Swine!" he spat at me. "You sleep with that mongrel bitch—"

"Hey!" Maxi yelled.

"And have the audacity to make light of Der Fuhrer's words! I wanted to kill you after you returned from the rally, but I dared not reveal myself."

Krafft was mixing some chemicals with a mortar and pestle and for some reason, that scared me more than the gun in Whitey's hand. The toymaker looked up from his work and gave that Geppetto smile that really made me have the heeby geebies.

"Hey, I'm just a working stiff," I said, "But there's a lot more where I come from who won't put up with your bull—"

"Funny you should use the term you did," Krafft said as he approached me with the mortar in his hands.

I could see a smoky mist rising from it, yellow colored and smelling like last week's Limburger. "You will be a lot more stiff in a very short time."

He put the bowl under my face and I tried to squirm away from the fumes, but had no luck. Like I'd had any good luck of late.

Then the two of them leered at me and stepped back.

"Moxie!' Maxi called out," What are they doing to you?"

"I don't know, Doll," I said. "But I've got better than even money it's not good."

Deadline Zombies

And I would have won if I had money down. Within minutes my head started to hurt like I'd gone rounds with Jack Sharkey. My vision started to distort and my mouth went as dry as a bone.

"I will explain, Mr. Donovan," the toymaker said. "You see, the alchemists were masters of transformation, searching for many centuries for the philosopher's stone to transmute base metals to gold. I search for a way to turn base subhuman forms into something that can be useful to the Reich. In your case, Mr. Donovan, I think your costume for the night suggested the perfect form for you to take: statuary for my shop." While he spoke, I could feel changes taking place in my body: changes I did not like.

My joints began to stiffen and my eyesight got even worse. My skin felt like it was starting to tighten, like astringent had been poured over my whole body.

"What's going on, Moxie?" Maxine called. "What are they doin' to you Honey?"

I wasn't sure myself and I was plenty scared, but I had to be the man, so I called back, "I'm just feeling a little stiff, Babe—don't sweat it."

"You get away from him, you Nazi weasels!" she called. Then she let loose with a string of curses that would have peeled the paint off a battleship.

Gotta love a girl from the Bronx!

My body was going through convulsions now, my spine felt like it was being pried out through my back and my skin was crawling like a thousand ants were makin' a home in me.

My two playmates were smiling and laughing at my pain and I wished real hard I had enough left in me to launch a kick to Whitey's next generation.

"You'll finally find your place in the journalistic world," Wilson sneered. "In front of the cigar store in the lobby of *The Star*!"

He and Krafft turned then and left me to my fate.

And what a fate—I could feel the changes coming more swiftly, and when I looked up at my hands, I could see the changes happening to my exposed forearms.

The skin was taking on a parchment-like appearance, turning color and darkening. As I watched with mounting horror as the flesh of my arm became almost petrified, but instead of turning to stone the cells of my arms became wood.

I could feel a similar change happening in my legs as feeling from them began to fade. I knew it was because my nerve endings were changing from flesh and blood to wood and bark. I could feel the process inside me happening as well, and with the vivid imagination Whitey had chided me for so often, I could see in my mind's eye the changes as I went from man to tree under the mad Aryan's magic spell.

My face had no feeling any more. I was aware that I had not breathed in a while and I doubted I even blinked at that point. My mouth was all but frozen, my tongue hard and leathery inside my dry mouth.

"I'm sorry I got you into this, Doll," I called to Maxi. My voice was like sandpaper and I had to work hard to make the sounds intelligible. If I was sweating from the fear and pain, I had no way of knowing it. I had no physical sensations from my skin at all, it was like I'd been coated with a thick shell of cedar, like I'd become my own coffin.

My neck was stiff and I found I couldn't turn my head any more. Fortunately, I was facing Maxi and had the odd thought that, even in the middle of all that, the kid looked sensational.

"I've always gone along for the ride with you, Moxie," she said in her bravest voice. She could barely hide her fear, but I could tell she was putting on a show for my sake. "And I don't regret a minute of it."

What a dish!

She was crying now, the look of horror on her face all I needed to know about what I looked like. My body had stopped convulsing and had literally stiffened up, so that I felt I must look like a wooden gargoyle outside some gothic cathedral.

I cursed toy makers and clock makers and editors and Germans and prayed hard that she got out of this all right, somehow. She didn't deserve any of the nonsense I'd put her through in the time we'd been dating.

"You are the best, Maxi," I forced out. 'When we get through this, I'm gonna make an honest woman of you if you'll have me: that's a promise."

I could barely see now, one eye was cloudy and dark, but she managed a slight smile.

"It took you being turned into a street lamp to make you realize I'm the right girl?"

I had to work my tightening throat against the encroaching dehumanization but I managed to force out, "I've always carried a torch for you, Kid. Just for now I'll *be* the torch." Then the words froze in my mouth, my jaw locked and the darkness encroached full on.

It was over for me and I couldn't even shed a tear about it. Not a single tear.

Deadline Zombies

Chapter IX: Deus Ex Machine Gun

Just when the final curtain was lowering on my peepshow, there was a noise like thunder and a scream. I couldn't turn my head anymore, but I could see Maxi turn hers and gasp. Then there were the sounds of gunshots, answered by the puff-puff sounds of Krafft's silent guns.

I heard Krafft scream," Schweinhund!" and then curse. The toymaker staggered into my field of vision, followed by the ugliest savior anyone could ever imagine.

It was the guy in the short leather jacket with a dark fedora on his head holding a Mauser automatic. But his face held my interest just as it had the night before: it was the Skullmask, made out of yellowed leather that allowed his lower lip and jaw to move freely. Beneath the sculpted bony-brows, his eyes were aflame with what I soon learned was a desperate need for justice. Spell that justice V-e-n-g-e-a-n-c-e!

Suddenly Whitey came into my field of vision with one of those air pistols in each hand. He tried to bring them to bear, but the skull-masked gunman was faster. He spun and lobbed two silver bullets into my former editor (I had decided to resign by that time), dead center.

Whitey went down and the already wounded Krafft tried to flee, but the death head avenger was right at his side.

"Reverse the spell!" the Skullmask rasped in a heavily accented European voice. "Now!"

Krafft sneered at him and shook his head.

My hopes rose and crashed as the evil Geppetto spat "Never!"

Skullmask didn't ask a second time—he just shot the old man through the thigh of his left leg.

"Arrgh!" Krafft dropped to the ground as blood spilled from the wound.

"Reverse the spell!" The masked man repeated.

This time Krafft looked up at the long barrel of the automatic and held his protests. He began to mumble and took some chalk from the edge of the worktable to scrawl some symbols at my feet. I couldn't see much of them but the few I could see seemed to be the same as the ones he's written before. Runes he'd called them.

"Hurry," the masked man said, "If you fail, you die." There was nothing in his tone that left room for doubt that he would carry out his promise.

"It might be too late," Krafft said.

"Too bad for you then," the masked man said.

And me too!

Krafft dragged himself to he workbench and began to mix some chemicals in his batter bowl. In a few minutes he had a steaming mess of something, and he waved the bowl under my now wooden nose.

I smelled nothing and felt nothing so I pretty much gave it up at that point. *"Nice idea,"* I thought to the masked guy. *"But you might as well get the cigars to put in my hand."*

Krafft looked horrified. He shook his head. "It is-too—"

The Skullmask raised his gun to point it at the toymaker's head.

Then I felt it; a twitch in my face.

A real feeling. Like an itch you can't scratch.

I would have giggled if I could have, but I didn't have that luxury at that point.

"See,' Krafft yelled, "It is working, do not kill me!"

"Like all your 'master race'" the Skullmask said. "Just a sniveling coward when pressed on it. I stopped your puppets at the Plaza: I knew you would try for so prominent a gathering—knew you set up shop here for that very reason. I confronted your man Dieter, but he was loyal to you to the end; he and his wife tried to shoot it out with me. Fools. I was able to make it look like a family fight. I had hoped his death would delay your plans until I could learn more; but after last night, I knew different. I just didn't count on this newspaperman getting on to you so soon."

Everybody was giving me credit for being a genius—so how come I was a lawn ornament?

I felt a tickle in my throat, deep down inside, a rasping sensation, but it was wonderful. It was like hot liquid dripping through my system in reverse, flowing upward through me from the center of my chest and outward toward my limbs.

Maxi was crying at this point, shaking her head up and down and whispering, "Yes, yes. Yes!"

I felt a pain in my chest and I was overjoyed for it. It felt like it was my heart restarting; a major 'thump' feeling, and then I took a breath! A real breath.

Even the masked man seemed captivated by my re-transformation. That was a mistake.

While Skullmask was looking at me, Krafft made a grab for one of the air guns on the workbench.

'Behind you!" I screamed. The masked man spun and put a bullet through the toymaker's head before the old man could bring the gun to bear.

"Thank you," the Skullmask said as I collapsed forward to my knees. He set Maxi free and she ran to my side.

Deadline Zombies

"I think you got that wrong," I wheezed, "You're the Tom Mix in this story."

The masked man moved to the back stairs of the workroom. Now that I could turn my head, I could see that several of the death puppets were piled near the store entrance, no doubt with silver bullets through their blank noggins.

"No," he said. "I am no hero; that is for ordinary people who live and love and make a difference. All I do is try to balance the scales."

"What will you do now?" I asked.

"Continue to fight these Aryan butchers that killed my family; I am German and they have sullied the word with their actions. The world must know what they are doing in Europe; the benign face they present is the great lie." He started up the stairs.

"I can promise you I'll do my best to make sure the world wakes up," I said. "And my typewriter can be louder than a cannon!"

I saw a smile beneath the horror mask then. 'It is all I could, ask," he said, "and congratulations on the wedding!" Then he was gone.

Epilogue:

I had a devil of a time making myself understood to O'Leary and his boys, but with the witnesses at the Keppleman party to back up the existence of the masked man, me and Maxi avoided any charges for the two stiffs in the toymaker's basement.

I wrote the story, which was picked up by the wire services and got me more front page space than I could have ever hoped for, and then I penned a series exposing the Bund movement in the U.S. that won a Pulitzer Prize.

The notoriety helped ease my way into the post of city room editor of *The Daily Star* with Fran getting the bump up to managing editor. We make quite a team and burnt the pants off a whole new generation of snot nosed reporters like I used to be. Now I'm the guy who yells at the typewriter hacks to make it real news with verified facts.

Over the months, there were whispers of the masked guy, or at least of a number of masked guys and some gals that wore that damned fright face, going toe to toe with the Fuhrer's boys in many corners of the world. Digger was always showing me a clipping from Casablanca or Harbin that mentioned a masked joker. It should have made me shudder, but somehow the mystery of it was not half the security of knowing he was out there.

The wedding went on, despite my protests that I was out of my mind when I promised Maxi—she's a tough girl and just don't take no.

I did have to limp down the aisle though: seems Krafft was partially right; I have a wooden left leg from the knee down and only Mrs. Donovan knows it's not an artificial one.

Hey, I think of myself as Ahab, and those Nazi jokers as the great white whale- only I ain't goin' down with the ship. With guys like the Skullmask out there fighting, and my typewriter, the good thinking people of the world are gonna win this one and that's a promise!

-30-

Even Hollywood Zombies Need Agents

Prologue: Casting for Parts

Charlie Bukowski was running for his life. It was dark and he was drunk but not so drunk that he did not know that the men in hoods wanted his life.

He was in the Jackass Hill area of Kingsbury Run and there was no one around to save him. The streets were deserted, the sound of his footfalls like thunder in the quiet August night. The air was heavy with the smell of rotting garbage from nearby tenements, and Charles stumbled in a pile of trash as he rounded a corner near East 49th and headed down Praha Avenue.

Charles did not know why the men had singled him out, could not think in his alcohol soaked state why anyone would want to hurt him. Yet they did want to hurt him, he could tell that because they had knives, big knives and they brandished them when they leapt from an alleyway blocks back and reached for him.

They thought him so drunk he could not escape them, but terror gave him strength and speed and he had fled.

That had been an eternity ago.

His legs burned with the effort, his chest heaved in an attempt to pump blood and oxygen to his body.

The sudden alertness of his mind was a curse, for he pictured all the things he had not done in his life: all the things lost, the jobs he had been fired from, the family he had thrown away because of his drinking.

Now he was going to die because of his drinking; if he had not been out looking for one more drink at three o'clock in the morning he might not had seen the hooded figure bent over the body of the woman.

If he had not been looking for one more drink, he might not be running until his legs burned and his heart near burst from the effort.

Then the second masked man caught up with Charles and plunged the blade into the running man's back.

He died still wishing for the one more drink: a drink he would never get.

Chapter I: The Gangs All Here…

Newspaper hounds are supposed to be grounded in the mundane and the everyday, blue collar ink slingers who never believe in things like the Tooth Fairy and Santa Claus and who would suspect the Easter Bunny of Homicide if it was even a vague fit for a headline. I used to live on those gray rain slicked streets but then I had a couple of encounters with things that go bump in the night and got a bum leg out of the deal and I became a believer.

When you've seen the sort of stuff that Bela Lugosi plays on screen running around in the flesh, it's supposed to make you unshakable, but when me and the lady on my arm, the Former Maxine Gladys Kellerman of the Bronx (now Mrs. Moxie Donovan of Manhattan) walked into the lobby of Carl Laemmle's mansion and I almost bumped into Deanna Durbin's derriere, I gibbered like a wino with the DTs.

"Uh—ah—excuse me Miss- Dur-dur—"

"Close your mouth, Moxie, you'll catch flies." Maxi just smiled at the teenage movie star and yanked me by my arm into the throng of Hollywood's elite.

I was in a monkey suit for her sake and I thought I could bluff my way through the party like I had at the theatre parties in New York, but theatre was just something I dipped a toe into occasionally, mostly to see the dames dancing (or now my wife's shows) but movies and movie stars were another story.

"Hey, is that—" I started.

"Hi Spence." Maxi blew a kiss to the star of *Boys Town*. "Did Louise come tonight?"

The short broad actor smiled from behind a wine glass and shook his head. "Naw, she stayed home with the kids so I could cut loose: save me a dance?"

"Not tonight, Spence," she said, "I brought my own ball and chain."

I felt the color rising and my height shrinking. I had a flipping Pulitzer for gosh sakes but here I was feeling like an *Orphan of the Storm*. This was Maxi's world—mine was a bunch of seedy alleys and hustling drunks for tips on break-ins.

"Stand up straight, Moxie," she whispered to me, "You act like I'm marching you to the gas chamber."

"That was in the church last year," I said.

She kicked me in the shins and waved to Randolph Scott.

"I was happy in the hotel bar," I whined. "I really do feel like a ball and chain."

Deadline Zombies

She pulled me into a little alcove before the main ballroom where there used to be some sort of statue, now it was just mister stiff-neck, me.

"Now you listen to me, Mister Michael Aloysius Donovan," she hissed.

(*She used my full name, I'm gonna die*).

"I am proud to be your wife and I wouldn't have married you if I didn't think you could hold your own with Kings as well as cons, so suck it up and smile or I'll crown you in your own right."

She leaned in and kissed me hard enough to make my hair stand on end and then, before I could say anything, pulled me into the ballroom of the Laemmle mansion that was big enough for the Hindenburg to land in.

The floor was polished wood and the walls polished marble with windows that were two stories high that looked out onto a vista of the town of Hollywood below and the stars in a clear sky above.

In the room were more stars than were visible in the sky: not just Universal stars but (as Maxi explained) RKO, MGM and some Warner stars since Universal often loaned out stars from other studios for its productions. Maxi explained the whole system where the studios ran their fiefdoms with absolute control and traded the stars under contract to them back and forth like kids traded baseball cards.

After her good notices in the film *Spenser's the Faerie Queen* for Producers Distributing Corporation, Maxi was in Hollywood to make a film with Universal. Another Queen picture, this time *Queen of the Zombies* with the guy, Tod Browning, who had directed Dracula with her friend Bela Lugosi back in '31. Marble mouth Bela had suggested her again for the lead role in it and his word and her reviews carried enough weight that she had come west the month before for screen tests and readings. She got the part.

I had been back in the big town all that time pulling my hair out as managing editor of *The New York Daily Star*. After it was confirmed that Maxi got the part, I made arrangements with Frannie Striker to take over for me. I grabbed a 'stringer' voucher from the paper and hopped a Clipper out to settle in with my blushing bride.

Now I was a Christian among the lions of the screen.

"So good to see you again, Moxie," The Hungarian vampire actor Lugosi said shaking my hand. (To me is sounded like 'zo ghud to zee you.'). He was looking older than just a little over a year ago though he was still tall and with enough of his matinee idol looks left to turn heads. His handshake was at least still firm.

"Nice to see you, Bela," I said and I actually meant it. He had saved my bacon back in New York from one of those 'bumps in the night' and was actually a pretty nice guy in person.

Only slightly creepy in a European way.

Maxi and he had adored each other since they'd done a show together years ago and I had to admit he was good for her career.

"When did you get permission to be away from the keyboard, you goon?" A raspy voice from behind me had me spinning to see Jimmy Sangster, a fellow word slinger. He was five foot five, built like a beer keg and with hair so red it was almost blond.

"What the heck are you doing here?" I asked. He and I had worked at a paper in Kansas City together years ago. He was a bulldog crime reporter and I was working the political corruption beat. I'd gotten an 'invitation ' from some local heavy hitters to relocate or be 'un located' and, knowing when to pick my fights, had gone to New York. I'd lost track of Jimmy, though I'd gotten a bottle of Scotch and a basket of flowers, when I got my Pulitzer, that had his signature on it. Back 'in the day' we had been pretty tight.

"I'm a flack for Universal, handling publicity for them," he said. "What are you doing here?"

"Jimmy Sangster," I said in a formal sort of semi bow, "May I introduce Mrs. Moxie Donavon, whom the world will soon know as the movie star Maxine Keller."

You could have knocked him over with a feather when I said that and he did his best to act like he couldn't be shocked. I loved the look on his face.

"Nice to meet you, Mister Sangster," she said.

"It's Jimmy, please," he said. "How the heck did that word butcher talk you into signing on with him?"

"I'm the one who trapped him," she said without missing a beat, "I plan to kill him for the insurance money as soon as he's a millionaire from his writing."

He laughed like a hyena, with a high-pitched wheeze I remembered so well. "He's going to be a married man for a long time then."

He said hello to Bela, who knew him from the lot and snagged a drink from a passing waiter.

"So we have two of the fabulous four of Queen," Jimmy said, "Have you met Todd?"

"No, he just flew out yesterday, Jimmy," Maxi said speaking for me. (It's what wives do and she had taken to the job with gusto). "Is he here already?"

Deadline Zombies

"And already three drinks ahead of you, Maxi, my dear," a new arrival said. He was a heavy-set guy with a little pencil mustache. He handed me a Scotch and water and kissed Maxi on the cheek. I liked him right away.

"Todd Browning," he said with a smile. "You must be the marvelous Moxie that our girl here keeps talking about." We clicked glasses and threw our drinks back.

"Guilty," I said. I was a little impressed that he was such a regular guy. I remembered him from his big pictures like *West of Zanzibar*, *Dracula* and *Freaks* but *Mark of the Vampire* and his last picture, *The Devil Doll*, were not big winners for him. With *Queen of the Zombies* Universal was taking one more chance on him with an attempt to recapture the magic with Bela in the lead.

We stood around for a while chatting like real people instead of movie cut outs and I actually began to have a good time. Todd had some funny stories about when he was in vaudeville and Bela some funny stories about touring in Europe. Jimmy did his best to keep his stories clean but Maxi got him blushing because she had the dirtiest jokes you've ever heard so I was feeling a little less alienated.

Two Scotches later I was even telling dirty jokes in an attempt to keep up with Maxi when the equation changed with the addition of two new people.

"Here comes her highness and her jester, fashionably late for the party," Jimmy said.

This caused all of us to turn toward the main doorway to the room along with many other eyes in the room.

There, standing in the doorway in a white and gold high-necked gown that covered her from chin to hips but showed off her long legs and curvaceous figure, stood the Great Greta, star of *Queen of the Zombies*. She had long jet black hair, blue eyes the color of the Mediterranean and a tiny bow of a mouth that always seemed to be in a half smile that was as 'come hither' as you could get. She was accompanied by the strangest figure I'd seen since my arrival in Tinsel Town.

He was taller than Greta and looked like he had stolen his frock coat evening suit from a scarecrow. He was a skinny figure with a shock of white hair and tiny circular glasses that looked as thick as coke bottle bottoms. She flowed into the room and he stumbled in looking like a demented lost puppy at her elbow.

"So that's her," Maxi said. She looked at the gliding figure with the same awe we all did; Greta had that 'something' real movie stars have and her presence, even in the midst of the other luminaries there, glowed. "I haven't met her yet."

"Yes, she has aspirations to be as aloof as the other Greta," Jimmy said.

Todd just grunted and stepped away to freshen his drink.

Bela, ever the gentleman simply said, "I met her in Berlin three years ago and found her very pleasant."

Jimmy pulled me aside to give me the lowdown. "Universal is hedging their gamble on the Browning-Lugosi team by bringing Greta Gardener back from Europe."

"Think the public will flock to see her?" I asked.

"You can see her;" he said. "Wouldn't you?"

"I'm married, chum," I said. "I'm not allowed to speculate. I go to see Baby Sandy films now."

But he had a point; watching the sleek form of the screen goddess glide across the ballroom floor greeting the famous and powerful, I had to agree it was a good hedge.

She had been a major force at the end of the silents in *Sister of Disaster* and *The Royal Siren*, before a car crash forced her into semi retirement in '26. She made a comeback in Deutsche-Universal-Film AG division in Germany under Joe Pasternak until they moved to Hungary in '36. She had come back to Hollywood and proved she still had it in *A Heart Afire*, last year.

"Rumor has it that she angled to do the film but only if her stooge there could do the design work and makeup. They wanted her so the powers-to-be had to say yes." He knocked back the fourth Scotch with no visible result and made a 'tsk sound. "Jack Pierce is on the payroll but she insisted she had to bring Mabuse with her… that horror show at her side."

"He her manager?"

"No, a personal make-up man and supposed genius." He said it with a strange tone to his voice, a hint of something darker. "She insisted he do not just her makeup but that of all the critters that are running around this picture.

"What's the supposed part?" I asked. "I know that look you ink whore—give."

"Oh no, " he said. "I work for Universal so no dirt on their employees—" He looked around and then whispered, " At least not here: I'm not drunk enough. Let's do a liquid lunch tomorrow and we'll talk."

I knew a golden source when I heard it so I nodded yes as the Great Greta slid up beside Todd and Bela.

"So very good to see you again, Bela, Mister Browning." She said. Her voice was like a muted clarinet and gave me goose bumps a married man shouldn't get.

"Please, Miss Gardener," the director said. "Todd."

"Then you must call me Greta." She smiled and I knew Universal had made the right move putting her and Maxine in the same movie. I knew she was to play my wife's older sister (by only three years) and the resemblance, aside from their coloring with Maxi being that pale glowing redhead skin, of their bodies was extraordinary. Same height, weight and with the best four legs I'd seen since Seabiscuit.

"Greta, may I introduce your 'sister,' Maxine Keller." Todd said.

The two women smiled as each other with that frozen moment that occurs when two beautiful women meet.

There was assessment, challenge and territory claiming all in their quick glance and the warm smiles that flashed with professional quickness on both their faces. Maxi squeezed my arm in silent signal that I was taken and Greta extended her hand in statement that she wasn't looking.

All this happened in an eye-blink and I'm not sure if the other guys in the group caught all of it but I've noticed, since I became married, how much better my understanding of women has become—and curses me with remembrances of past sins of miscommunication with the fair sex.

"So very nice to meet you, Maxine," Greta said. "I look forward to our scenes together."

"It is such an honor," Maxi said without missing a beat, "I have admired your work for so very long." I could see that the butter job wasn't believed by Greta, but she appreciated the attempt on Maxi's part. "This is my husband, Moxie. He's a newspaper editor."

"Mister Donovan is a Pulitzer Prize winning journalist as well," Jimmy threw in. He was trying to put up an extra fence between me and Greta for Maxi's sake and I guess he remembered my 'roving eye' days from K town. Sweet of him.

"*That* Moxie Donovan!" Greta said, "I thought that name unusual enough. I read your series of articles on the Bund in New York! Wonderful material; you must be very proud Mrs. Donovan!" Her smile was dazzling and seemed genuine.

"I am," Maxi said, her response seeming just as genuine. "I am." She shot me a glance that said I was in for a night of ribbing about my literary fame.

"I thought the articles very biased," the odd duck at the star's side said. He had a heavy German accent and I wasn't surprised he had a beef with an article that raised a hue and cry about the paper-hanger and his brown shirted monkeys.

"How is that?" I said sticking my wooden foot in the bear trap he offered.

"You seem to think that Herr Hitler would have the audacity to covet your country when he had so many difficulties at home to deal with." Mabuse had a disturbing habit of leaning his head forward and peering over his glasses as he spoke and I was reminded of a bird staring down from a perch at a mouse in a field.

"I don't think Hitler is audacious," I said with as casual and pleasant a tone as I could. "I think he's as mad as a bedbug and evil to boot."

Maxine almost spit her drink out, Todd choked on his and Bela stifled a laugh.

Greta's expression reflected a slight bemusement while her companion sputtered and wrestled for a reply.

"It is a wonderful thing that the world is full of opinions," Jimmy said calling on his full Irish charm to blunt my direct Irish pluck. "But that's no reason to darken the mood of the party." He gave his best flack smile and I knew he was working hard to keep his job so, for old times sake, I folded my tent.

"Of course I'm just a word jockey so don't take what I say so seriously." I smiled.

Bird Face squinted at me and then looked to Greta for a cue and she gave a slight nod.

"Yet they were well written pieces, I must acknowledge," he said. He smiled at me, a creepy thing to behold. "And since I have seen your work, you must stop by my studio during the shooting of the film; I will share some of my secrets with your readers.

Olive branch accepted.

"I'd be very happy to do that," I said. "I'm sure it will make a great piece for my readers."

The conversation went to less dangerous territory from that point on for an hour of casual camaraderie. We stayed in a fairly tight group with Todd as a ringmaster to the various Universal contract players that stopped by to say hello to him. Everyone seemed to know him and he was pleasant to them all. Maxi, to my surprise, knew most of them as well but explained that many of them had spent time on the New York stage before their journey west.

More than that, my head also spun as star after star drifted up to and away from the heavenly body of the Great Greta. I watched Maxi watch the 'Queen' as she held court, knowing that my dear wife was taking notes for her own future fame.

Bela regarded it all with a genial and cavalier expression the entire night and I found myself liking him even more. Marbles or no marbles, I could see how he charmed the ladies.

I also watched the sycophant Mabuse as he appraised everyone in the room like they were laboratory specimens. He was a queer bird indeed.

"He's supposed to be the greatest makeup artist that ever lived," Jimmy said to me while he swilled his sixth or eighth Scotch, "Greta had to throw a hissy fit to get him on."

"How come, if he is so good?"

"No history at it. Not a lick of film footage of this guy's work. But he did a whole bunch of imps in Hell this last week for the big crowd scenes and I have to admit they're even better than Jack Pierce's work on Frankenstein."

"So why do I detect a note of annoyance in your voice?" I said.

"Let's just say I have a clue where he was before Greta brought him out here, but I'll tell you tomorrow."

I was going to press him to tell me what was so mysterious but Todd raised his hands to attract the group's attention.

"We had better not stay too late," Todd said. "Tomorrow is the first scenes with the Queen of the Zombies herself." He smiled a directorial smile and waved a goodbye to everyone as he tottered off toward the door.

Jimmy took the cue and looked around at the group and toed the company line. "I have to agree," he said. "I have to be up bright and early to shepherd a herd of exhibitors from Milwaukee around the lot." He made his goodbyes to all and winked at me. "See you tomorrow, you prize-winning hack!" and headed out the door enjoying the air of mystery as he staggered to his car and drove off.

Chapter II: Stages and Stumbles

Morning came far too early because Maxi had a six AM makeup call on the Universal lot. Fortunately her loving husband could roll over and close his eyes for a couple of hours more.

It was near eight thirty when I drove through the gate using my press pass and headed to the soundstage where they were shooting *The Queen of the Zombies*.

I'd read the script when Maxi got it: it was not Shakespeare. Not even Maxwell Grant—it was more like Al Capp. A girl goes missing in the Brazilian jungle and years later when her younger sister goes looking for her discovers she has become the mistress of a mad magician and zombie master and the aforementioned Queen of the Zombies. Enter white hunter to rescue the younger sister (played by Dick Foran on loan from Warners) and in the last moment the older sister breaks the spell of the madman but is still killed by her zombie followers. The End. Run credits.

It was terrible but it was from Universal and Maxi was making more for her six weeks than I made in a year of pounding on my Smith Corona. And Maxi was having the time of her life so who am I to be a literary critic?

I spent my time making my way to stage eight where they were shooting, malingering along the star-studded alleyways and drooling over the exotically clad colleens walking around the lot.

The guard at the door of the stage knew I was coming, my presence okayed ahead with the director and the studio executives.

I got a good dose of Hollywood on entering the hanger-sized structure; in the center of the space a temple had been erected. It was something straight out of antiquity with large, apparently stone, blocks carved with snake reliefs on them. A convocation of figures was dancing around the altar in the center of the space.

Standing behind the altar was the star of the film, the Great Greta, attired in little more than feathers and silk, an elaborate headdress on her head and a wide collar of snakeskin around her throat. She was swaying to the beat of the drums and yelling commands to the figures who danced around her. She was something to look at (and I was struck again how much she looked like Maxi) but she was not the most interesting thing in the room.

Those figures in front of her were the most amazing collection of creatures I have ever seen; satyrs and donkey-headed actors, nymphs with gorgeous figures and the heads of cats and snakes. It was like some medieval painting of demons come to life. They writhed and squirmed erotically (within limits of the Hayes code) to the strains of booming drum beats.

Standing behind the cameras I could see Todd and a collection of crewmen including the pop-eyed Mabuse watching his handiwork. I had to admit, if those were his creations, he was everything advertised. They looked so real I had the creeps just looking at them.

I felt something touch my back and I jumped and spun around.

There was Maxi dressed in tattered jungle clothes and made up with artistically placed bruises on her forehead. When she saw the startled look on my face she stifled a giggle and threw her arms around me.

"Cut!" Todd called and the crew burst into applause as the dancers relaxed. "Print it!"

The anamorphed dancers all flopped exhaustedly to spots around the studio while the crew turned off the big lights that were blasting brightness on the set.

"You trying to give a guy heart failure?" I whined.

My darling spouse just snickered again.

"Big brave reporter," she said. "Afraid I was one of Mabuse's critters?"

"I was afraid you were one of the dancers," I said pushing her away from me. "I was afraid my wife would see me hugging a hot dame and kill me."

"You got that right, sucker."

I was about to say something witty and cutting back to her but Jimmy swept into the set with those exhibitors from the Midwest. They were a bunch of big bellied, balding guys wearing brown suits that looked like they'd slept in them—could have been reporters from their appearances.

Jimmy waved hello and came over to introduce them to Maxi. I was just background at that point. He gave her a big build up and they clustered around her like hungry wolves as she gamely smiled and let them take their picture with her—you can bet Greta wasn't going to put up with that much 'pressing of the flesh.'

I did my best to not run over and smack them on their bald pates and tell them to play nice. I suddenly had a cosmic insight of what I must have looked like at so many press conferences and the self-awareness made me shiver.

Jimmy stepped over next to me and whispered, "They make a lot of noise, kid, but they're harmless."

"Still hard to watch the feeding frenzy." I lit a cigarette and offered one to Jimmy but he waved me off.

"I finally quit," he said. "I want a long life to live off my ill-gotten gains." He gave a half smile that I recognized from Kansas City—we used to call him 'Sangester the Gangster' because he always had an angle on how to make a buck. Never a real crook, but he sure skimmed the edge of evil—which I figured made him the perfect guy for a movie studio publicity man.

"So what did you want to tell me from last night?" I asked.

"Nothing doing—I'll spill when you're buying the beer—but I'll tell you this—" he looked around to make sure no one was nearby to overhear and his expression got suddenly very dark. "I think I've grabbed a bigger tiger than I can handle, Moxie. I really need your help."

Before I had a chance to react to his out-of-character serious moment, the exhibitors finished drooling over my wife and he left me to herd them to the set of a musical in the next studio building.

He looked back and yelled, " See you at noon at my shack on the lot."

Maxi left her admirers and came over to stand beside me. "Uh," she said, "that's the part of the job I'm not so big on."

"Your public?"

"I think the term 'the great unwashed' applies to that group."

She looked so good I wanted to wrap my arms around her and carry her away from the circle of Klieg lights but she saw that look in my eyes and made the 'Not my makeup' face.

"Later, Bluto," she said when she saw my disappointment. "Momma has to go be brilliant now." She turned to walk into the temple set and I reflected on what lucky guy this key pusher was.

"You are going to fall over if you stare any harder," A silky voice from behind mind said. I whirled to find myself almost cheek and jowl with the Great Greta herself.

She was made up as the Zombie Queen with the high collar emphasizing the pale skin of her bosom below and her smoky eyes above. She smiled gently at me.

"You are a rare fellow," she said.

"How so?"

"You seem to actually be smitten by your wife." She said it with the typical Hollywood cynicism dripping from her words.

"No," I said with all the New York I could muster. "I'm just addicted to her perfume."

She laughed as gently as she spoke as if she were afraid to upset her makeup. "Hard-boiled to the end, eh? Well keep up the good work." She walked past me with a slink that almost dislocated my neck, though I was struck again from that view how much her body resembled my wife.

I spent much of the morning wandering around the set while they shot the same dance sequence from several angles and then close ups of both Greta and Maxi (who is carried in at the end of the number all tied up). I was soon bored out of my mind and found myself standing by the room that Mabuse was using for his makeup staging area.

The animal-faced actors who were not in use were resting in there and the makeup maven retired there between shots. Even in the normal light of the holding room and close up to the naked eye their makeup was flawless.

The beanpole German was going from actor to actor to supervise several male and female assistants who were touching up where wrists or necks on the body suits met the make up. He saw me standing at the doorway and I wasn't sure if he had swallowed a lemon or just disliked me from his expression.

"I am sorry, Mister Donovan. Today would not be a good day to visit me about my work- there is so much to do."

"Not a problem, Mister Mabuse," I said. "I was just passing by; and I have to say—great work!"

He cracked his façade with a toothy grin at my compliment but then snapped back to focus on a woman made up as some sort of human-bird hybrid.

After about a half-hour, I found watching the movie making process about as interesting as watching paint dry. I definitely preferred watching Maxi's rehearsals for the stage. I tried to fill the time by finding any crew members not occupied and chatting them up, notebook in hand for some background stuff—local color for the pieces I planned to get out of the trip.

By lunchtime I was very ready for the liquid meal that Jimmy had promised. Maxi went off to the studio commissary with some of the cast and I walked across the lot to the backwater area where Jimmy's 'shack' was located.

It was at the back of the lot where set pieces were stored, down a dirt road that gave one the impression of heading 'out of town' into the boonies. Parts of houses—wall panels, piles of doors and odds and ends of statuary—were scattered on either side of the road like the aftermath of a Kansas twister.

Who did you piss off to get exiled out here? I thought as I rounded a bend in the road to see the 'shack'. It was in fact a small farmhouse that was used in western productions where he had, he told me, appropriated the upstairs rooms, which were never used to shoot films. When he told me about the place, he said it allowed him the privacy to 'see a little action' with the contract players looking to butter up the publicity flack—like I said, Sangster the Gangster always worked the angles.

"Hey, Jimmy!" I called as I walked up on the wooden steps of the 'farmhouse.' "Have you started to get snorted without me?" I also remembered that Jimmy was a three-scotch lunch sort of fellow.

The ground floor was every bit the western farmhouse with a foyer that led into a living room to the right, a dining room to the left and a staircase up almost directly ahead and to the right. A corridor led straight ahead to the kitchen and a yard beyond was visible. I could see a dark sedan parked there.

"Jimmy?" I heard movement upstairs and so started up the narrow steps. My right leg doesn't quite keep up with the left as it ends in a wooden foot, so stairs annoy me. I wobbled my way part way up and called again, "Hey you souse, leave some Jamesons for me!"

The footsteps upstairs became heavy footfalls and suddenly two masked figures exploded down the stairs straight at me.

I had no time to move aside and the first of the figures slammed into me and knocked me backward. I grabbed a piece of him and as I flopped back butt over teakettle, I took him with me.

I've fallen down many barroom stairs in my day though I've seldom been sober when I did. Still, you can keep from busting your neck if you use the wall to slow the descent. I had the bullyboy with my right hand so I dragged my left along the wall.

It still hurt. Oh boy did it hurt, but from the curses coming from the hooded guy I was holding it hurt him worse. He was a thick bag of flesh so he helped cushion me some. We slid more than tumbled in the narrow space between the wall and banister with the other goon right behind us.

We smacked into the wooden floor and the second guy vaulted over us and then turned back to grab my dance partner off of me. "Move you idiot!" he yelled in a raspy deep voice.

By the time I got untangled, the two of them were out into the kitchen with the one who'd fallen cursing and limping. I watched them from the ground, not daring too move for the pain I knew I'd feel.

They jumped into the car outback and roared away at full speed.

I lay there for a moment watching them drive off before the thought struck me. "Jimmy!"

I pushed myself to my feet (foot really) and half crawled and half hopped up the stairs. "Jimmy!"

Deadline Zombies

When I got to the top of the stairs I knew why those guys were so anxious to get out fast and not be identified: the office was trashed, there was blood on the wall and Jimmy Sangster was nowhere to be seen!

Chapter III: Not so Happy Trails

I stood stunned in the mess that was Jimmy's office and cursed out loud that I wasn't a bruiser and hadn't been able to stop the two goons that had knocked me down. The room had been 'turned'—searched thoroughly. Papers were strewn all over the floor, drawers taken out of his old oak desk and turned upside down and all the pictures from the wall had been removed and the frames punched through to discover anything hidden there.

They had done a complete job of it. There wasn't seat cushion or container that had not been torn open anywhere in the office.

The most disturbing thing was there was a splash of blood on the wall behind where Jimmy's head would have been as he sat at the desk talking on the phone.

I felt my blood boiling; I don't like being pushed around and I don't like my friends being pushed around either. Somebody was going to pay.

"Don't go Irish on yourself," I said aloud. "Think!"

I tried to calm myself down and take my own advice. Somebody had taken Jimmy out of his own office and then come back to search it: so whatever they wanted was important enough to not just kill him until they had it.

"They might even have had him in the car out back while they searched," I said aloud; it made me feel less like an idiot to imagine I had a Watson to explain it all too. "Just in case some moron of a news hack wandered into the room while they searched."

Which meant that they didn't just want whatever Jimmy had—they wanted to make sure he couldn't tell anyone about it.

I turned my attention to trying to think like Jimmy. If I had something that might bring that kind of heat down on me I would *not* keep it in my office; at least not where it could be gotten with anything less than a secret decoder ring or fire axe. Neither would Jimmy.

And I could imagine not at his apartment either; not if it was the tiger by the tail that he had told me it was.

He'd been going to ask me for help and now he was going to get it in spades.

I walked around the room just as a matter of habit though I did my best not to put fingerprints on anything or disturb anything there; I knew if whatever the low rent Lone Rangers wanted was somehow hidden in some secret panel and I had interrupted them before they found it, I wasn't going to without a crowbar and axe—and I was sure the cops would be better at that than I could be.

Deadline Zombies

I tried to memorize everything in the room, made notes of the position of things and then, without wasting any more time, I tried the phone.

It was dead as I expected it would be, so I went back down the stairs and hobbled my way back up the road until I came to an office that had a phone.

I called the lot security, waited for them and rode back out with them.

The lot cop was a fifty-year-old ex-Los Angeles Police Captain who'd taken early retirement from a gunshot wound to his leg. His name was Shannon.

The two of us looked like a vaudeville act as we went into the farmhouse with matching limps.

"This how you found it when you got up here?" He lit a stogie while he looked around the messy office.

"As is," I said. "I made some notes but I didn't touch anything." I sagged against the wall as he walked around the room nudging things with his toes. The tussle with the thug had taken more out of me than I'd realized. He looked at the bloody spot on the wall and then up at me.

"And why should I not take you in for bashing in Jimmy's head and then concocting this story to cover it?"

I knew he'd seen the marks on the wall downstairs, I was bruising and my going to get him instead of just walking away spoke of my innocence, but I also knew he had to ask.

"There's too much heft to Jimmy for me to be able to carry him," I said. "Besides, I'm Irish, I'd never brain anybody before he bought me a promised drink."

He smiled at that and nodded. "'Bout how I figure it." Then he got a cagey look on his florid face. "And you're sure you have no idea what this is about?"

I could be honest for once with a cop. "No, not a clue," I said. "He said he wanted to take me to lunch because he wanted to ask me to help him with something but wouldn't talk about it on the lot."

"Okay," he said. " But don't leave town till we sort this out."

We both hobbled down the stairs and I'm sure it would have sounded to anyone downstairs like a couple of peg leg pirates attacking.

"I'll call the city cops, but they tend to follow our lead here on the lot," he said as we climbed into his car. "Where will you be?"

"Over on soundstage eight," I said, "My wife is one of the stars of *Queen of the Zombies*."

"Not Greta?" he said with an annoyed tone in his voice.

"No, Maxine Keller," I said using Maxi's stage name. "What is the problem with Greta?"

He made a face. "Not her, that nut job Kraut who came with her. The studio says I have to keep him happy but he and his assistants are all about secrecy: they always load in at night. A real pain. He has his own guards for his 'work room' at night too. I don't like it."

He dropped me at the soundstage and drove off with my promise to stop in on him the next day. The cast and crew were back from lunch and already getting ready to shoot the close-ups of the dance sequence that involved Greta and Maxi.

I watched the whole afternoon, not telling Maxi what had happened. I have to admit I was only half there, thinking about what was going on with Jimmy, that somebody might be squeezing him for—for whatever he had that they wanted.

It made me sick to think of it; and me with not the slightest clue; I knew I had to find him. Somehow.

"So how did you like watching me dance around with the undead?" Maxi asked me when we went to her dressing room after the days shooting had concluded.

"Only thing I saw all day, cupcake," I answered with no equivocation. She was a dish and a half.

"Don't tell me you didn't ogle Greta as well," she said with a sly smile.

"Okay, I admit she is good," I said. "But you had all my attention."

"Right answer, Romeo," she said as she took off her make-up. "But I have to agree—she has something—that star thing. Even doing the scenes with her I could feel it. She really is a star." Her voice had a touch of awe in it: one professional recognizing the craft of another.

"Okay, I confess," I said. "I remember her from *Sister of Disaster*: it was one of my favorite films when it came out. It's amazing to me how much she looks the same."

"I was thinking that too," she said as she slipped into a little green dress for the trip to the hotel we were staying at. "And I was kind of hoping to, you know, pick up a beauty secret from her but the funniest thing."

"What?"

"Once, between takes she snagged her collar on one of the light stands and when I went to help her get it loose she snapped at me and yelled for Mabuse to come and fix it. She apologized afterward, but…"

"Temperamental artist?"

Deadline Zombies

"No it was more than that," she said. She was looking prettier than she had in the glamour make-up from the set—fresh and natural like a sunset. "I saw a hint of something under the collar; maybe a scar."

"She was supposed to have been hurt in that crash in '26, "I said. "It would make sense she might be scarred. He is a make-up wiz."

She accepted that and smiled at me to change the subject. "So how was your liquid lunch with Jimmy? You seemed awful steady when you came back to the set; isn't Los Angeles booze up to New York standards?"

I had been waiting for the right time to tell her, and that seemed like the right time. She listened with that intent look she gets, her eyebrows knit and her piercing green eyes staring at me like live flame. We climbed into the car I'd driven to the lot and headed for the main gate.

"So you don't know what he wanted to talk to you about?"

"Not a New York clue," I admitted. "And no idea where he would have hidden whatever he was working on; he's a good reporter, even if he is a hustler. I suspect he found out something about somebody and that's what those goons were about."

"Do you think he's all right?"

"I don't know what to think," I admitted. We pulled up to the front gate and waved to the guard.

"Hey," Maxi said leaning out the window, "Where does a girl go around here to get a beer after work?" She beamed a million dollar smile at the old guy in the guard's uniform and he smiled back.

"That'd be Doolin's across the road over there," he said pointing. "Most all the crews stop there before they head home."

"Thanks," she said.

I headed across the road and, as we pulled in to a space in front, I suddenly had it.

"You are a genius, hon," I said. "I know where Jimmy had to have hidden his paperwork now!"

She looked at me, as she so often did, like I'd sprouted a second noggin.

"You usually talk like that after you've had a few," she said. " I think the sun has gotten to you!"

"Just follow me," I commanded as I exited the car. "You'll see you're not the only one in the family with smarts."

"Or the good legs," she said with a sassy smile. "Lead on MacDuff."

Chapter IV: History and Myth

I practically dragged Maxi across the floor of the watering hole and bellied up to the bar. I ordered two beers and two stiff Scotch and waters for the Donovan clan—no frilly 'girl drinks' for Maxi, she could drink me under the table when the occasion arose. We settled into a booth near the back of the room and I held forth with my hypothesis.

"Now here's the way I figure it," I said to her. "Where does an Irishman feel the safest?"

"The church?" She said to me.

"Spoken like a daughter of the desert chosen." I said. "No, a pub!"

She squinted her eyes as me and I held up a hand.

"Not all of us, it is true, but Jimmy is a reporter, doll, and you know he spent far more time in a gin mill than a soul saver shack."

She nodded at my logic.

"So?"

"So I figure whatever he was hiding, he left here with the barkeep for safety." I looked over at the burly gent behind the bar and waved at him.

He waved back.

I walked over and leaned in. "Hey, Mack, " I said. "I'm Moxie Donovan a friend of—"

"I thought you looked familiar when you grabbed your drinks!" the barkeep said. He thumbed at a photo that was framed on the wall near the end of the bar. It was a shot of me and Jimmy that had been taken at a Christmas Party in the newsroom of *The Kansas City Star*. Next to it, in the same frame was a headline that had the announcement of my Pulitzer Prize for my Bund articles from *The New York Daily Star*. "Jimmy was always talking about how he taught you everything you knew."

I felt choked up thinking of Jimmy sitting at that bar toasting and boasting about me with strangers. It made me determined to find him and help him no matter what.

"Guilty as charged," I said putting on a smile. "I was wondering if Jimmy left any of his files here for us to work on; I was supposed to meet him for lunch but got hung up."

The barkeep didn't even bat an eye and reached under the bar to come up with a briefcase. "Yeah, he left it yesterday saying you'd be in for it. He okay? He didn't come in for his lunch snort today either.

"Oh, he's just tied up," I said as I took the case and hustled over to Maxi.

"Pay dirt?" she asked.

Deadline Zombies

I grabbed her arm and nodded toward the door. "Let's go, I want to open this somewhere more private."

We made record time back to the hotel and up to the room. Maxi ordered room service while I opened the packet and laid out the contents on the bed. They consisted of newspaper clippings from back East, police files from the LA department and letters.

"What is it all?" she asked.

"It seems to be a file on those 'Torso Murders' in Cleveland that have been driving Elliott Ness crazy."

I read all the papers while Maxi waited for dinner to arrive.

When it did I filled her in on what I knew about the murders in Cleveland.

"It was one of those things we talked about now and then in the city room in New York, this series killer guy. Frannie Striker was convinced there would be more, kept saying with all the cars on the road killers could move location more than they used to and get away with more, but I didn't know. After all, at least a dozen deaths since '34 in a single area didn't mean the killer was all that mobile."

"How come I never heard about this?" she asked as she wolfed down a giant cheeseburger. It always amazed me she ate twice as much as me but had a waist I could almost get my hands around.

"You read the gossip columns, hon. I read the police blotter for entertainment." I nibbled at a so-so pickle while I continued to scan the papers on the bed and continued my lecture.

"The first was nicknamed the Lady of the Lake and was found near Euclid Beach on the Lake Erie shore on September 5, 1934, at virtually the same spot as victim number 7 was later found. The official toll of the murderer is 12 but I knew a newsy out that way who thinks the lady is the first victim."

"The victims seem to have been mostly drifters whose identities have never been determined, although there are several exceptions to this according to the news clippings: Edward Andrassy, Flo Polillo, and a woman named Rose Wallace, respectively. All the victims, male and female, appear to be from the 'working poor' who have nowhere else to live but the shanty towns in the Cleveland Flats."

"But how can so many murders go unsolved?" she asked. "And why?"

"I've told you, toots, people are crazy animals. Who knows?" I cleared the plates while Maxi ran a tub.

"What else is in that mess?" she asked as she slipped out of her clothes.

133

"He has some stuff on Greta's car wreck back in 26 and on a smuggling operation from South America during Prohibition. Just a hodge podge of cases."

"Wonder which one he wanted to talk to you about?"

"No way to know," I said. "So I'll follow up on each until I find the little Mick." She heard the anger in my voice and smiled at me gently.

"You will, ace reporter," she said. "You will."

That made me laugh. "Ace reporter and his Queen? We'll show Hollywood how we do it in the Bronx tonight."

"Do you mind if we don't do the nightlife tonight?" she asked as she slipped out of her clothes. "I'm really beat and I have to look top for the close-ups again tomorrow."

"Yeah," I said. "I wouldn't feel right with no word on Jimmy anyway. I'd hit the streets if it was New York, but I don't have many contacts out here. I'll read all this and formulate a plan for tomorrow."

"Well formulate in here and wash my back," she said." We are still technically newlyweds."

"Your wish, my queen, is my command."

Deadline Zombies

Chapter V: Strange Cargoes and Stranger Days

I stayed behind in the hotel when the Mrs. went off to dance with the undead so I could get at the paperwork that Jimmy had left behind. I spent a restless night thinking over all the stuff in those files of Jimmy's, trying to decide which of them was the 'tiger by the tail' he needed help with.

The crash of Greta's car in '26 was pretty straightforward. Here was a star at the height of her popularity out partying with one 'Jason Bartstow' when he lost control of the car on a curve and it flipped over. He was killed immediately and Greta was severely injured and had to go to Switzerland for a long recovery.

"Okay," I said aloud to the papers spread all over the bed and floor. "So if Jimmy is working an angle on this what is it? Was she driving? Did she hit someone and it was hushed up?"

No way to know.

Next were the police reports about smuggling of artifacts from Brazil into the states from Baja California. That seemed really far afield to have intersected his job at Universal but I couldn't discount it. There were some police names on the reports so I had someone to follow up on.

The Torso Murderer in Cleveland was the thing that really had me scratching my head. What information had he not put down about the case? Did Jimmy have a clue who the killer was? And how would he have found out: someone he ran in to in Hollywood or an old source in KC? Again no way to know.

What was sure was that the Torso Murderer always beheaded and often dismembered his victims, sometimes also cutting the torso in half: in many cases the cause of death was the act of decapitation itself. Most of the male victims were castrated, and some victims showed evidence of chemical treatment of their bodies though the paperwork in the files didn't say what kind of chemical treatment.

"Sounds to me like one of Bela's movies." I said aloud. "This is pointless—I need to get out on the street and burn some shoe leather on this."

I suited action to word and got dressed to head out and about in Los Angeles. First though, I realized I had to protect Jimmy's files so I made my notes then bundled them all up and took them downstairs to the hotel lobby. I knew the hotel had a safe so I watched while the clerk put the briefcase in it.

First stop, the coastguard station near the harbor.

"Sure, I remember that seizure," the officer of the day, a Captain George Williams, said. "It was early in twenty seven when I was an ensign doing Volstead interdictions. A boat foundered off the south coast of Catalina and we boarded to render assistance. There was this one crewman that was acting very skitterish about us going below to check for survivors so we got suspicious. We were expecting gin or whiskey bottles but the hold was full of shrunken heads, deadman's hands and all sorts of strange stuff. And books—all sorts of leather covered books with strange writing in them."

"What happened," I asked as I wrote furiously in my notebook. "Was the cargo brought ashore?"

"No, the boat went down and it was a full loss; one hundred percent pay out from the maritime insurance as far as I know," the Captain said. "But I remember it because of that strange cargo and that crewman who tried to stop me."

On a hunch I said, "that crewman, he wasn't German, was he?"

"Why yes he was," the officer said. "How did you know?"

"Thank you, Captain," I said. As I rose to leave his office I asked, "Did anyone else inquire about that wreck?"

"Why, yes," he said, " A little guy, built like a beer barrel; Name something like Singer or—"

"Sangster?"

"Yes that's it," he said. "Know him?"

"Yes, pretty well. I'm following up on his leads." When I got to the door I paused for one last thought. "What was the name of that boat; Jimmy didn't have it in the notes."

"It was the Lady Greta out of Santa Monica," he said. "Owned by some movie star."

* * * *

On the set of *The Queen of the Zombies,* the scene inside the temple had been completed in close-ups and filming had, after lunch, shifted to outside the 'temple of evil.' They were on what is called a 'green set' where an outdoor location is simulated inside a soundstage.

In the scene (which took place out of order in the story), the younger sister arrives in a carriage from civilization. Maxi looked ravishing in an elegant colonial-era gown (it was a period picture) as the carriage, pulled by a chestnut draught horse, deposited her in the midst of the natives. Out from the temple stepped a stunningly clad Great Greta accompanied by Bela, king of the marble mouth dialogue, dressed all in black.

I watched them shoot all afternoon, less bored because my subconscious mind was working on putting clues together. I tried not to bother Maxi, letting her focus on what she had to, but she pulled me aside when there was a long gap between her scenes.

"So? Give!" she commanded.

I filled her in on what I had learned and told her I had a bunch of calls in to the Cleveland department of public safety and Elliot Ness, who I'd had lunch with back in his Capone days.

"So it seems like at least two of those files—the ship—"

"Boat."

"Huh?"

"A ship is bigger."

"Whatever—so it and Greta, and maybe her car accident are connected?"

"Seems that way," I said. "And I am betting that, somehow, that third file folder is tied in."

"Creepy."

"This from the princess of the zombies?"

"Only an in-law of the zombies," she said.

"My brother is not that dumb."

"So what is next?" She was fanning herself with a script to keep her make-up fresh in the heat that spilled from the giant lights that were pointed at the faux jungle set.

"I thought I'd stop by the Mad Mabuse's workshop and see what I can stir up."

An assistant director came over to summon Maxi to the set and she air kissed me not to mess her make-up. "Be careful," she said.

"You're the boss," I said.

"Don't forget it or I'll turn you into a zombie."

"Three cups of coffee does that to me." I appreciated the view as she walked away.

The big chestnut horse from the carriage was standing near the door as I walked out and he stepped over to nuzzle me. I guess I just have animal attraction. (Or he maybe recognized a kindred soul from my brief stint in an equine form).

I gave him a pet on the muzzle and he whinnied in appreciation.

I still had it.

I headed out to find the workshop of the mad makeup genius and see if I could find any shrunken heads lying about.

Chapter VI: In the Chair

Newspaper men like me are a cynical lot. As a rule we don't buy all the fake glitz and glamour that showbiz has to order, but I had to admit being on the set of *Queen of the Zombies* on Universal's lot was making me feel a bit like a kid. In the course of my walk from the soundstage where they were filming to the studio of Milo Mabuse I saw Boris Karloff, Lon Chaney Jr., Buster Crabbe and Bob Baker! It was a bit much for even a cynic like me. (There were a lot of really sharp dames as well, but if I even gazed at them my own cutie Maxi would feed me to the alligators so I have learned to filter them out of my memory).

Maxine had a long day of close-ups and dialogue with the mysterious Greta Gardener.

I decided to take up the makeup maven Milo Mabuse on his invitation from the party to see how his wizardry worked and try and get a fix on him about Jimmy's disappearance. If he was dirty, I hoped I'd be able to find out something useful and, hey, I figure the legit stuff on his makeup was good for a two-column piece in the Sunday spread. I'll take any ink space I can find, Pulitzer or not. I'm not proud!

I wandered through a dizzying array of streets along the back lot: European villages, western streets and that New York street that doesn't really look like New York all crowded with an army of film crews. It was enough to melt the icewater (with a little Scotch) that we ink-slingers have in our veins and turn me into a six year old at his first magic show.

I had a fair idea of the lay of the fake land from my week on the lot and found my way to the little stucco building that served as the makeup shop of the 'Mad Mabuse' as the scuttlebutt called the German genius. It was right next to the building that was the on-lot abode of the Great Greta who had insisted on his presence on the picture. It did not make Jack Pierce very happy—he was relegated to doing the glamour make-up on everyone else on the picture—but delighted Chaney Junior who hated the creator of the Frankenstein and Mummy makeups.

I knocked a couple of times and could hear movement inside the building but no one came to the door. I was about to step away when the portal opened to reveal a scantily clad young woman with long blonde hair and a luminous smile.

"Can I help you?" she asked. She was a looker with long legs and almost boyish hips but there was nothing boyish about her upper body. She was in some sort of Greek get up with a golden silk scarf round her neck. As I stared at her I could feel the wedding ring on my finger singe my flesh.

Deadline Zombies

"Uh, Mister Mabuse invited me to stop by his shop," I managed to croak out. She had almost purple eyes and the longest eyelashes I had ever seen. I tried to think of Maxine's right hook to keep my eyes looking into the blonde's eyes and nowhere lower. "At the party the other night at Mister Laemmle's."

She looked me up and down like she was pricing me for a grocery market and the waved me in. "Follow me," she said. "And don't touch anything."

Oh brother, I thought, *I'm dead if I look at anything too long—if I touch anything, Maxi'll kill me and bring me back to life and kill me again!*

The girl led me in to a large inner room that looked like a demented Frankenstein's workshop with animal heads, arms and other body parts scattered around formed out of various kinds of clay, stone and plaster. In the middle of it all was the Mad Mabuse with his back to me dressed in a long painters smock and holding a small paintbrush.

In the chair before him was another nymphet but with a difference. She had the face of a cat complete with long whiskers and a light layer of fur. The fur faded out at her neck and the make-up artist was feathering strokes at the hollow of her long throat.

"Who was it, Gefion?" Mabuse asked.

"Just little old me, Milo," I said. My voice startled him and he turned to look at me. The effect was startling because his tiny round wire-rimmed glasses magnified his tiny blue eyes. His thinning white hair was askew so that he looked like he had been in a strong wind.

"Ah, ze newspaper man!" he said in that high-pitched voice of his. Then he smiled like the canary-fed cat. "You have come at a good time; just wait a moment and I will finish with Joan!"

He set himself for a few more minutes to applying the final touches on the cat-faced colleen. While he did, I took a gander at the strange surroundings. Besides the molds for body parts, there were sketches of the various makeups he had made for the diverse imps, trolls and zombies that were to people the exotic scenes in *Queen of the Zombies*.

I never spent much time in the museums, but I know art from a Dick Tracy cartoon—his drawings were good. There were costume drawings for the film, sketches of Greta at various angles and in various lights that were gallery quality or I ain't the next Randolph Hearst. He sure spent a lot of time looking at Greta, but then it was pretty certain he all but worshiped her.

"You like my drawings?" The make-up artist asked. He had finished with the cat woman and she had stepped behind a screen to complete her transformation to feline form.

"They look pretty good to me, but then I like Alley Oop."

He looked at me like I was a complete moron but before he could try to form a reply to my idiot remark, the cutie-cat reemerged in her full feline glory.

She was clothed head to foot now in a close fitting bodysuit that had a fur collar that blended perfectly with the make-up Mabuse had done on her head and neck. The effect was startling and amazing even close up. I could imagine it would truly be eerie on the big screen.

"Yes," Mabuse said seeing my expression. "It is better than that morticians' wax and cotton nonsense that Pierce fellow does."

The cat girl turned all around to show her swishing tail and fully realized suit. She wore gloves with claws and shoes that had cat-like toes and claws on the front of them.

"How do I look, doc?" the cat said with a very un-cat like Texas accent.

"You are ready, my dear," he said. "Hurry along to the set so that annoying Browning does not come looking for you."

The girl did a strange semi-feline curtsey and hurried out, almost catching her tail as the door shut.

"Now, Mister Donovan," the make-up artist turned to focus his whole creepy presence on me. "How can I help you?"

I whipped out my notebook to begin 'work.' "Well, Mister Mabuse, you said the other night that if I wanted to see how your makeup was created I should stop by and you'd show me." I gave him my best Gary Cooper smile. "If it's convenient I'd like to get that demonstration."

The skinny sculptor smiled a Peter Lorre smile back at me. "I think your timing is perfect, Mister Donovan. I have the afternoon free now that I have made-up the last of the imps for today's scene."

"I saw what the finished product was on her." I thumbed at the door after the cat. "And I have to say it more than the greasepaint and wigs I expected—very impressive. Could you explain a bit of it for my readers?"

He clapped his hands in sudden inspiration. "Perhaps I can do better than that, Mister Donovan, I can transform you into an imp, eh?"

I must have looked like I was not enthusiastic for the thought (I hate dressing up) because he pulled a trump card and had the scantily clad 'doorman' walk over and grab my arm.

"Come, come, where is your journalistic curiosity?" he asked.

She shuffled me to the chair in front of the makeup mirror and had me sit down.

"I'm afraid to be a cat," I said, "Curiosity kills them!"

Deadline Zombies

He laughed like a squeaky tire and opened a wooden box in front of him that looked like a fishing tackle box. Inside were collection of glass jars, brushes and glassine packets. He ran his fingers loving along the surface of the contents with the loving gesture of an artist for the tools of his art.

"I think we can go in another direction if ze kitty cats frighten you, eh?" He produced a brush and a small reservoir of dark liquid that he dipped the brush in. He leaned in and gave me a real close up look at those beady little peepers of his and the yellowing teeth of his smile.

He smelled of formaldehyde and strong beer.

"Uh, I am not so sure about this." I said.

He laughed again. "Certainty is not a commodity available to any of us, Mister Donovan. But I can assure you that you will have a wonderful story for your readers when you are done in this chair."

I did my best to relax as he began to draw on my face with the dark liquid but I had the galloping creepies every time the brush tip touched my skin. I could see beyond him to the mirror as he decorated my fine Irish kisser with cartoony lines that outlined my eyes and drew a strange looking muzzle over and around my nose and mouth.

I giggled at the absurdity of it and for some reason this made the artist grunt in annoyance.

"I must have a blueprint, Mister Donovan," he said, "One can not build a house without a plan and the new structure you will become must be made clear."

"When did you discover you talent for this sort of makeup, Mister Mabuse?" I asked.

"I have always been a student of the arts," he said. "Though I could never have imagined it would lead me to working in movies before I saw the first film with Greta."

His voice took on a truly reverent tone when he mentioned the Great Greta.

"I had been a student of certain ancient disciplines living in Brazil, you see. And when I felt the need to work for her in the business of movies, I was able to bring those disciplines into play."

He reached into his bag of tricks and removed a small shaped piece of rubber. "My methods are different from all those others who purport to bring about transformations for the camera, Mister Donovan," he continued. "I work not from the theatrical tradition as they do but from a more philosophical forum."

"I don't understand," I said. I got a bit cross-eyed looking at the odd shape he raised toward my face. It felt cold to the touch and seemed to fit as if it had been formed for me. It covered my upper lip and lower nose but with a pair of holes for me to breath through.

"It is simple." He took his hand away and the appliance adhered to my skin, a spreading warmth emanating from it. "The tradition I follow involves older traditions to effect the transmutation of forms."

I chalked it up to a bit of claustrophobia but it seemed as if the rubber pieces had warmed up with contact and were 'snugging' to my face.

"When did you first meet Greta?"

He looked at me oddly for a moment and the said in an icy voice. "It was after her unfortunate accident. It was dark time for her."

"Did you meet her here or in Europe?"

"It was when I heard she was in the hospital that I offered my services to her."

He was doing his best to ignore the direction my questions were going but I figured there was no better time for the hard question. "So, did Jimmy Sangster do any interviews with you for the studio publicity."

"You are the first such interview I have consented to, Mister Donovan," he said. "Partly because I met you when I did and Greta has taken kindly to your wife, Miss Maxine and partly because it amuses me."

The makeup artist was humming a tuneless song to himself as he added another piece above each of my eyebrows—protruding brow ridges that, combined with the muzzle piece, gave the impression of sunken eyes. As I watched in the mirror my face was transforming into a creature not quite human—it was sort of a demi-monkey. The separate pieces were different colored than my skin but the effect was clear.

"Wow," I said, "Even partly done this looks amazing." I looked like Tarzan was going to come calling for me any minute.

He made a little grunt of acknowledgement and then took a larger piece and fitted it over my forehead. It created a sloping appearance that truly gave the impression that my face was other than human.

It was easy to see that painted up there would be a completely other-worldly look to my face. As he fitted two big ears on the side of my head I murmured, "How did you know what sizes would fit my face?"

"All my pieces are the same size, Mister Donovan," he said. "I incant them to adapt to the size of the subject."

A little alarm bell went off of in my mind but before I could say anything he placed a second appliance on my cheeks, chin and lips, pressing it hard to adhere them to my face. He took out a wider brush and began to coat the appliances around my lower face. A new scent emanated from the two protrusions from my face and my vision began to swim.

I was being drugged!

I tried to rise from the chair but the near-naked Giofen had grabbed my arms and I felt scarves securing me to the arms of the seat. I tried to pull away but the smell I was inhaling weakened me and I could not find enough power in my limbs to break free.

"Alchemy seeks to transform base substances and elevate them; we feel that the physical world is but a manifestation of the spiritual one and thus we seek to influence one from the other."

I really was not paying very close attention to the German's ramblings as I tried to tug on my bonds. I had heard ravings about Alchemy before in that accent and I had a bad leg as a legacy from it. I did not feel like a repeat performance.

"You European whack job," I said in my usual way to endear myself to my captor. "You let me up and I'll show you how to transform into a monkey's uncle and a basket case!" It was all hot air though, I had no strength left in my arms and my legs were out to lunch.

He just laughed. "You Americans are so needlessly full of bravado: you all think you are Gary Cooper!" He opened a leather-bound book on the table in front of me and began to recite in some garbled language I knew wasn't German. "That fool Mister Sangster is much the same way."

A strange pins and needles feeling raced up and down my arms and legs. My heart raced and my skin itched like a bad sunburn.

"Oh I hate magic stuff!"

When my muscles began to twitch and I started to vibrate in the chair. "Why are you doing this?" I asked.

"Why?" he said as he flipped a page to run a bony finger along the text to find a new passage. "Because I can, silly boy." He mumbled the new quote and then turned to smile at me again. "That and you have been getting too close to the truth of things with you explorations of your friend's disappearance. So, as you Americans say, I can kill two birds with one stone."

I felt like the prize pigeon at that point as my body went into a twitch overdrive, and it was like I was having an epileptic fit. It hurt. Like heck!

"You German jerk!" I yelled. "My wife will lose her head and kick your Teutonic tush when she sees what you're doing to me!"

"Oh, I don't think so," he said with that odd laugh of his again. "In a few hours, she'll loose her head quite literally. Then it will not matter what information that annoying little man has; Greta and I shall leave this foolish country and she will assume the status she deserves in my homeland. There they will appreciate both our geniuses."

When he said that, I felt cold all over because he said it like it was a surety and I was helpless. The appliances on my face tingled and between bouts of blurred vision the mirror showed that they were changing as well, swelling and altering to fit the contours of my face.

Deadline Zombies

Chapter VII: Revelations and Rituals

While I was proving I wasn't the smartest tack in the barrel, Maxi was showing she was star material on the set. She had a scene with the Great Greta and she held her own, so much so that when their character's confrontation was finished both women got a round of applause from the crew.

"Well done, my dear," Greta said to her when Todd called "cut, wrap!" "We can both be proud of that scene; why don't you stop at my dressing room for a celebration drink, eh?"

"Thank you, Greta," Maxi said. "As long as you don't mind me calling the hotel to find out where my newshound has wandered off to."

"Not at all, dear heart, "Greta said. "But don't you know they are all 'hounds, except the ones who are jackasses."

Maxi laughed. "Not that ink jockey; I have him pretty well trained in only two years."

Now Greta laughed. "That's the spirit."

The two women were walking back to the dressing room bungalows. A warm evening wind was sweeping in off the hills and both actresses let their hair down as they walked, with Maxi opening her jungle kaki jacket.

"How can you wear that high collar in this heat?" My redhead asked.

Greta gave her a sad smile. "I am afraid, dear I have little choice. I'll show you when we get to my dressing room."

They arrived at the stucco structure that served as Greta's dressing room and suite on the lot when she had an early call. It was next to the larger building that Mabuse was using as his makeup studio.

"The phone is over there, Maxi," Greta said. "I'll go get out of this ridiculous gown and be back in a moment." She disappeared into the back room of the little cottage while my wife dialed the hotel.

"Hello, "she said to the clerk after she had tried the room to get me. "Is there a message for Maxi Donovan?" We were, of course, registered as husband and wife and she had gotten used to having three different last names much more easily than I would have.

"Oh yes," the clerk said. "A message from a Mister Ness from Cleveland."

She was about to correct him that the message was for Moxie, not Maxi but decided to hear it anyway. "Go ahead and read it, and then put it back in the box, if you don't mind." She listened patiently while the clerk read the short note to her and Greta reentered the room.

"Any luck locating him?" The star poured herself a brandy.

"No," Maxi said. She hung up the phone with a serious expression on her face. "But I just got a message meant for him."

"Something wrong?" Greta asked. She was in a silk dressing gown with a scarf wrapped around her neck and her hair wrapped in a turban-type wrap.

"Oh not really." Maxi said, "What are you pouring?"

"Whatever you'd like, dear," Greta said. "One of the perks of my 'status' is a fully stocked bar."

Maxi poured herself a Scotch and water and then turned to her hostess. "Greta, how well do you know Milo?"

"Fairly well," the star said. She sat down on a gold embroidered day couch. "Right after my—uh accident—he came forward and was helpful in helping me with my rehabilitation. He is more than just a make up artist, you know; he is a student of old healing disciplines of the East. It was his sanitarium in Zurich that I was treated at. "Why do you ask?"

"Did you know he spends considerable time in the Cleveland area?" My redhead asked.

"I know he has interests in a number of U.S. cities." Greta said. When she saw that Maxi was having trouble coming to the point she added, "You asked why I wore such a high collar; here is why." She pulled the scarf from her neck to reveal her neck from collarbone to chin.

Maxi gasped.

Stark against the white of Greta's skin was a jagged red scar like a bolt of lightening that raced around the whole of her neck. The skin on either side of scar looked shriveled and vividly white. When she saw the startled look on Maxi's face she re-wrapped it with the scarf and took another sip of he brandy.

"Now you know why I had to restart my career in Europe."

"Oh, honey," Maxi said, "I had no idea, but—"

The side door to the cottage suddenly flew open and two hooded men stepped into the room. Maxi recognized them from my description of the attackers the previous night.

The lead one pointed a gun at Maxi but before he could bring it to bear she snapped a fan kick to knock the gun from out of his hand. "Run, Greta!"

My red head grabbed at the fallen gun while the second hooded man sprang at her. She tried to roll over to point the weapon at the crook but he got on top of her and it became a battle of main strength.

Abruptly a lamp exploded on the back of the hooded man's head and he rolled off Maxi. Behind him stood Greta holding the base of the lamp.

Deadline Zombies

"Good shot!" Maxi yelled. She popped to her feet and reached for the star to herd her out the door when the first masked man grabbed her by the hair and yanked her off her feet.

"Go!" She screamed but Greta grabbed the gun off the floor and brought it to bear.

"Hold it right there, my dear" Greta said, "And don't bruise her, you dolt. If you resist too much, Maxi I will be forced to shoot you in the head!"

* * * *

While my cutie pie was getting blindsided, I was coming out a long stupor and thinking about what a dope I'd been in walking right into Mabuse's hands. The makeup was melding to my face and I felt it changing texture. In the mirror my features were looking less and less like foam rubber appliances and more like skin.

Monkey skin.

I am a dumb ape, I thought. *I should have known that Jimmy would not have put the files in one case if they were not related. Mabuse, the ship sinking and Greta were all somehow tied to the murders in Cleveland. And I was strapped into a chair in his studio under some sort of magic spell.*

I hate magic spells.

I'd been turned into a horse and a puppet by magic spells and now some sort of 'imp' makeup was taking over my body. Oh joy! *Oh I really don't want to know what I'm going to end up as.*

"What did you mean about Maxi?" I managed to squeeze though my tightening throat.

"You can see for yourself very shortly," he said.

Mabuse stepped away from me and smiled like an artist watching a picture dry on his easel. "You will be part of the ceremony where your wife will be the star, Mister Donovan."

The scantily clad woman assistant had been replaced while I was admiring my new kisser by a burly fellow in a dark turtleneck sweater. He had a peculiar pasty look to his face and a crooked smile with heavily lidded eyes that gave the impression he was half drowsing. He stepped up to me and bodily lifted me from the chair like I was a baby.

He set me down on my unsteady feet and held one hand on my shoulder to keep me from toppling over.

"Walk to the car, Mister Donovan," Mabuse ordered me.

My traitor body obeyed. I tottered out of the door and when he opened the back of the car, I threw myself into the trunk like a side of corned beef although I felt like a prized turkey. They closed the trunk but I could still hear them clearly.

My gorge began to rise when I heard the raspy voice from Jimmy's house say "I have the girl; she is unmarked."

"No thanks to this lummox," I heard Greta's voice say. "He almost hurt my new arms with his brutality."

I heard the sound of something being dropped onto the backseat of the car. "And we are closer to the time than we thought."

"She is still perfect, Dearest Greta," I heard Mabuse say. "We will have the ceremony in time; I promise."

"I will get the other one while you take him and her to the ceremony." The raspy voice spoke and I heard another car pull away.

Then came the sound of the doors of the car I was in slamming, and we moved off to some unknown destination. I knew for certain that the sons of blazes had my redhead prisoner as well.

Man I hate magic!

Chapter VIII: Ceremony of Evil

While I was in the trunk of the car, I kept going over all the information that I had about the three cases and still couldn't figure away to relate them to each other except that it was clear now that Mabuse was, or at least, fancied himself a sorcerer or alchemist or some sort. Have I mentioned I hate magic?

The ride lasted only a few minutes and then the trunk lid popped open and goon boy lifted me out again.

We were in a dark space that suddenly burst to brightness when a switch was thrown and I saw that we were in the soundstage with the temple set of Queen of the Zombies.

A burly guard stood on either side of me holding my arms behind me but when two more goons carried Maxi out of the back seat of the sedan, I made a moaning noise and lunged for her. The two on either side of me grabbed my arms and yanked me back. My hands were balled into fists in useless frustration.

I really, really hate magic!

I took advantage of my guards being distracted by the semi-conscious Maxi, squirming and stomped down hard on the feet of the two guys. I expected them to squeal and release me but instead the just gripped my arms harder and said nothing.

"Wooden feet?" I asked, being familiar with the condition.

The two men said nothing.

"Silence!" Mabuse was standing on the dais on the top of the temple by the stone altar. He wore a long golden robe with strange symbols sewn all over it in bright threads.

Why do these nut jobs always have to dress like my great aunt Maude at an Elks Lodge smoker?

Beside him, two scantly clad women in cat heads stood ready for his orders. Any other time I would have appreciated the show of female flesh but right then I only had eyes for my redhead.

Maxi was completely awake and when she looked up and got a gander at me, I saw first terror and then recognition wash over her features. "Is that you, Moxie?"

"Guilty!" I said in a deep monkeyish-sounding voice. It was hard to talk and it felt as if my face had fully become the half snout I'd seen I the mirror.

"Why do you always get turned into a merry go-round figure?" she asked.

All I could do was shrug; I sure felt like a monkey's uncle getting her into the middle of this again.

"You, Donovan, come to me." The robed madman ordered.

I wanted to run up to him and kick him in the gut but instead my traitor body felt compelled to move toward him at a steady pace.

The goon released me and I followed the directions of the makeup man sorcerer and climbed the temple steps. At his command.

"I can see from your expression that you feel my compulsion." Mabuse gloated at me with a sneer on his skinny face. "You see, the ancient herbal potions that I mix with my appliances allow not just for the transformation, but also let me completely control the bodies I create. You are mine to command now. As is that snooping publicity man."

Jimmy!

That's when one of the goons brought in the little fireplug and my breath caught in my throat; he was in pretty bad shape. His eyes swollen almost shut, his face mass of bruises and blood and his hands tied behind him. A goon was latched on him, but I had the impression that he was more to hold Jimmy up than to keep him from escaping. They had to have been holding him somewhere on the lot and working him over to tell them where he had hid his notes.

I could bet good money he still hadn't told them.

"Get your hands off me you two-bit, bag headed half-witted four-eyed creep!" Maxi started out slow but then the fire got into her cursing and soon I'd swear the paint on the stage walls would be peeling. The two men holding her started to drag her up the steps of the temple.

Behind her came the Great Greta walking slowly with her beautiful features fixed in a severe cast. Her eyes, focused on the struggling Maxi, held a hunger in them that was almost obscene.

"Greta, what are you doing?" Maxi yelled at her.

"I am truly sorry, my dear" Greta said, her voice strained. "But I need your body much sooner than I had hoped."

"What are you talking about?" Maxi asked. The three thugs who were holding her wrestled her to the altar top and secured her with leather straps.

"I have most of it pieced together now," I croaked from my alien throat.

The German madman turned to stop me with a gesture but Greta spoke from the top step.

"Let him speak while he can," she said. "Soon, like his colleague, he will be incapable." She dropped the robe and the scarf from her neck at the same time. The effect was startling; her naked form was very much the image of my captive wife's, gorgeous and seductive but my gaze was arrested by the ugly scar that ran around her throat at the base. The skin was puffy on both sides of the slash now and clear liquid puss was visible.

"That's the last piece of it all then," I said. "Mabuse was an obsessed fan who had skills; an interest in the occult and when you were nearly killed in the crash—were you driving? No matter—he whisked you away and somehow was able to save you; but he practiced his skills by murdering people in Cleveland For what—spare parts?"

"Not bad for a dumb ape of a reporter," the madman said with a little snicker at his own pun. "Though you got some of the details very wrong." He was circling Maxi, waving his hands in those weird conductor-like gestures these crazy sorcerers seem to love along with their robes. "I learned many secrets from the Bocour of Brazil, secrets to preserve and transform life. Like these statues here—" He gestured to the hideous carved figures that decorated the façade of the temple set. "They have power and those fools in the front office here just see them as 'texture and production value.' I was bringing some of the fetishes into the United States when Greta was injured in her accident—"

"I was deformed," Greta spat out. "Mutilated by glass and metal." Her voice held terror and pain in its tone. She stepped up to run her hands along Maxi's arm, making my wife squirm. "But doctor after doctor told me there was no way to hide the scarring or repair my body. Milo showed me he could. And no cost was too high to pay for it."

"Your neck," Maxi said. "It's not a scar from the accident?"

"No, her beautiful face was unblemished, but her body was..." Milo's voice trailed off as he recalled the horror he felt with the memory. "I found a way to transfer her perfect and unblemished head onto a new body; twice so far as the bodies tend to wear out."

"You are joking." Maxi said. "Tell me you are joking."

"I am German," Mabuse said. "I do not joke!"

He gestured at the goons standing at the four corners of the altar and they all removed their hoods to reveal neck scars like Greta's.

"I created my own group of aides in Cleveland salvaging the waste of humanity for my uses. You will be the new body for my dear Greta," he said as he leaned over Maxi's face. "So you see, you will be even a bigger star than you ever hoped to be, as the Great Greta's body when she once more reigns on the screen."

I tried to go for him then but he saw the movement and froze me with a gesture. "I control your flesh," he said. "And I do not wish it to move." His voice stopped me and I felt my traitor body stop cold.

At the foot of the stone pyramid, Jimmy Sangster threw back his head and cursed in anger behind his gag.

I knew just how he felt.

Deadline Zombies

Chapter IX: Going Ape

"I can feel the connections weakening," Greta said, her normally silky voice rough and raspy. She kept her hands at the scar line of her throat. "We may have waited too long."

"No, Greta, my worship," Mabuse said. "We had to wait for the moon to be in the right quarter and for them to shoot this set so we could take advantage of all the artifacts I convinced them to use. I will be able to severe her head and make the transfer with minimal loss of vitality. It was such a stroke of genius to persuade the studio to use real fetishes. The power here is almost what it would be at the actual temple site in the jungle."

"You really rigged this all for your horror show?" I gasped. My throat was tighter than a preacher at a Mummer's smoker, making it hard to talk.

"My time for another body was near," Greta said, "and we knew they would find a perfect body double for me for this film—they had to." She looked down at Maxi and pouted. "I wish it were not so, dear, but you do have the most wonderful body, so well toned. I promise to appreciate it for at least five years."

"I'd just as soon appreciate it myself for another fifty or so years," Maxi said. "But if I'd have known you were going to hijack it I would have had a second piece of cake last night."

Listening to Maxi puff it out tough made me choke up and made me angry. I wanted to smash that sicko scarecrow in the snoot so much I thought my heart would burst with the effort.

Mabuse kept up his mumbo jumbo over Maxi and I kept trying to attack him but his control over my faux ape form was such that I felt myself frozen in place.

Mostly.

It seemed that as I felt his mental control course through me, sliding from the facial appliances that hid my identity from casual view to my chest, limbs and groin. And down my left leg. It was like the tingle you feel as your leg starts to fall asleep.

I watched as the white-haired madman kept his arms stretched above him as he muttered over my wife and Greta stood in her birthday suit and watched like she was the big bad wolf and Maxi was a porkchop.

The goons standing around the altar were focused down at Maxi as well, their blank eyes vaguely watching my redhead. It occurred to me that if Mabuse were controlling them like a radio controlled bomb as well as keeping my body in check while also trying to mumble his spell he was a bit over-stretched.

Maybe that was why I could feel my right foot was different than my left. It didn't tingle.

Not a bit.

It felt just like, well, a foot should. And that in itself was odd because a nut job Nazi had put a spell on me once and turned it to wood. Real wood. Most people thought I'd lost it in an accident but I hadn't lost it at all. It had just been changed into a cigar store extremity.

Now I could feel it again. Why? What did I know about sorcery? The closest I'd been to magic before the adventure where I'd met Maxi on Governors Island was seeing Houdini twice at the Variety Theatre on Fourteenth Street in Manhattan.

Maybe one magic spell canceled another?

Mabuse was edging close to Maxi, eyeing her throat in a creepy way. He began making gestures with his empty hands that looked disturbingly like a cutting motion. Even with my face in full monkey mode I know I was pretty snarl-faced and Maxi, trying not to look up into the beady eyes of Mabuse, saw it.

She also saw my right foot twitching like Fred Astaire doing a conga and seemed to sense what I was up to.

So did Jimmy at the bottom of the pyramid. He was tethered near the door of the soundstage with his handler and watched helplessly as Maxi was set up for sacrifice and I was being an almost complete and useless Cheetah.

He had to feel like a helpless victim and I know that grated on him. Jimmy Sangster was nobody's victim. I could see he wanted to pitch in.

When I made my move, he and Maxi reacted as perfectly as I could have hoped though not like I could have predicted.

I finally took full control of my foot and shook it to test it.

Jimmy looked around him and snorted. He spun around and suddenly lunched forward to ram face-first into an electrical panel on the wall, which caused it to explode into sparks, taking out half the lights in the soundstage. The charge blasted through his body and caught the goon holding him so that both men did a horrid Saint Vitus Dance by the soundstage wall.

Everyone on the pyramid turned to see the sparks and I chose that moment to strike. I shot out the one limb that was still mine and struck Mabuse in his future generations. This launched him forward over Maxi with a scream of pain.

Deadline Zombies

My redhead seized the opportunity and as the mad makeup maven fell over her she reached up with her mouth, snatched his glasses off his head and snapped her head to the side to launch them out into space.

Mabuse made a second gasp and tried to reach for them as his glasses clattered down the stone side of the temple.

This all happened in a blink of an eye. The naked Greta screamed when she saw what was going on and reached for Mabuse to pull him off Maxi.

I re-cocked my one weapon and snapped out again.

I think I overdid it.

My right heel struck her squarely on the side of her temple. There was a sound like a suction cup being pulled off a pane of glass and the head of the Great Greta Gardener separated from her body. It arced off, spinning over the altar, rolling end over end to hit the steps where it bounced twice.

Blood sprayed everywhere.

I will never forget the sound of the head as it struck each of the steps or the look on the face of the zombie woman, a mixture of rage and startled shock.

The four guards at the corners of the altar watched their mistress's demise with frozen horror until the head came to rest upright at the base of the pyramid. Then they turned as one to face me with looks of rage on their oddly attached heads.

Mabuse screamed like a gutted porker and spun to lunge toward me with a face twisted by a hideous fury. He made unintelligible snarling sounds.

The effect was dulled somewhat by the fact that he was so blind without his glasses that he missed me by a mile with his mad grab. I helped him along by lashing out with my killer clog.

I kicked him into one of his goons. The two of them rolled backward down the pyramid steps end over end yelling in terror as they did.

The two women in the cat makeup seemed stunned. From their body language, they were incapable of deciding whether to come to his aid or run.

Mabuse's scream stopped abruptly with a cracking noise and at that same moment the three remaining 'assistants' dropped abruptly to the stone of the dais as if they were puppets and their strings had been cut.

I guess, in a way, they actually were.

At the same moment the two women screamed. Free of Mabuse's influence, they raced out of the temple set into the night.

My strings to the mad Mabuse ended at that moment as well and I could feel all my limbs—even my right foot. It wasn't wood any more.

I didn't wait for the goons' reactions but ran to Maxi's side the second I was in full control of my body and started to work on the straps that held her. It took a bit but I got her loose. She rolled off the slab and threw here arms around my neck and kissed me on my faux muzzle.

"You cut rate King Kong!" she said. "My hero!"

She held on tight as a shiver sped through my body. She could feel it too and tightened her hold on me, shivering herself with the aftermath of horror to what had occurred. It was suddenly damn good to be alive and standing next to her near-naked form. I nuzzled her neck, albeit with a face full of rubber monkey snout.

I reveled in the feel of her and the thought that we were safe and then I had a horrible thought. "Jimmy!"

I pulled away from her and we raced down the pyramid to where my friend lay by the electrical panel.

The flesh on his forehead and cheek, where he had collided with the panel to sacrifice himself to save Maxi, was singed black. The other side of his beat mug seemed almost at peace with a wry half grin on his lips. Even in death he seemed to be working the angles.

Sangster the Gangster to the last.

I held him up to my chest and rocked back and forth while my redhead leaned her head against my back and joined me in a salty memorial to my friend.

Deadline Zombies

Epilogue: Falling and Rising

In the firmament of the Hollywood sky, stars rise and fall with regularity with those that fall likely to have been pushed and those that rise doing so usually with deals, favors and lots of luck.

After Shannon's security guards found me and Maxi in the midst of the blood bath on the movie set, I talked myself blue explaining to him what had occurred. Jimmy's notes and the physical evidence proved it all out but behind the scenes, official forces made sure I couldn't write it up the way it really happened.

If I had, they never would have released *Queen of the Zombies* which now stared Maxine Keller as the queen after some re-shoots (which were able to use all the previous longshots of Greta though the close ups were now Maxi in that role. Another actress replaced Maxi as the younger sister—a final irony).

The bosses liked Maxi's performance so much in the reshoots that they offered her a three-year contract and we accepted.

I left *The Daily Star* to Fran Striker—who was a much better editor than I was anyway—and took over Jimmy's old job for Universal. I kept all his notes on the case and in my spare time I worked on a book about it all that I bylined with both our names.

I was gonna get that little fireplug a Pulitzer that had his name on it or die trying.

He had.

Teel James Glenn

Circus Moxie Mess

Prologue: Rome-ing Around

The peroxide blonde perched nervously on the chair in my wife Maxine's bungalow on the Universal lot and sobbed, "I know something horrible has happened to Joey!"

"Go ahead, Chloe." I offered her a Scotch on the rocks. "Just tell me the whole story in your own way."

She took the gum out of her mouth and, after looking around for someplace to put it, stuck it behind her right ear.

"I was hired to dance at one of Mister Kokavich's parties, you know," she said between sips.

"That big deal Russian director who did that film with Ramon Navarro and Markovika last year?"

"That's the one; he has a big place up in the hills. It's like a castle or something."

"Up in North Hollywood?" I asked. I was still getting used to the geography since I moved out from New York when Maxine signed her contract with Universal Studios.

"Yes," she said. "It's like the entire top of the mountain and you can only get to it up this long road. Anyway, I got Joey—Joey Calvera, my boyfriend, a job being a waiter at the party; he is really pretty... I mean well built. " She smiled recalling her boyfriend. "And so they were really happy to have him with all the waiters dressed in these little skirts and togas and such."

"Skirts?"

"Like in Roman times," she corrected. "With little helmets and all. The whole place is made up like old Rome. I was dressed in this little hanky skirt and—well, anyway, me and the girls danced twice, once before diner and once during. Afterward, Mister Kokavich had some acts like jugglers and stuff and then—" she started to sob, chucked back the full drink and then pulled the gum from behind her ear to start chewing it again all as deftly as if it were choreographed "—then he stepped up and said, 'my friends, I will now demonstrate skills I learned at the feet of my friend and mentor the great Grigori Yefimovich Rasputin in my homeland of Mother Russia.' He stood so tall and straight with his pointy beard and fire in his eyes."

"Mister Kokavich did some more talking about things I didn't quite understand bout things like 'the depths of the human mind' and all sorts of strange stuff and then called for a volunteer to step up 'so he could show the true power within!' At first no one would come up to him with everyone in the crowd a little frightened—I admit I was—but Joey raised his hand and Kokavich told him to step up."

She was clutching the empty booze glass like it was her best friend so I gave her a refill. She repeated her gum routine and continued speaking when she had sipped half of the Scotch. "Joey sat in this big throne-like chair and Kokavich—who was in these purple robes—started to wave his hands in front of himself like an orchestra conductor and suddenly Joey's eyes went all strange and glassy. That kind of scared me too. Kokavich whispered to Joey and then my guy stood up and Mister Kokavich handed him this horse costume."

"Horse costume?" I asked with a creepy feeling shivering through me. Guys in robes and animal costumes give me nightmares.

. I was trying to give her a sympathetic ear but her story was starting to make me hope that maybe she had been sipping a bit of Glenfiddich before she had come looking for Maxine and found me. I really didn't want to be involved with more horse and magic shenanigans.

"It was sort of like a rubbery thing, white and covered his whole body and even had a little head that slipped over his like a hood. Joey put it on with this zombie look in his eyes and then Mister Kokavich stepped back and ordered him around like a ringmaster at circus. He had him sort of rear up and then stand up on all fours like a real horse and then lead him around the room and had him jump over a chair and had one of the women from the party climb on his back and ride him around. It... it was so humiliating. I didn't know how Joey could stand it but then I saw his eyes and he looked so empty- so lost."

"Sounds like Joey was just trying to make the boss happy."

"No," she insisted. "He told me afterward that it was like the mad Russian had made him into a robot; he was awake and aware of what Kokavich was saying but he had no power to refuse. His body did just what that guy commanded him to do. Kokavich paraded him around for a half hour like he was a horse before he did the strange arm movements again in front of Joey and then he took the horse suit off and was back to himself. Everyone applauded, but Joey looked so confused."

"Is that when Joey disappeared?"

"No, Mister Donovan—"

'Moxie," I said. "My dad was Mister Donovan." I gave her my best charming smile and got a ghost of one from her in return.

"Moxie. No; we went home together but he had terrible nightmares that night: he woke up screaming twice. He told me he kept seeing himself as a horse being controlled by Kokavich. It was the same for two nights in a row, waking in a cold sweat and he was jittery all day. Then last night he wasn't at home when I came back from the serial I was shooting over at Republic. He didn't leave me any word at all, not a note or nothing."

"Could he just have had a late night out," I suggested as gently as I could. "Maybe trying to drown the nightmares in a drink and slept at a friend's place."

"No, absolutely not," she said. "Joey is a physical culturist: doesn't drink or smoke and works out all the time. It's why he got the job at the party, he is in such good shape. He's always making fun of me for not eating right or—or for drinking." She started to lose it again, sobbing in a deeper, more desperate way than even when she had first told me Joey was missing. "I just know something terrible has happened to him."

I didn't want to refill her glass a third time since she was already slurring her words and if I was going to try to help her I needed her capable of speech. Instead I sat down on the day bed next to her and put a hand on her shoulder.

"Have you talked to the police about this?"

"Yes but they would not listen to me, they kept saying that I was imagining things, just a hysterical woman and that Joey just left me for— for another woman."

I knew that cops could be very cavalier about missing persons, at least in the early stages, and an actor taking a powder on his girlfriend was not the rarest of things either. But Maxine had often talked about how solid she thought Chloe and her boyfriend had seemed. I wanted to give the sobbing girl the benefit of the doubt, but my natural inkslinger's cynicism—despite my experiences with guys in robes- made her story a hard sell. So I forced myself to ask: "Could he have, Chloe?"

"No!" she jumped to her feet and for a second I thought she was going to bolt for the door or take a poke at me for impugning the faithfulness of her man. "Joey's not like that!"

Before I could apologize or react the door to the bungalow opened and an Indian maiden in full buckskin dress walked in.

"What's all the yelling about?" she asked. Then she saw who was in the room and her made-up features went pale.

My wife of a year, Maxine Keller had as much Indian blood in her veins as this son of the old sod (unless you believe the lost tribe of Israel story), but she made a very fetching Pocahontas knockoff, if I must say so myself.

Deadline Zombies

Maxi was making a western with Dick Foran and that day was shooting some interior scenes on studio sets. It was how come we had made plans to meet at the bungalow at lunchtime. I had come to the lot and found Chloe at the door in tears.

There was something in the shocked expression on Maxi's pretty face that was more than being surprised by seeing me and a woman in her little dressing room. There was some very specific horror in seeing her friend Chloe.

"Oh Maxi!" the girl said, racing cross the room to throw herself into the startled squaw's arms and start a whole new waterworks display. "Joey's missing; something's happened to him, I know it!"

Maxine got even whiter beneath her redman's makeup, her eyes pleading with me in a way I didn't understand until she said, "I know, honey, the guard at the gate just told me. The police found Joey's body up in the hills."

That did it, Chloe collapsed to the floor, taking Maxi with her.

I guess I was going to miss lunch.

Chapter I: No Second Takes in Death

"I thought I'd seen it all working the Hollywood beat," the police detective said to me, "but this one is new to me."

We were standing at the foot of a hill off Cahuenga Boulevard that the Sheriff's department had roped off. The body of Joey Calvera was lying partly covered by brush at the foot of a steep slope. He was wearing tight fitting light gray slacks that seemed like they were made out of cow or horse hide and naked from the waist up except a leather harness and wide collar that resembled nothing so much as a horse's tack.

"How did you know who he was?" I asked the flatfoot in charge.

"He used to teach physical fitness at the academy when he got out of the marines," he said. "So the patrolman who found him knew him. It sort of makes it one of our own."

"Cause of death?" I asked the detective.

He was a middle aged cop, a little soft around the middle but with a hardness hidden behind the folds at the corners of his eyes that spoke to his years of seeing the worst the world had to offer. His name was Mahoney so I spoke to him Irishman-to-Irishman rather than newsy to cop.

"Nothing stands out from first looks." He was chewing the stub of a cigar and from the looks of it he must have been working on one since The Volstead Act was repealed. "Seems straightforward: most of his injuries look consistent with taking a tumble from up top there." He pointed to the crest of the hill were there was an abrupt drop off just short of being called a cliff.

I moved in as close as I could to look at Joey's body. It was a muscular physique, a regular Apollo type though it was hard to tell if he had been pretty of face like Chloe said. His head was canted at an odd angle and his features were pretty mashed up, but it could have been from the fall or from before. The thing that caught my eye and stood out were a series of marks diagonally across his back. "Those scratches on his back?"

"They interested me as well." He scratched his balding head and got a philosophical look on his face. "Made me think of somewhere I'd seen the same; I went to a Jesuit school, " he said, "and you know what that means; Discipline."

"I had nuns myself," I said. "But I expect the Jesuits swung the ruler even harder than Sister Mary Joseph."

This made him chuckle. "Father Mike used the rope from his robes on us when we didn't conjugate properly." He pointed at the parallel lines on Joey's corpse. "They're just a bit different, but I'd say those are whip marks on that man's back."

Now that he said it I could see clearly that the deep gouges were too regular to have been made by a fall down the hillside. "You might have a future in this police business," I said. "I think you have something there —see how they are deeper at the upper right, as if each one was where the tip of a whip swung by right handed man might strike."

"About right," Mahoney said.

We walked back up the path toward where the cars were parked as the morgue guys came for the body. "I did the walk around at the top of the hill, no sign of a struggle; I think the stiff was running all out in the dark and just did a Brody."

"The question is," I said, "what was chasing him?"

* * * *

I didn't drive directly back to our apartment where Maxi had taken Chloe (after we had gotten her drunk enough to pass out), but I did call Maxi to tell her it really was Joey. I got his address from her and went over there, using skills learned in my near criminal youth to slip into the apartment to look the place over.

It was a neat place and showed that Chloe must have spent as much time there as at the apartment she shared with two other girls. There were pictures of the two of them everywhere and some medals of his from service time in the marines. He seemed a regular Horatio Alger and I could find no dirty magazines or lovers' letters or anything to make him out to be anything but what Chloe thought him to be.

Next I went to the gymnasium he ran, which was in full swing with muscle men in sweat clothes lifting more weight at one time than the sum of every beer I had ever imbibed.

I talked to half a dozen men there, some of them I was sure walked on the other side of a certain line—if you know what I mean—but none of the swishers had a bad thing to say about Joey. In fact, they were pretty broken up about his death and you know, I didn't see any difference in their pain from my own when my buddy Jimmy was killed.

I had some figuring to do, so I went to my favorite house of intellect, Doolin's Bar across the street from the Universal lot.

Mike, the barkeep, who used to be a stuntman until a horse did the Tarantella on him, waved to me as I entered and had my 'regular' sitting on the bar by the time I reached him.

"Hey, Moxie," he said. "You look naked without that doll on your arm."

"Mind your manners you west coast heathen," I said as I scooped up the shot glass and beer mug. "Lest I shall have to chastise you with manly fisticuffs; that doll is my wife!"

"No accounting for a woman's taste," he said with perfect deadpan delivery. "Or lack of it."

"*Et tu, Brute?*" I said. I took my drinks over to my favorite booth and slid into the torn leather seat to think.

I knew that Mahoney had a bulletin out on Joey's car, but I could feel it in my gut that it wouldn't matter; what mattered was, why would a guy who lived south of the studio be up in North Hollywood? Where was he overnight? And why was he dressed in the strange leather harness? That's what I had to find out. I looked up at Mike and waved to him: "Set me up again, this is a three shot problem!"

I got up and went to the phone booth and found a directory for North Hollywood and looked up an address.

"Close enough," I said aloud to myself after comparing the address to a map of the area in the phone book. I made a phone call to a friend at the *LA Times* and made an appointment to see him in an hour then picked up my two other shots.

By the time I had downed the three shots I had a plan of action all worked out. First stop was the *Times* and Danny Carter, an old crony from Kansas City who had landed a beat reporter job and had helped me adjust to the new turf in Los Angeles.

"Hey, Moxie," he said extending a meaty hand. Despite his last name, he was an Eastern European bear—one of those whose family names had been changed by Ellis Island. You know the type, he has to shave three times a day just to keep his beard down to a shadow. "You here about that actor in the horse harness?"

"News travels fast," I said. "Bad news anyway."

"One of my stringers saw you talking to Mahoney. What's your interest; he's not under contract to Universal."

"My wife is friends with his lady."

He led me to his desk in the bullpen and slid a chair over for me to drop in to. "You said something about that leather thing he was wearing?"

"Yeah," he said. "They traced it to a harness shop that makes tack for horses. They had a bunch stolen a month ago; it had been altered to fit on this Calvera guy, but it still had the marks from the original maker."

"Any ideas on it?" I asked. I slipped a bottle of his favorite bourbon into his bottom desk drawer and watched his broad face split into a grin. "Could it be some sort of strange sex game or something like that?"

Deadline Zombies

"Well," he said leaning back in his chair. "I talked to a couple of my sources, one of them works out at the same gymnasium as your guy. He says Calvera was a straight shooter and not even a rumor of anything out of the ordinary."

"That's what it seemed to me when I talked to a bunch of them up there." I tapped my fingers on the desk and then asked, "What can you tell me about Josef Kokavich?"

This made Danny sit up and lean in to me as if he wasn't sure he heard me correctly. All round us the bullpen was a beehive of mad activity working to get out the evening edition and was a steady noise like a babbling brook. We were both so used to the noise we generally ignored it.

"What does that whacko have to do with this?" He got that *'I smell a story here'* look on his face.

"Maybe nothing," I said. "But word you won't break anything until I give you a heads up?"

"Got it."

"Okay—" I told him about the strange party story that Chloe had given me and all the while he nodded his head. When I was finished he gave a little chuckle.

"What, you don't believe it? " I asked.

"Oh no," he said, "It just confirms rumors I've heard but could never substantiate."

"So," I said, "give!"

"First off," he said with an evil cast sliding over his features. "Did you ever see *Ben Hur*?"

"Yeah, I saw the reissue in thirty one, but what does that have to do with this."

"Well, Kokavich, born in Russia, emigrated during the revolution to Italy and worked in films there until he was given second unit direction for the galley fights—"

"Wasn't there some trouble with that?"

"More than trouble, " he said, "There were deaths when he loaded one ship with fascists, one with communists and then armed them with real weapons!"

I tried to give the facts proper reverence but I'm afraid I laughed.

"Yeah," he said with a barely suppressed chuckle. "Me too. But it didn't make the studios happy, they scrapped all his footage and re-shot it all at great expense back here. Needless to say- he was off the picture and blacklisted. They covered it all up but everyone in the industry knew it.

He eventually got to direct some films over there and one of them, *The High Seas*, got him good notices. He was finally 'redeemed' and got a contract with RKO back here but he won't let it go about *Ben Hur*—when they re-released it with the sound track in thirty one he tried to get the studio to let him re-shoot some sequences."

"Wow," I said. "Can't let it go, huh?"

"Yup," Danny said. "He has his place fitted out like a set from the movie to the point where his guards are dressed like Roman Centurions and is constantly trying to talk to any one who will listen to remake it 'correctly' to his vision. Like anyone would ever remake that big mess of set pieces."

We both had a laugh at that. "So," I said. "What do you think?"

"I don't see how Kokavich ties in with your body builder; you said he was at the party two days before so what's to connect the death and the mad Russian?"

"Well," I said. "If you look at where the kid was found, it's just a quarter of a mile over rough wild land to Kokavich's mountain-top retreat." I'm willing to guess that when Mahoney's monkeys find Joey's car it—"

"They found it," he said, "It just came in before you got here. It's all the way on the other side of town from where Joey's apartment is in Pasadena."

"I was sure it would be found near Kokavich's place. This might blow my theory."

"Not necessarily," Danny said. "If there was something hinky at Mount Olympus there and they did have something to do with this guy's death, don't you think they'd dump the wheels somewhere else?"

"And not near his apartment necessarily; they wouldn't need to bring it there."

He looked at the notes he had on the death and then nodded again. "So you could have something there, Moxie; almost makes me think you learned something about reporting back in New York. Maybe the Pulitzer didn't ruin you at all."

"So what else can you clue me in on about this Russian guy?"

"Kokavich's parties are known for their wildness. He also goes on at length 'bout how he studied at Rasputin's feet—"

"I thought that had to be kidding, really Rasputin?"

"Is this the face of a kidder?" he said when I just stared at him.

He continued, "Okay—but this time, no. He likes to put on those hypnosis displays at every one of them but its getting hard to find takers with people in the know—he makes people chatter like monkeys, squawk like birds, you know like a bad vaudeville act."

"Sounds like the guy I need to scope out," I said. "But I have to do it on the sly."

"Well," he said. " He has parties every weekend and always needs staff; I have a buddy who hires people for these parties. I even tried to get one of my guys in there once, but they found him out."

"I'm not that well known out here," I said. "And I sure as heck have done that sort of thing."

"I'll see what I can do," he said. "But you go in as my stringer, okay?"

"Done deal, Danny," I alliterated. "But I better get back to Maxi. Give me a call when you got it arranged."

I left *The Times* with the hope that at least I might be able to tell Chloe something positive in the midst of all the pain. It was not a conversation I was looking forward to.

Chapter II: To the Manor Not Born

Chloe was a basket case for the rest of the week, but Maxi had to go on location for her film, so I sat with the distraught girl the next day. Mostly, I kept her stewed and let her sob; I didn't have any phony philosophy for her but I did tell her that I would find out what happened to Joey. It seemed to help.

Her sister came up from San Diego to take charge of her care and that freed me up to do some sleuthing (and do some of the flack work I was drawing a salary from the studio for).

Thursday, I got a call from Danny to meet him at the office of the party company that supplied the staff for the weekend affairs at Kokavich's. The guy who ran it was reluctant to let me go in undercover, claiming 'the reputation' of his company, but Danny had some dirt on the guy (don't ask, I didn't) and blackmailed him into letting me in.

I spent an hour learning my 'duties' as a butler and he put together a faked resume that I memorized so I had a pedigree.

"You owe me, Donovan," Danny said as we left the company with my marching orders for a party at the Kokavich Castle on Friday night.

"I'll let you dance with Maxi at the next Correspondence Dinner," I said. "But not a slow dance."

"You are a cold man, you Irish hooligan," he said. "But I accept your terms."

That night when Maxi came back from location, exhausted and ready for bath and bed I told her what I was doing the next night and she hit the roof.

"Are you insane?' she said. "Kokavich's parties are supposed to make Caligula's shindigs seem tame!"

"I'm going in as a butler, honey," I insisted. "Not to ogle the local talent."

"You're male, aren't you?" she said. "That's your license to be King leer!"

"Why look at hamburger when I have steak at home?" I said but I knew immediately it was the exact wrong thing to say. She got *that* look on her that meant the argument was over but I knew I had one trump card.

"I promised Chloe I would find out what happened to Joey," I said, wearing my virtue like armor, though I knew nothing could stop her right hook if she swung for me. "This is the best way to do it."

I saw the fire in her eyes spark but the kettle didn't boil over, I had caught her with a perfect block to her fury.

Deadline Zombies

"You promise me you won't look at other women?"

"Doll," I lied like a judge. "Ruby Keeler could flash her gams and I'd look the other way. You're it for me, babe." She was it for me, but Keeler's legs would make the Pope turn his head.

"You are the best, Moxie," she gushed and threw herself into my arms. She got her bath that night, but by then I needed to wash off a lot of faux-redman color myself.

* * * *

The Castle Kokavich was perched on the flattened top of a hill whose sides were dense with trees and could be reached only by a winding road. It was like stepping back into some medieval dream. Even with all the strangeness I had yet found in Hollywood, it was a whole new level of weird.

The building was not medieval at all: its multi-storied exterior was vaguely Spanish in style, having been built in the early twenties and rebuilt in nineteen thirty when Kokavich bought it. He had added Roman-style columns along the outside of the structure and statues on the four corners of the man made plateau that looked like Roman gods.

I looked a bit like a Roman god myself, if I do say so, having gone to the studio make-up man to have my auburn hair darkened and curled to give me a more Mediterranean look since Kokavich preferred Italian butlers. I knew how poor J. Carroll Naish felt—the black-Irish actor gets to play every ethnic group in the world except Irish. I was hoping my high school Latin and pizza parlor Italian would help get me by.

I was in the back of a truck with the catering staff, having gone to the hiring office to be picked up together for the trip to the fortress-like home. There were two dozen of us and we were hired to work until Saturday afternoon with everyone knowing that the mad Russian's parties ran until exhaustion.

I didn't join in the chatter of the others, most of them, like me, never having been to one of the parties before; the guy who ran the agency said that Kokavich didn't like the staff to be 'familiar' so that only the supervisors were repeaters.

The truck pulled up to the tall gate of the 'castle' and two guys dressed like Roman Legionnaires passed us through. That's when it got really weird.

Inside the fence, the grounds had been transformed into an Italian garden and the strangest creatures I had ever seen were roaming around. I saw a unicorn, a guy with furry legs and goat horns, and one big guy who had a single eye in the center of his head. The costumes were realistic and for a second I thought somebody had slipped something in my lunchtime Scotch or, worse, I was having a déjà vu' of Mabuse et al. Then I saw the zippers, well hidden on the Cyclops headpiece and I relaxed.

We were led into the back of the massive mansion where the building was dug into the mountaintop and so that we entered at ground level but I had the sense we were in the basement. The large room we entered was lined with lockers and changing booths and already had others in it in the process of becoming faux Roman citizens. The head butler, a red head guy with a gut, called us all to attention.

"You are going to a very special place," Big Red said when everyone was in the room and looking around curiously, "You all signed contracts that state you cannot talk about what happens here; there will be severe financial repercussions if you do; but on the other hand, should a guest approach you for anything within reason and not terribly illegal, you may participate if you wish. You will be compensated."

I couldn't believe my ears, but even to my jaded squawk catchers that sounded like he was pimping for the Russian.

"Your costumes are in lockers with your names on them," he continued, "and you will put them on and then meet by that door over there. Do a good job and have a good time; this will not be the worst job you ever got, I can promise you. It just might be the most fun!"

I went to a locker marked with my name and took out the costume I was to wear for the night. I was suddenly really glad that no one I knew was going to see me in the outfit. I hate costumes.

Thank God it wasn't a toga; it was a long coat and short pants with high boots, sort of a George Washington sort of get up; to make me stand out from the regular run of the mill servants.

And there was a wig.

I almost bolted then: a wig? But I did promise Chloe. And besides, my reporter's nose was smelling a hell of a story so I sucked it up and plopped the white curled thing on my head.

I took solace in the fact that there were three others in the same butlering garb as mine, complete with wig.

Of just as much, or perhaps more interest to me were the dancing girls and waitresses who were beginning to gather at the doorway out of the room. They were wearing little more than the suggestion of descent clothes and my wife's earlier condemnation was ringing in my ears.

Oh boy, I thought as I touched the spot on my finger where my wedding ring usually sat. I had taken it off at home since it had mine and Maxine's name engraved inside. *I sure hope this spot doesn't burst into flame based on my thoughts.*

Deadline Zombies

I joined the others at the door and waited with them, listening to the buzz of actor talk from all of them. All were anxious for what was ahead of them, but one or two seemed to know—confidentiality agreements or not, rumors about the parties at the Kokavich castle painted a wild picture.

Big Red met us and opened the double doors and let us all up a wide set of stairs to scene that would have indeed have done Caligula proud; The first floor of the mansion was a huge open space separated by slight steps up or down into multiple areas of debauchery. The floors were marble with frescoes of orgy scenes and sylvan glades painted onto the walls and expensive curtains draped artistically around to give the feeling of great antiquity.

To our left was a sunken area with founting water and rising steam that simulated a Roman bath and mineral springs. To the right, in an area raised two steps, pillows had been spread around with low tables in the manner of an old Roman orgy hall. Between was a long wide space that was clearly a performing area and beyond it the foyer and main entrance to the mansion.

"Man alive," I said aloud. "Fatty Arbuckle had nothing on this place!"

Musicians took up their spots and began to play a low sensual tune that soon filled the room. The dancers all fluttered about, finding their spaces, rehearsing their steps in a sort of shorthand

Big Red came to the head of the group and began to send everyone to their various 'posts' around the large room. He conducted each of us 'butlers' and brought us to our posts, explaining briefly our overlapping 'field' of responsibility.

We were basically glorified maitre des for that area, though in charge of the servers—waiters and waitresses—and our job was just to keep the booze and food flowing. Big Red—his name was Hiram but I couldn't think of him like that—was in charge of the entertainment. He would orchestrate the night like a ringmaster.

My assigned area was a semi-circular space in the center of the house's first floor near the stairs that led up to the second floor of the mansion. There was a serving station, an intercom to contact the kitchen directly and a large throne-like couch.

As I stood there in my ridiculous wig and breeches, the lord of the manor put in his appearance, and I realized I had pulled the prized assignment of the night; I was the go-for for the grand poobah himself!

Josef Illya Kokavich was an impressive sight in his purple robes. He was a tall man with thin, hawk-like features, longish brown hair streaked with grey and a spade beard that would have given him a scholarly look if not for his wide, staring eyes. They were electric as he surveyed the scene downstairs, almost glowing with an inner fire. He had a laurel wreath on his head and looked the perfect image of one of the guys that might have given the shiv to old Julie Caesar.

The only anachronism to his Roman attire was a monocle in his left eye. It magnified his eye to almost make him seem like one was bigger than the other; the effect was unnerving.

He stood for a long moment at the top of the stairs impassive, his piercing gaze taking in all of us below and I had the sense of him being apart from us 'mere peasants' by his physical attitude.

He smiled but it was clearly from an internal motivation and was cold and distant.

Then he slowly descended the steps, obviously comfortable in his robes and flowed down like a regular Theda Bara. When he got to the bottom of the stair he walked over to me and regarded me like a lab specimen.

"Name?" he asked.

"Gianni Scotto, sir." I said. I'd worked out my cover identity but hoped he wouldn't probe too deeply.

"Well, Gianni," he said. "I am not too demanding a master; just keep my cup filled, make sure there is a pretty girl at my side and we shall get along fine."

"I shall do my best to serve, sir," I said with my best, 'oh I am not worthy' attitude. "And to anticipate your wants. Your choice of beverage?"

"Red wine for an orgy, my dear, Gianni," he said with a chuckle. "After all, there will be a great deal of meat on display!" He laughed at his own joke and I poured him a goblet full of wine.

Two scantily-clad women slithered to either side of the purple-robed Russian and arranged themselves artistically on the couch. I poured goblets for each of them. Both of them, who probably had been jerking soda the week before, looked at me as if I were little more than an accessory with their evening wear. It was a condescending expression that made me want to take them over my knee to teach them manners.

Just as he took his first sip, the doorbell chimed and the wide main doors of the mansion opened; the first of the guests had arrived.

They stopped in a pair of anterooms inside the outer doors where they changed from their mundane clothes to more period appropriate robes before they entered the foyer of the mansion.

Deadline Zombies

Even my news-hound's cynical attempt at stoicism was a little shaken by the variety and magnitude of the guests who walked through the doors of the Kokavich mansion. Politicians, both city and state, a few former bootleggers who had attempted to cloak themselves in respectability and some that hadn't bothered, civic leaders, a pastor who had a national radio show congregation (!) and a number of movies stars both new and old came through the doors dressed in Roman garb in the next half hour.

Kokavich seated himself on his couch and waited for each of the guests to trek across the foyer for his 'royal' blessing. He greeted each one of them personally without rising from his couch and I had the impression that they had all been there before and knew the routine. It was as if he were a real emperor.

The guests wasted no time in either moving to the hot springs area or the couch area where food was laid out. It was a sumptuous feast of fruits, cold meats and various finger foods.

Others moved to slow dance near the band or slipped off to the shadowed areas made by the strategically placed tapestries. I was pretty certain that at least one of those pairs—a congressman and a socialite—were married to other people. It was a sure thing that the Kokavich castle was used for many of those assignations on regular basis. Too bad I wasn't working the gossip desk instead of the crime beat.

The opulence of the whole thing was amazing and the atmosphere so decadent that it almost made my head spin.

"If this guy is so obsessed with re-making *Ben Hur*," I thought," why the heck doesn't he stop throwing parties that cost this much and just finance the thing himself?"

But I realized that he was also accumulating contacts and information that would give him influence far beyond the film industry. Doing it the way he was he might get his remake and a lot more.

I had just finished topping off the faux emperor's cup again when another couple entered the foyer of the mansion. They were like many of the pairings that had come through the door; he, a middle aged pair-shaped, balding man and she a much younger, attractive pippin.

She was wearing an obvious blonde wig that concealed red hair and had long, shapely legs.

It was the legs that made me look twice as the mismatched couple ankled toward the 'emperor.' Those gams were eerily familiar.

I followed the legs up past the curvaceous hips ignored the blonde wig and stared directly into the over-made up face of my wife!

Chapter III: Showtime at Apollo's

Maxi let her eyes slide past me and I could not tell if she recognized me in my Italian disguise or not as she walked up to the couch where Kokavich reclined. Her companion, who I could see was wearing make up and eyeliner, extended a meaty hand to shake the Russian's.

"So very good to see you again, Mister Cohen, " Kokavich said. "And who is this lovely dear with you?"

"Josef," the chubby man said. "Allow me to introduce Maxine Keller the newest star at Universal, recently come out from New York."

I recognized the name Cohen as one of the studio production people, a musical director whom Maxi was friendly with.

I looked at his beady little eyes and double chin and suddenly felt an unreasoning dislike for the butterball. It was all I could do to not crack a bottle of wine over his thinning pate.

"I've heard so much about you." Maxi flashed her devastating smile at the Russian.

I shifted my target options from Cohen to Kokavich's noggin but stayed my hand and just poured a cup for the studio guy.

"I hope, my dear," the Russian said, "that Hershel has at least lied in my favor when he spoke about me."

"He said you were a great director," she said coyly. "And you knew how to waltz like Nijinsky!"

The Russian laughed so hard he spilled his wine. He threw the cup aside and sprang to his feet yelling, "Play the Blue Danube!" at the band.

He grabbed Maxi by the hand and as the musicians struck up the tune began to lead her across the marbled floor and dance her around the room.

I ground my teeth so hard it's a wonder I didn't drown out the music.

The monocled masher waltzed Maxi in spinning steps round the dance floor for the whole song and when they finished did an exaggerated old-fashioned bow to her.

She curtsied, showing more of her dynamite walking stems and a bit of her cleavage and sending my blood pressure skyrocketing.

Everyone around the room applauded and Maxi, ever the performer, took a bow.

"He did not lie, Mister Kokavich," she said as the two of them walked back toward the couch. "But he did understate your ability."

"You are too kind," he said. "And a fabulous partner; I see that with such poise and presence (and perhaps the right director), you will indeed become a star!"

Deadline Zombies

I swallowed my bile and had a new goblet ready for the Russian. Then I stepped up in front of my twinkle-toe mate and asked through tight lips, "And what would the lady like to drink?"

She looked me straight in the eyes, smiled and said, as if I were just a service flunky, "A beer if you have it. My husband has gotten me really used to the low things in life."

My ears began to burn as my blood pressure threatened to blow the top of my head off.

"Oh no, my dear," Kokavich said, "Pour the lady some champagne, Gianni; such a stylish dancer deserves much better than mere beer!"

I did as directed, handing the flute to her. At which point she gave me a quick flash of a smile and a glance from beneath half closed eyes that let me know she was enjoying torturing me.

The first of the performing acts erupted onto the dance floor then, six women wearing almost nothing and gyrating in synchronized choreography to the exotic strains of the band. Their performance was both exotic and exciting in an erotic way. I could see that their perambulating pelvises had an effect on the watching crowd as more couples became entwined in non-connubial lip lock or rose to make for the shadowed niches with their intent quite obvious.

I split my attention between my host, who was nuzzling one of his two decorative assistants and Maxi who was talking and giggling with her escort while watching the dancers with a chorus-girl's critical eye. I was giving equal consideration to murder and divorce when she caught my eye and tapped her wedding ring with a finger of her right hand.

I tried not to reveal myself to the entire room and just outright yell at her but she compounded my problem by leaving her companion and walking over to me.

"Oh butler," she said. "I need more champagne, my glass is empty." She held out her glass for me to attend to and then whispered under her breath, "I see you're not wearing your ring; I found it when I got home from the set early."

"I'm undercover!" I whispered.

Aloud I said, " I'm glad you like it, miss."

Under my voice I said, "You are going to get me thrown out!"

"I just have to be careful I don't drink too much," she said aloud, "It tickles my nose."

In her whispered voice she said, "Just stay undercover but don't get undercovers."

"You're the one who came with a date to an orgy!"

"Herschel is an old friend from New York; he's more likely to make a pass at you. By the way, nice wig!"

Then she turned and, with a bubbly laugh, headed back to stand next to her friend.

I went back to the work station and watched with a slow burn while she and Herschel walked off toward the hot baths area. In no time he had taken off his robes and slipped into the bubbling water. For a moment I thought she would disrobe and that would have been it as far as my undercover reporter career, but she just hiked up her robe and sat on the edge of the shallow pool to slip her legs into the water.

She chatted with several people in the pool (most of whom were nude or close to it) while keeping her eyes half on me. I had to work very hard to pull my focus back to Kokavich.

Fortunately, he had been busy nuzzling his own companions and apparently took no notice of my exchange with my soon to be ex-love of my life.

An animal act took the center performance area after the dancers finished their incendiary dance. It was a trained dog act and was a sudden 'cute' factor after the sensual display. It had the effect of 'cooling the room down.' Even the mad Russian came up for air and I refilled his cup.

That set the pattern for the evening as one sensual or erotic performance was spaced with dance music and a 'cooler' act. By twelve o'clock I had witnessed many pairs disappear into the shadows of the tapestries in different combinations. I was also certain I had seen a number of 'back room' deals being made between various studio executives, politicians and gangsters there 'incognito'.

Attendance at one of the Kokavich events was discouraged or frowned upon by the moguls who ran the major studios for fear that moral turpitude clauses in many of their stars contracts would be violated. But as long as no word of what happened left the walls of Kokavich's estate, they availed themselves of the chance to burst through the caste system that was in effect outside of the mansion's no holds barred atmosphere. As far as they could, they turned a blind eye.

My eyes were anything but blind, they were focused mostly on Maxi. My firecracker redhead amazed me with the deftness with which she fended off casual and not so casual interest from those around her with no apparent effort; I guess all those years of theatrical boarding houses on the road had given her the knack. She was also very good at not revealing my cover with any errant glances or gestures though once or twice when she got a refill of fruit juice from me we made eye contact. I felt like grabbing her and just running straight from the madhouse of the mansion.

Just after the one o'clock performance of a fire-eater, Kokavich was deep in conversation with a buxom actress that I had seen last on a soundstage at Columbia. She was wearing one of the exotic dancers, a dark skinned Asian girl draped over her lap. Occasionally the two women would kiss and then the actress would go back to her conversation with the Russian.

Finally Kokavich stood up and called the attention of the gathering. 'My guests," he said, "I Josef Illya Kokavich have been challenged again to show the abilities that the great Grigori Yefimovich Rasputin taught me in our village in Siberia."

The band had stopped playing and the murmur of conversation around the room faded as he took center stage. All eyes focused on him as he stepped out to the center of the dancer's performing space.

"Our lovely friend has questioned whether I can truly alter the patterns of a mind with my own; but many of you have seen that my superior intellect has in the past overtaken and controlled that of others." He swiveled his head like a searchlight, his monocle continuing the illusion as he fixed each face in the room. He seemed to make contact with everyone directly including mine with an intensity that was, in the true sense of the word, mesmerizing.

"So I will show you all, who may doubt." He snapped his fingers and his two couch companions stepped forward with the strangest thing I had ever seen, a rubberized horse costume.

It must have been the one that Chloe had described Joey wearing at the last party. It was eerie; it should have been just a costume, an adult version of a child's Halloween masquerade suit but it was more; I couldn't explain why, but I knew it was the key to the death of Chloe's lover.

I also knew that the only way I was going to unravel what had happened to Joey was to go down the same path that he had traveled: to take the chance.

I know it was insane and risky, but that pretty much defines what I do for a living. And I figured that with my past experiences, I would be better equipped to deal with things than Joey might have.

Maxi and I made eye contact and I could see that she knew what I was thinking; I'd told her that's why I had to marry the crazy redhead, she always seemed to have me figured out and knew what I was thinking. I couldn't take a chance on her selling that information to *The New York Tribune*!

"So, my friends," Kokavich said. "I will demonstrate how I can reach into a soul and shape it; why I am the greatest director that ever lived. I can mold anyone who gives themselves to me to be whatever role they are destined to play." He turned around and took in all those who looked at him with rapt focus.

No one moved or spoke.

No one dared to.

"Who will step forward and be brave enough to entrust their soul to me?"

I could hear the water gurgling in the baths, the rustle of cloth as some of the guests emerged from their shadowed alcoves to see what the silence was.

Maxi opened her eyes wide and subtly shook her head 'no' to try and discourage me. I wanted to agree with her, my gut telling me that this was a scary road to go down, but I'd never walked out on a hard job before and it seemed like the best, quickest way to find out what had happened to Joey so I stepped forward.

"If you will, sir," I said, "I'd like to play your game."

"Game!" he said turning to look at me with his exaggerated eye aflame with indignation. "Not a game, my dear Gianni," he said. "But an experience I am sure you will not ever forget for the rest of your life." He motioned for the two women to approach me and before I could stop them they had slipped my jacket and shirt off me and grabbed for my boots.

"I'll get them, ladies," I said. I snuck a glance at Maxi and I could see she was ready to race across the room but I wasn't sure if she was going to club me or Kokavich.

I took off my boots myself but drew the line at taking the breeches off. This last garment didn't seem to deter the damsels and the two nymphs came forward with the horse suit to help me to slip my legs into the hind legs of the rubber horse suit. The zipped the horse legs up tight at the ankles and smoothing them out as I climbed in to the rest of it. I can't say that their attentions weren't pleasant, but it could have been more so if Maxi wasn't slicing them up with her gaze from across the room.

I slipped the upper/fore arms on as if it were a jumpsuit and they zipped up the belly to seal me in. The head hung behind me like a hood.

I felt oddly helpless since I had no way to use my hands, encased in the sleeves of the suit completely with the lower part of them blocked off with an extension that ended in hooves.

Deadline Zombies

"Well, Mister Scotto," Kokavich said as he stepped before me. "Tell me, have you ever been hypnotized before?"

I wasn't sure how to answer him. I thought about the weirdness that had happened to me on Governors Island back in New York where I had been changed into the shape of a horse, and then another weirdo Nazi back there who put me under a spell and I'd ended up with a wooden leg (now gone) and could have gone on reflecting but what point? My wife was right, every time I got involved in any heavy story I seemed to end up as a carousel animal. But I'm not sure you could call any of those occasions as hypnotism.

"No, sir" I said. "But I have faith in you."

"Very well, Mister Scotto," he said with a wide smile. "You are good to do so." He held my gaze with his and said, "Now look into my eyes and open your soul to me; we are about to go on a journey together!"

Chapter IV: Win Place and Scream

His eyes were like whirlpools of power, drawing me in to them.

I felt as if I were falling down into a well filled with warm liquid. The sensation of spiraling into darkness and the muffling of all sounds around was overwhelming.

The light of the room seemed to dim and the sounds to fade so that all I could hear was the sound of my own blood pumping in my veins and *his* voice sharp and strong. I felt like it was crawling under my skin and into my brain.

"Hear me, Gianni." His voice was musical and mysterious, like a saxophone playing in a distant mountain pass. "Know that you are a thought, a moment in time and no more. You are only what you believe and you will believe only what I tell you to believe."

There was no other sound but his voice; every word was like a wave on a beach washing over me, submerging me to his will. I tried to look away from him, to see Maxine to find strength to pull my gaze back. But I could not.

I was frozen, trapped by his stare as surely as if I had been staked out on a beach waiting for high tide to drown me or bound against some dungeon wall. My limbs were unresponsive to the point where my neck was locked and it felt as if I could not even blink. My breaths came in shallow gasps and it felt as if I had a weight on my chest.

"You will wonder, all of you," he said, " why I have placed him in this outer casing if I am just going to show you my talent to hypnotize? It is because I do not merely do a vaudeville act, my guests, but actually alter his thoughts so that he becomes the thing which I wish him to be." He walked around me as if he were examining a horse on an auction block.

"I can hasten the process by allowing him to focus on this outer shell. A weak mind must have its symbolism to grasp on to. A mold, if you wish, to pour its unformed thoughts into to be reshaped by my will."

I felt it was true; it was if my insides were jellied and the flesh that had confined me before was being reshaped by foreign thoughts that were seeping into me. I was in another world than the one I had come from. I felt separated from all I had been, adrift within myself and yet completely aware of that separation.

I didn't feel it as the two women slipped the rubberized horse head over my own, pulling it down tight. I could still see my tormentor through the eyes of the equine mask, still hear his voice whispering to me in his native tongue. All other sounds were muffled by the suit save his voice with came to me more clearly, more intensely. His whisperings slipped into English and He said, over and over. "A horse you will be."

He stepped away and for a moment broke eye contact with me and I felt as if air had been taken away, as if I were plunged into darkness. I craved his stare and that fact, more than anything else, frightened me to my core.

"My friends," he said to the assembled and enraptured crowd, "In Mother Russia I was an officer in the ranks of the Czar's cavalry. This is why the chariot race in my version of *Ben Hur* would have been and *will* be the greatest action sequence to ever be shown upon the silvered screen!" His voice and tense posture betrayed his anger at the very thought that he had *not* shot the chariot race in 'twenty-five, but he controlled himself quickly and his tone became playful. "So I thought it appropriate to show you my skill with the equine form at the same time I demonstrated my mesmeric skills!"

He fixed his eyes on me again and I felt as if I had surfaced from the depths of the ocean and breathed air or felt the sun on my face for the first time. His voice was a warm and comforting embrace that made me want to do whatever he asked.

"My young friend Gianni here will aid me in this demonstration, will you not?" he asked me.

I wanted to call out to him and say 'yes' but I could not find the word in my throat.

"Answer me as you are," he said, "I know you want to, to discover the beast within you."

I felt as if I were standing on the edge of cliff, swaying in a strong wind. It was the dividing line between my own free will and falling over that cliff into the abyss of submission to his will.

"You know it will be better for you," he said. "Become what you seem, assume the form you will become; surrender to the hope of the beast; answer me."

I tried to resist his will one last time; *damn finding out what Joey went through, damn any story I could get or promise I had made*; I had to fight to regain my own mind. I had to fight to be free. I had to hold onto my humanity. I could not reply!

I could not!

I whinnied and I was lost in the vortex of his spell and I was lost.

I dropped forward at a gesture from him so that I was on all fours, but in a way I had not been before (unless you count that time on Governors Island) so that I was moving like a real horse.

It was like I was in at the end of a long corridor watching myself at the other end of it, shaped differently than I remembered my self. I was not a man in a horse suit any more; the thing I was looking at *was* a horse.

Kokavich acted like a real ringmaster, exhorting me with wide sweeping gestures to make me move in front of him. It was strange that I moved so smoothly in the costume with my arms extended by the cleverly designed sleeves.

The tight-fitting horse head allowed me to see out of the equine eyes as if they were my own and I glimpsed a horrified Maxi standing near the bath area, her hand to her mouth in shock.

Kokavich fitted a halter over my horse head so that he could lead me around. I tried one last time to exercise my 'free will' but it was a futile gesture.

I tossed my head in a horse-like gesture that startled even me. I was 'thinking' horse-like in just the moments since Kokavich took over my mind. I tried to shrug it off, a physical shiver going down my whole body but it seemed to delight the watching crowd and they applauded the equine nature of the gesture.

Somehow the applause humiliated me and seared into my soul in a way like no embarrassment I had ever felt before. And the fact that it was in front of my wife made it even more horrible.

"In my Mother Country," Kokavich said, "I was a master horse trainer and now I will show you how we prepared a fine stallion for the front lines!"

He had gotten a long riding crop from somewhere and he used it as a combination pointer and prodder to move me around the elongated performing area. He had me 'trot' first one way then by voice command had me reverse. All the while he held the lead rope and 'conducted' me with his crop/pointer.

This also delighted the crowd and my 'public' clapped and cheered as the Russian put me through my paces. It was a demeaning performance worse than anything I could have imagined possible for a hardened street reporter like me, a kid from Brooklyn who never took no guff from anyone. Now I was nothing but a puppet for the Russian and I understood, like I could not have before, how Joey had felt—a man who had worked hard to be disciplined and master of his body had lost all that control and had his body completely taken over.

I trotted, I capered, I was made to rear and buck like a circus horse in the bigtop in ways that should have been impossible for my human body. I functioned perfectly as if I were a four-legged creature.

Deadline Zombies

I felt none of the physical limitations that I should have; my muscles responded to the outside orders better than to any I had ever given them, heck, if I could have run half as well on two legs as I was on four I might have tried out for a college football team!

All the while the crowd laughed and jeered in delight and my humiliation deepened.

This went on for a full half hour with the rubber suit causing me to perspire profusely and I was getting dizzy from the exertion and dehydration.

Just when it seemed I could not raise a leg again and would surly fall over, my 'horse master' held up his hands and laughed out loud. "I think this old fellow has been an excellent stallion, eh? Shall we send him to the glue factory or put him out to pasture and let him rest?"

There were laughing cheers from the audience of "send him to the glue factory!"

For a moment I had the unreasoning fear that he would have me put down and I could see the same thought flash across Maxi's face.

"Oh now," Kokavich said. "I think the old fellow has earned a carrot and a rest." When he said that he waved his hands before my masked face and whispered, so that only I could hear, "Be free to be who you were and always remember who I am!"

Suddenly, it was like a cork had been removed from a bottle or a bubble burst; the distance of the sound the and the sense of being removed from my own body were gone and I was just a half-in-the-bag beat reporter wearing a rubber horse suit.

I dropped to the ground and rolled onto my side so tired I could not even attempt to get up. I had no strength at all. Now my muscles wouldn't listen to me because they just had no power to, not because they had been 'stolen' from me.

After a time one of Kokavich's couch companions took pity on me and gripped the belly fastenings of the suit to open them. The rush of air was cool against my sweating skin and it revived me enough to push my way out of the costume.

It was like I had been reborn.

I lay on the ground, like a fish out of water, gasping for air for quite a while as a singer stepped up to the performing area and belted out a blues tune. The crowd shifted their focus from me and the couch companion went back to her job of rubbing herself against Kokavich.

"You did well, my boy," Kokavich said to me, "There will be a bit extra in your pay envelope; I think you are effectively done for the night, you can go home.

Maybe he said I could go home but the thought of even standing up was beyond me. I was dripping with perspiration and breathing hard and not likely to get home under my own steam. At that point a redhead came to my rescue.

"All right, boy," Hiram, the big red haired major domo said. "Come along with me." He reached down and pulled me to my feet and half dragged, half carried me back to the wide stairs to the basement changing room.

Over his shoulder the last thing I saw before I was carried through the wide doors was the terrified face of my wife left alone in the middle of the mad Russian's orgy room.

* * * *

"I've never been so scared in my life!" Maxi screamed at me the second she came through the doorway of our bungalow. "Or so angry!"

I had poured myself onto the couch when the cabdriver that Hiram called dropped me off. I didn't even have the strength to pour myself a drink so I had just opened the bottle of Scotch and slugged it back. That was how Maxi found me with the half-drunk bottle attached to my right hand.

"I wasn't angry at all that you tried to get me caught by showing up where I undercover," I said. "Or scared that my wife was in the middle of a bunch of perverts and whackos and there wasn't a damn thing I could do about it; so why should you be scared?" I could barely look at her and was so weak I couldn't get up and walk away from her.

She stood in the doorway, a lovely ball of fury backlit by the moonlight spilling into the open door. She kicked the door shut and kicked off her high heels with one graceful motion then somehow managed to lose her evening gown in the time it took to cross the distance to the couch. Then she was kneeling next to me in a slip and crying her peepers out.

"I was so scared!" she said through the sobs. "I sat here thinking of all the things that could go wrong with you at that madhouse—thinking of all the things that Chloe told me about it—and I just had to go." She nuzzled her head into the hollow of my shoulder. "I didn't know what I could do, but I knew I couldn't sit here and do nothing."

"You weren't there to keep me safe," I said with more tang to my words that I should have, "You were there to keep me on the leash because you don't trust me."

She snapped her head up to stare me in the eyes. "And you trusted me? Herschel went with me because I begged him and left with me a half hour after they put you in taxi." Her green eyes were rimmed with red and wet with tears but they still were the most beautiful things I'd ever seen.

I tried to stay angry with her but it was harder than it had been to resist Kokavich's horse show.

"I was scared too, toots," I said. "When I saw you in that snake pit I wanted to run screaming from there; why did you risk yourself like that? I'm the one who promised Chloe I'd find out what happened to Joey, you're supposed to be home and safe; how could I live if you got yourself hurt?"

"You—you big lug!" she said. "If we're not a team we're nothing."

How could a guy argue with a redhead that made so much sense?

I pulled her onto the couch with me and we settled in to sleep right there.

Sometimes it's really good to be married.

Chapter V: The Night Mare

I didn't have Joey Calvera's physique or stamina, so, unlike him, I was not up and around Saturday or off to a gymnasium to 'work out the kinks.'

Au contraire, I was a horizontal squid lying bonelessly on the couch while my devoted and amazing redheaded wife kept my whisky glass and my arms full.

By Saturday night I was feeling human and had enough of my wits about me to begin worrying again about what had happened to Joey. I knew for sure it had to do with the Tsar of Zooey, Kokavich, but I couldn't figure out why or how Joey ended up at the bottom of a ravine dressed like Ken Maynard's Tarzan.

I put in a bunch of calls to my contacts and Danny stopped over so we could talk face to face about what I had seen Friday night. I downplayed my horse impersonation but gave him all the other high and lowlights.

"I'll get all my street sources working on it," he said as he left. "I still haven't been able to trace the leather harness after it was stolen from that shop, but even the police don't believe that Calvera's car was driven to where they found it by the kid himself."

"Why am I not surprised," I said.

"But here is a little tidbit for you," he added as he went out the door. "I did a little checking around about Kokavich's parties and it seems that at least four other guys who worked for him at his parties—all muscular types—have gone missing in the last six months. Might be nothing: actors are always coming and going but—"

"Yeah," I said. 'I'm with you on that. I believe in coincidence as much as I do the tooth fairy." Even as I said it I realized I shouldn't be so glib about it considering all the strange things I had seen in my recent reporting career. Still, Kokavich smelled like fish and I had a hook out for him.

Maxi called Chloe's sister and spoke to her about her friend. There was no good news; the little faux blonde had been having bouts of uncontrolled sobbing and ranting about Joey and the party at the Russian's. They'd had to keep her sedated most of the time to cope with things.

When she hung up the phone Maxine cried for a time herself; it made me feel useful at least that I could hold her.

She didn't have to be back at the studio until Tuesday to start her next picture so we made plans to get out of town for a couple of days to

Deadline Zombies

a friend's beach shack in Malibu. It was a pleasant drive and I was feeling more myself but preoccupied with the why and wherefore of Joey and Kokavich.

I just couldn't understand why Joey would go back to the place where he had been—where we had been—humiliated.

At least I couldn't until the nightmares started.

After midnight on Saturday night, they began.

I was on a sunny field somewhere but I was different, strange. I could see the shadow of me on the ground but it was not a shape I recognized, at least not at first. I had a long face and ears and a neck that... I was a horse! It was clear; a long necked, broad-chested horse.

When I glanced further down I saw my forelegs pounding the ground, my hooves clomping up wedges of earth as I raced along.

"Not again!" I cried out loud but my voice was different too. It was deep throated and alien. Not quite a whinny but close enough to give me chills.

I was getting so sick of playing horsy.

The sunlight in the dream (and I was aware it was a dream) burned brighter than it should have been and there were other things wrong with the world in this nightmare, but what horrified me was the unsettling sensation that I would never be right again.

There was an awareness that I was not alone and then I saw the shadow of another horse running beside me, only it was not just a horse. It was a horse with a human face. It was a face I knew: Joey Calvera. He looked over at me and I had the sense that he was pleading with me, but I couldn't understand the words.

He was wearing a harness and then I was aware I was wearing a harness as well and the two of us were pulling a wagon of some kind.

I turned my head to look back and saw him; Kokavich riding in chariot dressed as a Roman Emperor.

He was yelling commands in Russian at me but I couldn't understand what he was saying.

I woke up screaming twice and startled Maxine both times.

By Monday morning I was almost as big mess as I had been Saturday morning.

"You have to find a way to deal with this," Maxi said to me as she cooked breakfast. "Or I'm only going to get old lady parts; I need my beauty sleep."

"I know, doll," I said. "I just can't seem to get that horse thing out of my head." I had told her on Sunday about the nightmares as much as I could remember and understand of them. We tried to just chalk it up to anxiety over solving the case about Joey, but I was beginning to think it was more.

"Do you think this kind of nightmare may be what happened to Joey?" she asked me.

"That's it!" I yelled as I jumped up from the table.

Maxi spun with the frying pan in her hand ready to swat whatever I was obviously yelling at, but when she saw no circus bears had invaded the house she put it back on the stove.

"What's it?"

"If you were having these nightmares and you didn't know that the nut job who did it to you had maybe hurt someone else, what would you do?"

"I don't know." She made a pout face and looked like Shirley Temple pondering the size of the universe. "I guess go ask someone about it."

"Like maybe the guy who claimed to be a hotsy-totsy hypnotist?"

"You think he went back to Kokavich?"

"Sure, why not? He had no idea the guy was maybe connected to other strange things like other disappearances; if he thought his nightmares might have been caused by the hypnosis session he would have gone back to have the guy undo whatever he had done."

She looked at me like maybe I wasn't crazy for a change and nodded. "And so he drove up there when he couldn't sleep that night when Chloe was at the studio, and—uh—"

"Whatever happened, happened, " I continued. "Somehow they got him to put on that harness and pants and when he got away on foot and went over the cliff, they had someone drive his car across the city to try and throw off suspicion."

"You might be okay at this reporter stuff, Moxie," she said leaning cross the table to plant one on my cheek. "So what now?"

"I think I have to go back there." It scared me a little to say it but I knew I wouldn't get rid of the nightmares until I had an answer to why I was having them. And the only place to get that answer was within Kokavich's madhouse mansion.

She shook her head furiously. "No; *we* have to go back."

I thought about arguing with her for a moment, but only for a moment. The secret of married life, I was discovering, was knowing when to give in to superior forces. And one redhead dancer/actress always trumped a beat reporter—whether or not he had a Pulitzer Prize on his mantel. She swings a mean skillet.

Deadline Zombies

We enjoyed the day at the beach (though I missed the Nathan's Hotdogs from back home on Coney Island) but before dinner we packed up early to head back for a little night sleuthing at the Kokavich castle.

We left our car hidden in the brush at the side of the road at the base of the hill leading to Kokavich's place and hoofed it up through the woods. Maxi wore slacks and a dark jacket and I looked like a low-budget lumberjack in a flannel shirt and blue jeans.

The moon was setting when we broke through the foliage at the outside wall of the building and crouched down to consider our options.

"I don't think we are very good burglars," Maxi whispered.

"How so?"

"We don't have any ropes or masks or any of the stuff like Dr. Shadows uses in the serials." She was looking all around us as she whispered, afraid a squad of policemen was going to pop out of the darkness and nab us.

"Most people are really sloppy about security," I said as I led her along the base of the wall to the entrance the performers had used. I checked each window as we came to them. "I noticed he didn't have dogs last week and those are the only real problem if you want to burgle; we don't need to make like Tarzan and climb anything."

Sure enough an open window near the performers' entrance allowed us to slip into a utility room.

Maxi wanted to go first, more afraid of being caught outside than of what she might find inside but on that one I overruled.

The house was quiet and we did our best to keep it that way, tiptoeing out of the utility room intending to slip upstairs to look around.

We barely started up the step when we heard strange noises from behind a door off to the side of the stairs. They were muffled sounds alternately sharp and dull punctuated by a giggling laugh.

We looked at each other, shrugged our shoulders and then changed course. We two headed for the door sounds seemed to be coming from behind. It was a plain red-painted wood door that was slightly ajar. There was heavy hasp lock on it but that hung open on the frame.

As we approached it sounds became more distinct; the sharp sound was a whip crack and the laughter was definitely Kokavich's.

We looked at each other again. I assumed my face was as pale as hers.

She nodded and we opened the door. Inside was a set of circular steps. As I went down them, I witnessed the most bizarre sight of the many bizarre sights I had seen in the Kokavich castle.

Huge arc lights were flooding the space as to make it as bright as day. In a cavernous space that looked to have been made by enlarging a natural cavern in the mountain, Kokavich had constructed a scaled model of the Circus Maximus from the movie *Ben Hur*.

On the track itself a chariot was racing around on which the mad Russian himself, dressed in his Roman robes, was snapping whip and cackling at the top of his lungs. That was remarkable enough but what was drawing him around the arena was even more so.

Harnessed to the chariot were two men dressed as Joey had been, wearing the leather traces and sweating profusely. Their upper bodies were as muscular as the dead man had been and from the look of the healed scars on their backs had been whipped by Kokavich for a long time.

I'd seen enough and was ready to get Maxi out of there when I heard a grunting sound behind me and whirled. I was just in time to get the vague impression of someone with their arms wrapped around Maxi before a boot connected with my head and I took a long hard tumble into blackness.

Deadline Zombies

Chapter VI: Not so Merry-Go-Round

I crawled up from the black pit into a world of pain. I felt like the Nicholas Brothers were doing a duet on my head.

The first thing I saw when I pried my eyelids open was Maxi's face, pasty white and with her green peepers fixed on me with horror. Then I saw that she was bound hand and foot to a stake in the ground and remembered what had happened and where we were.

I tried to sit up but discovered then that I was bound as well. Worse, I was dressed in the leather traces and horse-hair pants like the men pulling the chariot had been.

"Ah, my newest trusty stead is awake," Kokavich said from behind me. "I was hoping you would return last night; the post hypnotic suggestion I gave you should have brought you to me then." He stepped up in front of me and reached down to my bound form to grabbed my chin in his thin hand. "Yes, a stronger will than I thought."

He stayed face to face with me, his enlarged monocle eye cartoonish up close.

"Get your hands off me you cut-rate Stroheim," I said, "I'm a reporter and I'm making a citizen's arrest!"

Kokavich stared at me for moment and then roared with laughter. "Oh my," he said between wheezes of mirth, "I do love a spirited mount!"

"Moxie!" My wife called to me, "The police you left the message for should be here any time; hold on!"

Good girl. She knew I hadn't told anyone where we were going.

"I know, Maxi," I faked, "Mahoney and his boys should be here any time."

"Oh please," Kokavich said, "Don't you think a director of my caliber can tell bad acting when he sees it?"

"Bad acting?" Maxi yelled at the Russian, "I got two notices in *The New York Times* that called my work 'Stellar!'" She tugged at her bounds and ground her teeth. "You let me loose you pantless loon and I'll show you me acting Medina on your head!"

That's my gal!

"I think not, dear lady," he said, apparently not bothered at all by her fury, "I'm not quite sure what to do with you—I was not prepared for a matched set; but I do so want to try out my new pacer!"

With that he turned back to me and fixed me in his stare.

Once more I found his mind worming its way into mind and now all the nightmares made sense. I understood why Joey came back—drawn by the implanted thoughts. I had thought the idea to come back was my own, but perhaps it was in the orders I didn't even know I had been given.

Suddenly Kokavich released my hands and feet and stepped back.

I could see that I was on the track of the faux circus Maximus. A chariot rested beside me where another man was harnessed and stood, eyes fixed forward and vacant.

I immediately tried to jump at Kokavich but I barely got to my feet before he stopped me with a word.

"Stand!" he said and my traitor body froze in place. My legs locked in place and I hung there swaying forward almost overbalanced but unable to move.

I could see that my feet had boots on them that gave the impression of hooves.

Oh not another carousel animal!

But it was too late to protest; the mad Russian began to gesture in front of me as if from my nightmare and mumbled "Become."

"I'm so tired of this!" I thought. I tried to call to Maxi, to yell at Kokavich but even my voice was under his control.

Then I began to 'become.'

I felt my belly curving outward, my face elongate and my chest broaden. My thighs thickened and I stooped forward.

Kokavich moved behind me and I felt him pulling on the lead lines to the harness on my back.

"You have not the haunches of my other horses," he said as he worked, "but I think your spirit will make you equal to them."

I tried to show him some of it and turn toward him but, held fast by his command, I could barely move my head.

I felt the weight as he stepped back and got onto the chariot.

"Now, my steeds," he raved, "I will continue to perfect my exact shot sequence for the chariot race in my sound and color production of *Ben Hur*. It will be the most perfect sequence ever filmed."

He snapped the whip.

I felt the sting on my hindquarters and lurched forward. The harness creaked as my shoulders took the weight of the chariot pole. I looked over to see a grey horse also straining at the harness.

The whip snapped again and Kokavich called, "On my steeds!" We pulled onward and then suddenly a second chariot with Hiram, the Major Domo shot past us.

"Don't let him win the race," Kokavich yelled, "I am *Ben Hur* this time around: he is Messalla!"

Deadline Zombies

I tried to resist but his voice and the whip forced me to move with the other trapped animal/man.

Behind me Kokavich kept calling phrases like "close up, Hur; Long shot both, special the whip cracks." As we wheeled around the quarter scale track under the blinding arc lights.

"Let him go!" Maxi screamed at the top of her very capable lungs, "You'll run him to death!" She was struggling at her bonds at she yelled and when he didn't respond, upped the ante with a string of curse words that would make Frank Nitti cover his ears and blush.

The mad Russian took no notice, pushing me and my fellow transformed horse harder in an effort to pass the other chariot.

I don't know how long this went on but my body was covered in sweat and my breath was ragged. It felt oddly right to me pulling the two-wheeled cart, oddly right to feel a tail bobbing behind me. When I looked down and caught sight of my shadow it blurred for a moment but then there is was with the long nose and ears and it too seemed oddly right.

Even Maxi's screams and curses faded into the background and seemed normal as I went around and around the track.

Then the sounds changed and Maxine's voice changed tone as she yelled, "Michael Aloysius Donovan stop it this instant and get me out of here!"

I faltered in my stride and swiveled my head to see her staring at me with flaming eyes. I felt a surge of pride that this amazing woman had chosen to let me be the one who took her home every night, that I was the one she had agreed to spend her tomorrows with.

Then anger swelled up in me that I was also the yegg who got her into this stupid circumstance, tied to a pole in the middle of a studio set of Roman arena while her supposed protector galloped around playing Seabiscuit.

Kokavich snapped the whip into my back and it made me snort and come up short. I spun round, tearing the reins from his hands and breaking free of the traces holding me to the wagon tongue.

"Get him, Moxie!" she yelled.

"Stop him," Kokavich called to Hiram.

I sent a hard kick into the bucket of the chariot, which jarred him hard enough that he stumbled back out of it.

"Behind you Moxie!" Maxi yelled.

The red hired Major Domo came straight at me with a cudgel raised over his head.

I dodged his first swing and whirled to 'mule kick' him in the breadbasket, putting him out of the game.

"Way to go, Babe Ruth!" my wife called. "Get me out of here!"

I raced over to her and bit at her bonds.

"Untie me, silly, you're just hypnotized," she called, "Don't slobber on me."

Since I was having no luck chewing on the knots I tried to use my front hooves that kept flashing into hands and back again. It was all so confusing, I just spun and kicked the base of the stake so that it broke.

Then Maxi slipped her arms off it and with her dancer-flexibility she stepped her legs through the arms to pull the hands up in front of her. Then she started to work on the knots with her own teeth.

Her eyes went wide in alarm but the warning didn't come quickly enough and I couldn't avoid the full impact of the club that Kokavich swung at my head.

I staggered back and tried to get my arms up to block a second strike and slipped down to my knees. Good thing, too, because there was an abrupt explosion and the Russian flew back to slam into the wall of the circus.

"You killed my Joey!" Chloe yelled and fired the second barrel of the shotgun to splatter Kokavich into an impressionist painting.

Epilogue: Happy Trails?

Fortunately for Chloe, Hiram caved in and confessed to Mahoney about how he had helped Kokavich kidnap 'practice' subjects.

The cops accepted that she had 'diminished' capacity and were fine with her having shot the director to save our lives.

After that, uh, things got complicated.

It seems that Kokavich was a better hypnotist than director. Without him to 'un-hypnotize me and the other prisoners, we had problems.

So until Maxi can find some cut rate Mandrake to make me completely normal, I'm eating a lot of oats.

But the up side is that maybe I can work with her on her next western; I've always wanted to meet Johnny Mack Brown!

The End

Teel James Glenn

Inky Dinky Death

And now a special extra bonus preview of the next Maxi and Moxie collection: **The Morgue File Blues:**

Prologue: A Death with Brush

Being a flack for a Burley Queue house as opposed to a movie studio is like the difference between a vampire bat and a mosquito: one only of degree. They both suck.

So after a sojourn plastering the walls of glass houses to defend the honor of aging stars that had none, I switched sides from Universal Studios and started to work for *Hollywood Secrets Magazine*. I guess the blood that ran through my veins was pure yellow ink.

That's right, I, Moxie Donovan breathed the same rarified air as Hedda Hopper and Walter Winchell. Although it was more like hot air most of the time. There were more false fronts on the Hollywood elite than on the buildings on the old western towns they shot horse operas at.

I know, gossip guru is supposed to be below the purview of a real reporter, but, hey, a paycheck is a paycheck and if you turn over enough rocks you sometimes find a pot of gold along with the creepy crawlies.

One of those creepy crawlies was Abner Mantly, (we called him Mental Abner), a one-time studio publicity man who was so strange that even the corrupt studio system had to admit it and canned him from the inner circles. But he still had contacts and for the moolah I could sling his way, he came out into the sunlight of an October afternoon to meet me at a hash joint on Cahuenga Boulevard in North Hollywood.

"Moxie, pal," he said, half rising from the diner booth. He was so painfully thin that his clothes hung on his frame like a second-rate scarecrow. He had watery blue eyes and a tick on his left cheek that made it seem as if he was winking all the time.

His hair was longish and stringy and his teeth looked like they hadn't been brushed since grade school. His hand had long fingers and long nails that made me want to not touch it, but I sucked it up and did my best to give hearty handshake.

His grip was like a dead fish.

"So what's so urgent that you had to come out in the scorching sun?" I asked. I hoped he didn't see me wipe my hand on my pant leg.

I needn't have worried; he was preoccupied with adjusting the hearing aid in his left ear to hear me better. At least I hoped so, he might have been dialing in a baseball game for all I knew.

Deadline Zombies

The waitress came to the table. She was a dish of a disher, hoping to boost her tips by wearing a little pink waitress outfit two sizes too small for her. She had my voice for a few extra cents.

I ordered a coffee and a side of fries to munch on. I flashed her my winning smile that got a wink from her and felt my wedding ring heat up.

Abner kept his own council and fidgeted more than usual until she left then leaned in a theatrical version of a whisper.

"Danielle Scarlini," he said. He slid a copy of *Hollywood Reporter* across the table at me then sat back as if he had given me the secret files of the Salem Witch trials.

The gorgeous brunette on the cover was the aforementioned Italian beauty wearing almost enough to be legal with a headline 'The New Flavor from Rome!'

When I failed to react, he scrunched up his bush eyebrows and hissed, "Lexi Collins!" As if it would explain it all. Then he dropped a copy of *Hollywood Nitelife* with a stunning blonde on the cover.

He started to make me nervous because he kept looking around, his glance darting to the door and watching out the windows to survey the street.

"I'm sorry, Abner," I said with a shrug. "But I don't see how mentioning two starlets is even worth the price of lunch, let alone any real Jack."

He got an annoyed look again and leaned in. "You ain't no genius of journalism then," he hissed, "Cause if you ain't noticed, they're all suddenly the latest craze."

It was true; the two European starlets had burst on the Hollywood scene, all curves and eyelashes to wow the cameras. They didn't seem to have much pedigree but they were stunners so most camera jockeys didn't care.

"Why is that news?" I asked. Just two more dames looking to make a splash. Probably both really from Des Moines.

"Because in Europe they both did films before the war as female leads under the names Renee Korval and Alicia Simons."

"So?" I was feeling like my time had been wasted by an old hophead who was too ashamed to put a touch on me for cash without an excuse. "Child stars sometimes actually have careers as adults!"

He shook his head so violently I thought he might fall over. "No, No!" he said, "They were adult leads."

"That can't be, "I said. "Neither one of them look over twenty two."

He nodded and got a Jack O'lantern grin that showed off his yellowed teeth. "Now ya see." His voice dropped to almost a whisper. "And I know how they did it; and it ain't no plastic surgery!"

I was about to quiz him when my coffee and fries showed up so I clammed up. He looked around as if any moment the IRS might storm in and check his pockets for change.

"I gotta powder my nose," he said springing up and heading for the men's room at the back of the diner without waiting for any comment from me.

I found myself wishing I had something a bit stronger to flavor my coffee with than cream. My mind was whirling about all the appointments I had that day and a cocktail party I was supposed to attend with my special gal Maxi and her pal Kiki Gold over at Milton Berle's house. The last thing I needed was to sit and wait for a washout like Mental Abner to do a line of cocaine in the John.

I sipped my coffee, munched my fries and steamed while wearing the face off my wristwatch with my eyes until I heard a scream from the back of the diner.

I was on my feet and running, java juice flying before the scream was finished.

Mental Abner was sprawled awkwardly in the small hallway outside the lavatories with the sexy dishette doing a Judy Canova impersonation hopping around and squealing.

He didn't look any less grotesque in death than he had in life but one thing did look more interesting; there was a big fat paintbrush sticking straight up out of his right ear.

I guess it's true, you never hear the one that gets you!

To be continued...

Made in the USA
Charleston, SC
14 November 2016